ROGUE OUTLAWS:

YEMEN WAR, BOOK 2 of 2

(Book 15 of the Rogue Submarine Series)

By John R. Monteith

BRAVESHIP BOOKS

PROLOGUE

A week before the *Xerses* and *Wraith* had escorted its first humanitarian aid shipment to Nishtun, Yemen, Danielle Sutton was on Ascension Island, feeling at home in the Royal Air Force Station's officer's club.

Though she missed wearing her nation's uniform, she appreciated the inquisitive stares and whispers of the British officers around her. On the tiny island, a woman commanding a warship was rare, but Danielle recalled plenty of gawking when she'd commanded the *Duke*-class frigate, *Westminster*.

What made her stand out–and notice herself standing out–was her uniform as the newest commander of the world's most unusual warship within a unique mercenary submarine fleet.

Her beige khaki pants and starched white shirt served as a uniform uniting her with the comrades seated at her booth, but loneliness distracted her. She was no longer a British sailor, but she considered herself less than a mercenary.

She hadn't killed anyone yet.

Across the table, Jake Slate lowered his diet cola. "What's wrong? You look like your dog just died."

She hoped he was addressing someone else, but the elder Frenchman by his side wore a face of dignity under his impeccable silvery hair, and her executive officer sat beside her with a wide smile. She cleared her throat. "Me?"

"Yes, you."

"Can't I just relax?" She sipped her London Original bitter beer.

Jake continued the assault. "Not with a sour puss face like that."

"First my dog died. Now a sour puss? Who talks like that?"

Next to Jake, the silver-haired Henri clarified. "He likes cats."

"I can name every species."

Appreciating the distraction, she played along. "Seriously? Every species? How many are there?"

"Something over forty. Closer to forty-five, if you count tigons and ligers, but I don't think God ever meant for tigers and lions to mate. That's why he put them on different continents."

She almost asked him if he believed in God, but she knew the answer. When not commanding a mercenary submarine, he was studying the Bible in some university back in the States.

The last thing she needed was another sermon.

Dmitry Volkov had given her plenty.

Instead, she wanted companionship. She wanted to feel like she belonged with the mercenary fleet, but having negotiated herself out of a one-for-one certain-death torpedo exchange with a Turkish submarine had imparted the opposite effect.

Emotional isolation.

Only fellow commanders within her fleet could understand, and they were all men.

No woman understood her plight.

None could.

With the abnormally high mortality rate during the mission in Yemen, she saw some commonality with Margaret Thatcher's plight four decades earlier in sending the Royal Navy to the Falkland Islands. Thatcher had sent hundreds of men to their deaths, and the mercenary fleet's newest commander respected the pressure the decision had placed upon the deceased stateswoman.

But Thatcher only had to do it once, and nobody was shooting back at her.

Danielle expected to make repeated mortal decisions with each mission, and she wondered if her lengthy standoff with the Turkish submarine had scarred her.

Something had stirred a deep fear within her–deeper than she dared look.

She changed the subject. "Speaking of continents, here we are on a rock between two of them. Maybe that's why I have a sour puss, as you say."

Jake looked away while sipping his beverage. "Fair enough."

After gulping the remainder of her beer, she excused herself. "I'll be in the ladies' room."

Her stroll across the club twisted rubbery necks, and whispers abounded as she walked. Surprising herself, she enjoyed the attention. After sixteen years crafting a path to commanding the *Westminster*, suffering a career-ending political attack, and then rebounding within a Frenchman's fleet, she took the looks of admiration as validation.

Her legs wobbly from ocean travel, she muddled through relieving herself and washing her hands. When finished, she braced herself for more stares while exiting the restroom.

Instead of curious eyes, she saw Jake blocking her view. "Feel better?"

"Uh... yeah. Thanks for checking, but I'm a big girl."

"Okay, big girl. Let's go outside."

Unsure of his motives, she followed him into the evening's humid air. To appear strong, she withheld her questions.

As a moist breeze blew his hair, he sat at a table in the patio's farthest, isolated corner. "Sit. Let's talk."

She lowered herself into the chair opposite him. "What's on your mind?"

"Your ass."

"Excuse me?"

"It's wound tighter than a top. If I stuck coal up it, I'd get a diamond back in five minutes. You've got to chill out, or you'll burn out before we get to Yemen."

Her ire rising from the uninvited criticism, she counted to five and calmed herself before responding. "I haven't heard the ass-diamond metaphor in a long time."

"I don't use it much, but it's what came to mind. I wanted to use a little humor to share a point."

Assuming his intentions charitable, she let herself be analyzed. "It's appreciated. So is your point. But wouldn't you expect some tightness from me? After all, I'm the newest commander on our most complex mission."

He examined her. Apparently content with what he'd seen in her face, he looked towards the beach. "Yeah, there's some truth to that. You should be the most nervous of all the commanders, but…"

She wondered who'd conceived this conversation. "But? Are you sharing your thoughts, or are you the messenger?"

He looked back to her. "A little of both. Ultimately, it's self-preservation. I need you at your best while our lives depend upon each other."

Accepting the claim, she welcomed his criticism. "Well, then. Tell me what you recommend."

"Become comfortable with being watched. Everyone has eyes on you, and it feels like they only watch you. But we all watch each other. That's part of the tightness of submarine life."

"So, this is my pep talk? Telling me to become comfortable with being on stage?"

He locked eyes with her. "We've seen the nerves. Me, Pierre, Mike, Henri, Antoine… we all noticed, even over video chats."

"I'm… uptight?"

He nodded.

"And your advice is to become comfortable in my own skin, more or less."

"More or less."

She ruminated over his counsel. "Okay."

"Okay? Okay… what?"

"Okay, I will."

"That's it? You don't want to claw out my eyeballs?"

"Not at the moment. Shame on me if I made it this far and don't have thick skin."

"Huh. Good point." Again, he stared at the beach. Then, abruptly, he looked back to her and spoke with gravity. "You're still worried about killing, aren't you?"

She gasped and then recovered her composure. "I'm not dodging the question, but why do you ask?"

"Because you haven't killed anyone yet, and the rest of us have. I think it merits an answer. Just my opinion."

"You're in charge of two warships. Your opinion counts." She reflected upon the accusation, which rang true with her earlier thoughts of the evening. "I admit, I was hoping that Dmitry and

Terry had taken care of the nastiest parts of it."

"Fair answer. I'd be concerned if you weren't wary, but since you're admitting to hoping not to kill, I'll take that as a healthy respect for life."

"It is."

"Good. There was some method to his madness, if I give Pierre credit in retrospect."

"How so?"

Jake's tone was pensive. "We'd let the world forget that we have real teeth. The slow-kills are fantastic for winning without killing, but if your enemies expect humane treatment, they stop respecting you. So, Pierre had us flex our muscle by killing a few Iranian submarines. Nobody will care outside a few intelligence circles, and we've regained our street cred."

She wondered if she had the mettle to kill. "Yeah. And no matter what Pierre strategizes about, we can all be called to kill when a battle turns deadly."

"You're feeling the weight of it now."

"Bloody hell, Jake, I feel it all the time. That's why you think I've got a stick up my ass."

"There you go. Snuffing out one life is hard enough. When you imagine taking out entire crews of ships, it's crushing."

She realized she was having the right conversation with the right person at the right time. "Yeah. So, how do you deal with it?"

"For upcoming combat, I try to remember that death isn't the end. We can't say what brings our spirits to life. Therefore, we can't say what kills them. I believe the spirit is eternal."

Groaning, she lowered her forehead to her hand. "You've said that before, and I don't want another religious sermon. I get them all the time from Dmitry."

"Well, are you afraid of dying?"

She reflected in silence. "Yes."

"There's the problem. You're casting your fears onto those you would kill and letting that false fear reflect back on you. It's all happening in your head. But what if you could convince yourself that everyone you might kill is ready to die?"

"I'd say..." She paused in thought. "Hell, Jake. I don't know."

"Well, if you ponder that, I bet you'll make progress on that diamond factory between your butt cheeks."

She snorted. "You have a way with words."

"Eh. Sometimes."

Replaying portions of the conversation in her memory, she found an unanswered question. "You said you deal with combat by looking at death as not the end. What about the people you've already killed? How do you deal them?"

"How do I deal with the dead I've created?"

"Yeah."

Again, he looked away, and a gust added a menacing tone to his answer. "In my nightmares."

CHAPTER 1

A refueling stop in Cape Town, South Africa behind her, Danielle braced for ugly seas.

Notorious for winter storms and mammoth waves, the infamous passage around Africa's southernmost tip, off Cape Agulhas, was dangerous. Warm eddies from the Indian Ocean mixed with cooler water from the south, and the dense Antarctic Circumpolar Current mashed against the hot African Agulhas Current. Then high winds whipped these waters into a frenzy atop the shallow Agulhas Bank.

As a ten-foot wave approached, Danielle altered the *Goliath's* course to take the incoming crest thirty degrees off the transport ship's hulls.

Standing beside her, the former British submarine commander sounded nervous. "That wave doesn't worry you?"

She snorted. "Which North Atlantic Ocean did you steam in?"

"The same as you, but I enjoyed it from underneath the swells."

"This is nothing." She reconsidered. "Well, it's something. Hold on to the railing." Lifting her chin towards an open microphone, she raised her voice. "All stations, make sure you're rigged for sea. We're facing heavy seas. A big wave's coming for us."

As the words left her mouth, the starboard prow rode up the incoming water.

The deck titled back and then leftward as the aquatic undulation traversed from her starboard keel to her port.

She held her breath and gripped a railing during the roller coaster ride. When it was over, she exhaled with a slight smile. Having taken wild rolls in the North Atlantic Ocean, she'd seen worse. "See? That wasn't so bad."

Taylor agreed. "Yeah. Not too bad." Her executive officer looked at the video screen showing the *Specter's* control room. "Are you guys okay?"

In the display, Jake replied. "Fine, other than the usual shit falling everywhere. You should know how submariners hate stowing for sea. Unless we're taking some fun diving angles, it's like an admission that we're on the surface."

Taylor snorted. "Right. I hear you."

Danielle was more concerned about her ship's discipline than her cargo bed passenger's sea stowage. "Mike, walk the ship and find out who wasn't stowed for sea. Get them stowed. We'll see other big waves before we pass the cape."

The balding man of average height lowered his head as he turned, revealing the sheen of his scalp. "I look forward to it. I'm not so sure I like the view outside the dome yet. Give me circular ribs and a room of welded steel."

His footsteps echoed as he descended the stairs into the ship's submarine-shaped section.

Alone, she reflected upon her mission.

With the *Xerses* and *Wraith* assuring the influx of humanitarian aid against UAE and Iranian forces, Danielle anticipated her first taste of battle against new enemies–Houthi rebels and Separatists of the Southern Transitional Council.

She intended to help the ragtag Yemeni Navy and its family members recapture their overrun hometown of Aden before Houthi rebels could cement their stranglehold on the port city.

Expecting to succeed, the *Goliath's* commander ignored her disadvantage in raw firepower. Though the combined Houthi-Separatist fleet outgunned her and had a nine-knot advantage in top speed, she had a half-century technical advantage, and her ship could hide under water.

And she had the *Specter*.

And depending on the political alliances when she'd arrive in theater, she might have Saudi allies.

Then again, she might have Saudi enemies trying to fill the

power vacuum the UAE had left behind.

Regardless of Saudi support, her challenge was parking the *Goliath* off the port of Aden and providing naval gunfire support. Per plan, it sounded easy and surgically innocuous.

But the weight of possible lives lost burdened her.

From the submarine in her cargo bed, Jake seemed to notice her pensiveness. "Hey, Danielle?"

"Yeah?"

"It's getting near dinner time. Can you please keep the deck from bouncing and rolling?"

Appreciating the levity, she played along. "Sure. Just as soon as Pierre gives me hover-drive to fly over big waves."

In the display, Jake smirked. "All we need are some huge turboprops, and we'll be the world's first flying, submersible, submarine-carrying destroyer."

"If it's within Pierre's budget."

"Be careful what you ask for. He's surprised us before."

The comment piqued her curiosity. "How so?"

"Adding the MESMA plant to the *Wraith*, for starters. After we stole it, he sent it off for the upgrade. And he also splurged for that beefed up gearing you've got on your shafts. I know Terry's appreciated it while running from a torpedo or two."

"I hope we don't have to run from torpedoes."

"Nobody wants to, but we've got to be ready."

She recalled the endless lessons Jake had shared with her and her new, growing crew as he'd taught them tribal knowledge of the mercenary fleet's past tactics. The group had lived life on a razor's edge of near escapes.

Nobody's luck could endure much longer, she reasoned, and she wanted to make her upcoming trials look easy.

When Taylor returned, his climbing steps echoed with enthused levity. He reached her side. "Not bad, really. Just a few pencils and books knocked over. The galley was especially well stowed."

"Did you check the port side?"

"Uh..."

"It's alright. I know you didn't. You came back too fast."

"I'm happy to..."

Sniffing a teaching moment, she treaded lightly. They'd both been British officers of equal rank who'd commanded warships, and she wanted to treat him like a former commanding officer. "Mike, is invading a woman's private space going to be an issue for you?"

"Well, not when I have to."

"Go pay the port hull a visit."

He showed her his shiny crown as he turned. "I'm on it."

For a moment, she questioned her decision to staff the port hull with all the *Goliath's* women. To minimize the temptation of sexual encounters, she'd maximized the gender segregation between her port and starboard crews.

Although she'd needed two men with specific experience for running the far hull's MESMA systems, she'd staffed the rest of her port team with females who could keep its engineering space humming and its railgun ready.

Alone again, she scanned the rough waters ahead and saw another oversized wave arriving, except this one looked larger than the recent roller coaster ride.

Lifting her jaw, she yelled. "Control room, bridge. Can you see a wave on radar, about a mile off the starboard bow?"

Overhead speakers issued a man's deep voice. "No, ma'am. But we've got something brewing two and half miles out. It's... long."

"Long?"

"Covering a wide swath of azimuth. I thought it was a storm at first, but... wow. It's big."

Concerned, she lifted her binoculars and studied the distant water. The white caps seemed small for a ten-foot wave.

They seemed small for a twenty-foot wave.

Although she'd never seen a fifty-foot wave, she thought the white sections of the incoming wall framed a crest of such height. "Bloody hell. That's a big one."

Tapping her rudder's icon, she adjusted course and aimed the

Goliath thirty degrees off the monstrous crest's incoming motion. "Coming to thirty degrees off the incoming wave."

Grateful to have a submariner in charge of the tandem ships, she welcomed his warning.

Jake issued his order. "Get a camera on that wave."

Obeying, she rotated one of the *Goliath's* external cameras towards the incoming wall of water.

As he looked away from his webcam, Jake narrated his actions. "I'm aiming my periscope towards it and seeing how many divisions tall it is... doing some quick math in my head. Uh... shit. This can't be right."

As she watched the wave grow taller than any she'd seen, she expected it to appear within arm's reach, but it remained distant. "How big?"

"I've got it at fifty feet."

"Shit, Jake. That's a rogue wave!"

His voice rose half an octave. "Get us under it!"

"Should we crash dive?"

"No, that's for the *Goliath* alone in combat, not a safety maneuver with cargo."

Thankful her destroyer could submerge, she employed the feature. "I'm going to slow us and start flooding my tanks, Jake. You should get ready to flood yours."

"Agreed. Let's start submerging. Where's Mike?"

Having waited for Jake's approval, she tapped keys to bring water into the *Goliath* and slow her vessel's speed. "I sent him to the port hull. I'll get him on a circuit." She tapped an icon and lifted her chin. "Executive officer, contact the bridge asap."

Seconds later, Taylor's voice came from the speakers. "Executive officer, on the line."

"Mike, Jake and I are assessing a fifty-foot wave. It's about two miles away now. I wanted you in the discussion."

"How big, you say?"

"Fifty feet. Jake measured it."

"Holy shit."

"I know." She found it haunting.

"We should slow and submerge, unless you want to turn back and try to outrun it. Maybe come back around it."

"I don't want to lose a day running from a wave, and I don't see a way around this monster. We're slowing and submerging."

"Has Jake weighed in?"

Through his inter-ship connection, the *Specter's* commander replied. "I already agreed with slowing and submerging. I don't see a better way."

Taylor's tone remained serious. "Have you ever been underneath a hurricane, Jake?"

"Yeah. A couple times in the South Atlantic. We were rocking as deep as three hundred feet."

"I've got a nasty feeling that we're going to be rocked no matter how deep we go."

"You're thinking about detaching me?"

Taylor's tone became thoughtful. "Maybe. We'll have to keep a close watch on hydraulic ram stresses. Danielle, I'll come to the bridge and watch the stresses myself."

She appreciated having two men with submarine command experience at her disposal. "Sounds great, Mike. Get back here."

"On my way."

Danielle lifted her chin and raised her voice. "Listen up, crew. We've got a rogue wave, fifty feet tall, coming our way. That's why I've slowed the ship and am taking on water to make us heavy. We're going to submerge, and we'll release the *Specter* manually from the bridge if the rams fail. I'm shifting propulsion to the MESMA systems. Prepare to submerge."

She tapped an icon silencing her microphone and then worked through menus to bring the air-independent power plants online.

Jake added his insights. "I know you're supposed to take a thirty-degree angle when you're driving over a wave. But I'm pretty sure those rules change when we're going under one."

She chuckled. "Are you quizzing me?"

"Maybe a little bit."

From her ongoing crash course in undersea tactics, she recalled that submarines could mitigate damage from warheads by facing the blast with their bows or sterns. Exposing a smaller cross-sectional area to an incoming blast minimized the energy transfer, and she assumed the same logic for a wave. "Turn towards it."

"Correct. Once I'm deep enough to take in water, you should turn. No later than when you see my decks awash."

She filed the new but self-evident phrase, 'decks awash', into her memory. "Got it. I'll keep an eye on you."

As water lapped her bridge windows, she checked the distance to the rogue crest.

One nautical mile.

She expected more violence in the seas so close to a rare wave of massive power, but the sensation was like being on a calm beach before a tsunami.

"I'm registering movement through the water now."

Hungry for knowledge, she risked exposing her ignorance. "Is that how you verify that you're immersed?"

Jake shrugged. "That's how I'm doing it. It's nothing I learned in the real navy, but it works. It means water's flowing over the pit swords that measure my speed. But I'm not taking water into my tanks until I see my decks awash."

As water formed a translucent hemisphere around her, the views from the *Goliath's* cameras showed the murky shallows. She switched views in a nearby display to see the world above through the *Specter's* exposed periscope, giving her the sensation of looking through the world's tallest periscope.

"Decks awash. Turn us toward the wave, straight towards it. I'm flooding my tanks."

"Understood. I'm turning us towards the wave." Tapping keys, she adjusted the *Goliath's* course.

"I'm going to stay lighter than normal. In fact, I'm going to stay ten thousand pounds lighter than you."

She recalled that normal cargo operations required the immersed submarine to outweigh her transport ship to create friction between the ships. "You'll be harder to hold that way."

"Right. That's the point. I'm deviating from the normal weight distribution. You want me to be a balloon instead of a rock, in case I fall off. Well, more like... get ripped off."

Heightening her disadvantage of undersea ignorance, another submarine commander interjected his ideas in a French accent from a display screen. "Jake's right, Danielle. I've been listening after learning of your rogue wave."

"Understood. Thanks, Pierre."

"I'll lose you when Jake's antenna's immersed. Stay calm and use your wits. You're all charmed, as far as I–" Renard's face froze.

"We lost him. My periscope's under."

With all cameras covered, Danielle found the opaqueness eerie and flipped her affected screens to their main menus.

Bounding up the steps, her executive officer returned to the bridge. He stepped beside her and examined displays. "This could get rough. I'm calling up controls for the hydraulic rams."

Danielle injected her surface warrior's mindset. "Very well. Announce your intentions before releasing a ram, if you release one. Give me one second to confirm or deny. If I say nothing, assume you have permission."

"Command by negation... one second. Understood, ma'am."

"Also, Jake's making the *Specter* ten thousand pounds light. Not heavy. Pierre concurred."

"Huh. In case we need to let him go?"

She appreciated Taylor's independent thoughts confirming those of the American and the Frenchman. "Yeah. Exactly."

"That makes sense. We should also take an up angle."

"Up? Not down, so the wave presses Jake into us?"

"Up. To avoid getting driven into the bottom."

From the display, Jake interjected. "Yeah. Good idea, Mike. I'd say fifteen degrees."

The artificial lighting cast a glare off Taylor's scalp. "Fifteen up sounds good to me, ma'am."

"I concur. I've got it." She tapped keys to let the *Goliath* adjust its stern planes and water movement from aft to forward. The deck tilted backwards.

As the deck reached twelve degrees up, the tidal wave hit.

Like a nightmare, the consoles in front of her face moved towards her, and she sensed herself moving in slow motion. She held her breath and extended her arms, but the metal bar she'd grasped collapsed them. The railing hit her chest and knocked out her wind. Wincing, she dropped to a knee.

Hurting, she endured a wave of insecurity. Defeatist thoughts flooded her mind, telling her she shouldn't be here. She's not capable. She's a woman in a man's world... a surface warrior in a submariner's world. Weak.

Two feet away, Taylor was folded over his consoles. With greater arm strength and muscle around his ribs, he'd fared better and backed his weight over his feet. "Are you okay?"

Unable to speak, she nodded.

He moved towards her. "You're sure?"

Loud metallic groans rose in rounds of choruses, with each hydraulic arm protesting its strain on its own timing.

She waved him away and squeaked a word. "Rams."

"Right! Shit." As he turned towards his panels, one of them sent out a chiming alarm. "Six... seven rams are in the danger zone but still within limits."

Her gut hurt, and she folded her arms over it. "Use your judgment, Mike. I can't see for myself..."

"Ram seventeen is above the alarm limit, but not yet at the specified design limit. Wait... still going up. Damn it. I'm folding it back." He glanced at her.

She nodded her agreement. Impressed in her executive officer's technical memory under stress, she appreciated the ingrained nuclear-trained paradigm, which had conditioned him to memorize tons of information.

Today, the design limits of the rams allowed him to keep the pressure on despite alarms from multiple arms.

She rolled to her feet, grabbed the railing, and stood.

Taylor continued narrating his work. "Folding back rams twelve and sixteen. Torques on all rams are rising... but now steadying."

Jake interjected "Do you need to let me go?"

Danielle climbed up the console to her executive officer's side and saw the raw data. Red flares showed the dangerous stresses, but they stopped rising. She shook her head.

Taylor answered. "No. I think we're good. I'm reengaging the disengaged rams."

"Looks like we made it. Are you guys okay?"

Danielle locked eyes with Jake, forced a smile, and nodded.

Taylor spoke for her. "She got her wind knocked out, but she held her ground."

Finding her voice, she added her colorful commentary. "I took it in the stomach. That really hurts."

"I've been kicked in the gut enough times that I get it. It sends you right to the ground."

She acquiesced. "Duly noted, Jake. Mike, walk the ship and check our status–people and systems."

"I'll walk the ship, ma'am. Excuse me." Taylor departed.

In the silence, she inspected her hands. They were trembling, and she resented her hidden fears while the submariner officers around her seemed calmer, stronger.

Alone with the *Specter's* commander, she sought his advice. "Jake?"

"Yeah?

"Can you think of anything I should be doing now?"

He chuckled, and his tone was reverent. "There's nothing in the submariner playbook about a rogue wave. You just dived face-first into one, and I think that puts you in a minority."

The fleet's prototypical commander helped repair her confidence. His words encouraged positive thoughts.

Maybe she was in the right place. Surrounded by world-class talent, maybe everything would work out for her. Maybe even a romance with a Bible-thumping Russian submarine commander. Maybe a new identity as the first and only female mercenary submersible destroyer commander.

"You talk about it like it's a badge of honor."

"Hell yeah, it is. If you do something submerged that few people have done, you get bragging rights."

"I guess I should feel honored."

"Yup. Congratulations, Danielle. You're one step closer to becoming a submariner."

CHAPTER 2

Stooped over the *Specter's* central charting table, Jake checked the ocean's depth.

Four hundred and twelve feet.

He judged the water shallow enough for the next huge wave to drive the *Goliath's* prows into the bottom, if the ship had to escape underneath the storm's crests again.

To evade the rough waters, he considered the slower undersea transit around Africa's southern tip.

But the *Goliath's* length and simple trigonometry left little room for error in depth control if another surge forced a steep angle.

A submerged transit implied no promises of safety.

Jake faced a decision to either stay submerged and limited in transit speed, or to surface, endure the tempest, and hope for reasonable wave heights. And in either case, he risked the damage and delays of bottoming.

Wanting to talk it through, he strode to the semi-privacy of his elevated conning platform's console. "Danielle?"

The *Goliath's* commander walked into her screen. "I'm here. I was just talking to Mike."

"How's your ship?"

"Fine. Looks like I was the least prepared for the wave. Everyone else has a few bruises at worst."

After receiving reports from his crack mechanic, Henri Lanier, after his walk about the *Specter*, Jake knew his crew had endured the wave without serious injury. He agreed that she'd suffered the worst of it. "Looking out for everyone else first, huh?"

"Yeah. I suppose."

"But you'll be fine?"

"I'm fine, Jake. What's on your mind?"

"Surfacing. Or not. That's the question."

"Are you asking my opinion?"

He wasn't sure if he was coaching her, leaning on her, or building consensus with her. Perhaps all three.

As he assessed her visage, he saw quiet strength.

Renard had done well finding her, and she'd proven herself witty and resilient in the encounter against the Turks. Her face also had a jaded edge, the type Jake liked, for having endured harsh injustices within their prior fleets.

Long ago, foul play had dashed Jake's hopes of commanding an American submarine, but he'd recovered from that loss.

Though he commanded a vessel less capable than a frontline *Virginia*-class, he'd seen more combat than all his submarining countrymen combined. His freedom to act with the approval of a lone Frenchman, for motives of a small team's choosing, had allowed it.

His regrets seemed few, upon shallow examination.

Now forty-one years old, he was aging beyond the standard years of a warship's commander.

After leading the prior mission from the control center, he'd tasted the fleet's high-level leadership role.

Although he still preferred commanding a warship, he'd enjoyed the wider view from above. He also enjoyed coaching his teammates through challenges, and it boosted his confidence to know he had experience doing so.

After a slight hesitation during which he questioned his skill in jousting with a former commander of a British frigate in ship handling, he embraced the responsibility. "Yeah. I'm interested in your opinion. What do you think?"

"I'm a destroyer girl at heart. I kind of like the rocking and rolling, and we're on a tight schedule."

"But that's a big storm above us."

"We'll probably see big waves again, but nothing half as big as that last behemoth."

"I'm not so sure my submarine could stay inside your cargo presses with a twenty-five-foot wave. Maybe not even twenty."

"We can always dive again if we have to."

Jake drew motivation from her confidence and agreed to risk the surfaced journey around the cape. "Yeah. Good point. Let's..."

Across the *Specter's* control room, the sonar ace's wide, toad-shaped head curled forward into his chest.

Seeing Remy move from the corner of his eye, Jake withheld his order to surface. "Hold on, Danielle."

"What's wrong?"

"Not sure. Ask Mike about surfacing, as a third opinion. I need to check this out." Jake walked from his elevated conning platform, across the tiny space, and to the sonar guru's shoulder.

Sensing his commander's presence, Remy raised a finger to order silence.

Concern rising within him from the sonar ace's gravity, Jake obeyed and kept his mouth shut.

Remy broke the silence with a gravely tone. "Fifty-hertz tonal, coming from our towed array sonar. Possible submerged contact."

"Seriously? We just deployed the array."

"Seriously. Bearing is either zero-nine-two or one-six-eight."

Surprised to encounter a submerged contact south of Africa, Jake shifted to tactical mode. "If it's one-six-eight, it's not in our path. We'll assume it's zero-nine-two and see if it holds true. Any idea whose it is?"

Remy shook his toad-head. "No idea. It's just a fifty-hertz power plant. It's clean, coming in bottom bounce."

A hyperbola of bearing appeared in a tactical display above the sonar ace's screen of raw sound data.

"We just announced ourselves with a nice symphony of groaning metal." Jake looked across the room to his mechanical expert. "Henri, find out the latest intel we have on submarines in the area. Anybody's. Friendly, neutral, enemy."

The silver-haired mechanic tapped his way through a menu.

"I thought they were all enemies, except our clients."

"No time for joking. See who's out there."

Henri finished reading the latest intelligence report from Renard and then looked at his commander. "Jake, nobody's got a submarine in the area unless it's local operations."

Jake checked his mental list of global submarine ownership. "South Africa has three *Type-209* submarines, all about fifteen years old. Formidable. Comparable to our capabilities."

Henri shrugged.

Jake looked back to Remy. "How loud is it out there?"

The sonar ace slid a muff behind his ear. "Like a storm. The background noise is horrible. Either this fifty-hertz tonal is covering a surprisingly long distance, or the contact is close."

Jake strode to the elevated conning platform and addressed the *Goliath's* commander. "Danielle, we've got trouble. An unidentified submerged contact bearing zero-nine-two."

Her frown cast a shadow over her eyes. "Any idea whose? What's the range? Course and speed?"

"Nothing other than a fifty-hertz tonal."

The *Goliath's* balding executive officer moved beside his commander. "Fifty hertz, and nothing else?"

Jake appreciated the British veteran's expertise. From his minimal encounters with him, he found the former *Astute*-class commander a respectable specimen of his nation's submarining lineage. "Yeah. That's it. Clean, but no other sounds."

"I imagine in this environment that you wouldn't hear much except the lower frequencies. Our towed array isn't deployed. You were bloody smart to get yours out as fast as you did."

"Smart or lucky. Or charmed as Pierre says. Doesn't matter. If we can hear their electric plant, they can hear ours. And we have more than one, and we just gave them a ton of metallic transients underneath the rogue wave to announce our location."

"Yeah, those were nasty creaks."

"Whoever they are, they know we're here, and they were ridiculously close to our charted course."

Taylor shrugged. "Could just be the local South Africans out on ops. I imagine they train a lot around the cape."

"If you were in charge of this two-ship tandem, would you write them off as disinterested friendlies?"

Looking down, the balding officer snorted. "No. Good point." He met Jake's gaze again. "The question is, do we hunt or do we run."

Jake knew the desired answer. "Our mission isn't here. If they weren't so close to our track, I'd say that we run. But given–"

Remy interrupted. "Torpedo in the water!"

His stomach knotting, Jake twisted his neck towards the sonar ace and yelled as he marched towards his guru's station. "Bearing? Bearing rate?"

A pallor caked Remy's face. "No bearing yet. It's coming in bottom bounce and then bouncing off the surface. It's a mess out there. I need more time!"

Jake hoped he'd stumbled upon a South African naval exercise, but his gut said otherwise. "What type of weapon is it? What do you hear?"

"Nothing useful while you're talking."

"At least give me a swath of ocean to avoid."

Scowling, the sonar ace spread his arms and aimed his fingers slightly left of the ship's heading.

"Understood." Jake darted to the nearest console showing the *Goliath* commander's concerned face. "Danielle! We need to turn right one-hundred-sixty degrees. Full rudder, and bring us to maximum sustained submerged speed."

She shouted her response. "I'm coming right with full rudder to course... course two-nine-zero, making turns for thirteen knots."

"Very well, Danielle." Expecting the world to tilt, Jake was impressed with the level-deck stability the transport ship provided its cargo through a rough turn.

The sonar ace called out. "I've resolved the bearing. The weapon's coming from bearing zero-nine-nine. Bearing rate is zero, maybe slight right. It's a good shot–at us."

Jake mentally translated 'good shot' as well-aimed destruction and death. He crouched between Remy and his top apprentice, Julien, seated beside him. While the pair of sonar technicians discerned data from the sounds, the *Specter's* commander studied the information on their screens.

Adjusting for Doppler effect, he tried to match the weapon's seeker with his mental inventory of known frequencies. The numbers misaligned against his expectation of a German-designed South African weapon.

That disconnect strengthened his suspicion that someone beyond the local navy was trying to kill him. He voiced his thoughts. "There's no reason for the South Africans shoot at us."

His composure reestablished after discerning the weapon's bearing and rate, Remy replied. "I have no idea. Maybe we have prices on our heads. I recommend evasion course two-three-zero."

After verifying the geometry as an optimum of running from the torpedo and sideslipping its seeker, Jake yelled. "Danielle, settle us on course two-three-zero."

Thick, odorous air carried her response across the control room. "I'm on course two-four-eight, shifting my rudder left to two-three-zero. Jake, shouldn't we surface and run?"

The *Specter's* commander stood, stooped over the tactical chart, and pondered his plight.

Danielle snapped. "Jake?"

"I'm thinking!" He glared at the chart showing a questionable solution to the incoming torpedo. "Antoine, do you have a counterfire weapon ready?"

"Julien does, but it's a terrible solution."

"I don't care. Which tube's ready?"

"Tube one, a slow-kill."

"Henri, is the ship ready to launch?"

"The ship is ready to launch a torpedo from tube one."

"Shoot tube one."

As the pressure change of the pneumatic impulse launch popped Jake's ears, he reexamined the chart.

Remy announced his improvement to the solution on the incoming weapon. "I have bearing rate and a loose range. I'm updating the system."

Jake watched the hostile weapon's icon hop farther from his ship than the sonar ace's original estimate. After tapping boxes on the huge touchscreen to examine evasion scenarios, he noticed he had time to run, but he was still trapped within the torpedo's reach.

The weapon had the speed and endurance to catch the *Goliath* and *Specter*, no matter what course they took together, surfaced or submerged.

But at the very least, he wanted to maximize his time to think. He yelled towards the nearest microphone. "Danielle, surface us and sprint at the best speed."

If fear gripped her, her strong voice hid it. "I'm surfacing... preparing to shift propulsion to the gas turbines."

"Very well."

As the deck angled upward with the climb, it started to bob, rock, and roll in the rough swells.

Jake clasped the railing around the central charting table and studied the danger. He then decided and announced his order to carry out the task they'd rehearsed ten times more frequently than the average naval vessel. "Henri, Danielle... prepare to abandon both ships."

Obeying without question, Henri reached for communications equipment by his station to share the order within the *Specter*.

But a protest issued from the *Goliath's* display–from its executive officer. "Jake, Danielle's getting ready to abandon ship, but hear me out."

The *Specter's* commander checked the timing until detonation, subtracted the time required to exit the ships, and then concluded he had two minutes to talk. He yelled while walking to his elevated conning platform. "Go ahead, Mike."

In the display, the *Goliath's* executive officer wore a dire expression. "We've got an underwater mountain four miles away. We might be able to hide behind it."

Jake recognized the tactic's theoretical soundness. Theoretical. "Hide behind it?"

As Taylor nodded, his scalp reflected artificial light. "Or next to it or on top of it. Whatever. It's our only chance.

"You'd take our chances on gnat's ass navigation around a mountain of rock and coral?"

"We've got the sidescan sonar."

Jake had forgotten the sidescan sonar. "You're a genius. Make it happen. Tell Danielle."

Her voice echoed through the *Goliath's* bridge dome. "I heard you both. I need to come right to course two-six-four."

Jake concurred. "Do it. And still prepare to abandon ship, in case this doesn't work. I'll get my propulsion warmed up, too, in case you need the extra boost."

As the floor's bouncing and angles became more pronounced atop the water's surface, Renard's face appeared on a monitor. "I see that you're surfaced. What's going on?"

As the tandem's senior officer, Jake replied. "Someone just shot at us. We're running from a torpedo."

"Dear God!"

"We don't know who. The weapon doesn't sound South African."

With his impeccable hearing, Remy entered the conversation and yelled his contribution. "It's a Russian USET-80 torpedo. Adjusted for Doppler and verified."

Renard complained. "What did Antoine say? I couldn't hear him."

"He said it's a Russian USET-80. Shit, Pierre, that's an export weapon. It could be any Russian client."

"Think man. You know who it is."

Jake agreed. "Iranian *Kilo*-class submarine. I thought we had a ceasefire with them."

"We didn't. The Yemenis did. And since when do you trust the Iranians? Assume it's an Iranian *Kilo*."

The gravity of his adversary's deadly intent struck Jake. "Shit."

Renard's tone was grave. "Can you evade?"

"Maybe. Mike had an idea to hide behind the Twelve Mile Bank. It's steep and jagged enough to provide sonar reflections."

"Dear God! That's your evasion?"

The *Specter's* commander beat back an encroaching inner iciness. "We were ambushed with a facial shot, and we're not getting away. The *Goliath's* sidescan sonar can paint the mountain for us, and we can find a place to park and hide."

Blushing, Renard had to agree. "That's a terrible plan, but I can't think of a better one. I can only pray that you're still charmed. Hopefully, Danielle has some charm to spare as well. Perhaps some lady luck."

Letting her forceful tone protest the gender remark, Danielle answered. "I've got us making thirty-two knots in a bloody minor hurricane. I'll get us to the bank's far side, slow with a backing bell, and then dive. A crash dive is too risky for losing the *Specter*."

Jake waved his hand. "Agreed, no crash dive. We'll have to dive slow and shallow since that bank's peak is only eighty-five feet deep. Once we're under, we'll use the sidescan sonar to find our berthing."

Reasserting herself as a commander, Danielle kept talking. "I've got us six minutes from the bank, eight minutes to torpedo impact. Do you concur, Jake?"

"I concur. Let's do it."

Five minutes later, Jake's heart raced as the readings from the *Goliath's* fathometer climbed. Checking the chart, he suspected the undersea mountain's base was below him. As he hoped to see the water depth rise shallower than one hundred feet, it trended back down after approaching two hundred. "I think we're off the bank's center. We need to submerge and figure it out."

Danielle grasped the situation. "I'm coming to all-stop. Shifting propulsion to the MESMA units to submerge."

"Very well."

"We're below twenty knots... I'm flooding my tanks."

As Jake watched the seas rise around the dome behind Danielle, he gave his French boss a last chance to advise him. "Any parting words, Pierre?"

Renard bid his team farewell. "I would wish you luck, except that I know you and Danielle are both charmed. Keep my ships from being–"

The Frenchman's face froze, and the *Specter's* commander tapped the screen to invoke a tactical display.

Another minute later, Jake was a spectator watching the British officers maneuver the *Goliath* towards the green hues of the jagged mountain their ship's sidescan sonar painted.

Danielle narrated. "We're making twenty knots, draining the battery. Jake, can you give us some propulsion?"

"I'll make turns for twenty-five knots to help us along." Jake raised his voice. "All-ahead full, make turns for twenty-five knots."

Danielle was hopeful. "That should do it, Jake. It's enough to get us to the mountain in time."

"If Antoine's solution to the torpedo's accurate."

Displaying his aural prowess, Remy interjected from across the room. "It's accurate."

"Then we'll make it." Jake watched the greenish hues of the bank grow larger as the *Goliath* escorted him towards it.

As the crags and gullies forming the undersea mountain became discernible, Jake worried about a collision. "Don't you think we're coming in a bit fast?" Hearing no answer, the *Specter's* commander glared at Danielle's quarter profile.

Looking offscreen, the *Goliath's* commander said nothing.

"Danielle!"

"I'm driving!"

Jake clenched his jaw shut and let her drive.

Carrying out his order, she snapped hers back at him. "Get ready for all back emergency, both ships, on my mark."

Conceding to her tenacity and judgment, Jake obeyed. "I'm awaiting your mark."

Motion in the sidescan sonar display caught Jake's eye–a school of fish marking his proximity to the underwater edifice.

"Mark! All- back emergency!"

Jake echoed Danielle's command. "All- back emergency!"

The deck shuddered, and speed gauges flipped downwards.

When momentum ebbed to five knots, Danielle extended her ship's four precision motors. "Deploying outboards."

Remy announced his concern. "Torpedo impact is in ninety seconds, if it still has us."

Jake yelled over his shoulder. "You don't know?"

"It's coming our way, still behaving like it has us, but I can't tell what it's doing with all the reflections off the bank."

"Keep monitoring it." Jake looked back to the *Goliath's* bridge. "And get us as close as you can."

Danielle's face revealed her weariness of being micro-managed. "I am. We've got thirty meters to go. All-stop, both ships!"

Jake placed his faith in the British woman. "You heard her. All-stop!"

Oozing confidence, Danielle described her actions. "Out-boards are full back. Slowing to two-point-five knots. Fifteen meters from the point of impact."

The *Specter's* commander understood the term as the distance between the *Goliath's* prows and the cliff of rock. He found it logical but disliked its use of 'impact'. "What's happening with the torpedo, Antoine?"

"I'm seeing an increase in bearing rate to the left."

Jake recognized the desired geometry. He glanced at the tactical display showing the hostile weapon drawing to the bank's opposite side. "We're good. Slow us down, Danielle."

She remained silent while the distance to the rock tapered.

Judging himself safe, Jake checked his position and speed. With the four outboard motors holding the vessels steady against the ocean currents, the *Goliath* and *Specter* were unmoving over the nearby ground.

Remy announced the ship's safety. "The hostile torpedo is tracking away from us."

"Very well."

During a silence, the sonar ace voiced his future concerns. "What now, Jake? There's still a hostile submarine out there."

The *Specter's* commander straightened his back. As panic drained from him, he ran scenarios through his mind.

Attack blindly.

Hunt diligently.

Sprint furiously.

Or hide.

He said a quiet prayer of thanks for surviving and then announced his decision. "Danielle's going to park us on this mountain. From there, we'll hear everything, and we'll go ultra-quiet and listen for that bastard who shot at us to press his luck."

CHAPTER 3

Yemeni Commander Andi Amir doubted the feasibility of his *Tarantul* corvette riding in the *Xerses'* cargo bed.

But his commodore had overruled his protest, and with only hours to plan the assault, the *Tarantul's* commander had acquiesced to his boss' order.

They'd try a test.

With his warship dead in the water, he stuck his head out the window and ogled as the mercenary transport ship inched through the surface swells below him.

Coming up with a steep list, the *Xerses'* dome rose through the water first, followed by its starboard weapons bay in the rear.

Hoping to avoid damage during the controlled collision, Amir felt helpless as he trusted the mercenaries and their calculations.

The seas groaned with metallic creaks, screeches, and bangs as, below the waterline, the cargo bed lifted his keel.

His ship's gentle rising from the water bothered him less than its list counterbalancing that of the *Xerses* below him. As the starboard hull glided up, the transport ship's outboard motors pushed the cargo bed laterally to the left to rotate the *Tarantul* over with a starboard list onto the retracted starboard presses.

As the corvette rolled farther to the right, pencils, markers, and navigation instruments clanked onto the deck behind Amir. Given the steepness, he judged the bridge's securing for sea satisfactory.

Joining him at the opened window, Captain Damari examined the beast's starboard hull below them. "I never thought I'd see such a sight."

"You don't sound worried, sir."

The captain scoffed. "Even if we fell face-first over the *Xerses'* side, we'd hit the water on a nasty angle, but I'm sure the ship would right itself."

As the corvette's commanding officer, Amir agreed. "I'm sure, too, sir. In theory. But I'd prefer to leave that untested."

"Agreed. It's impressive what the *Xerses* can do. Let's leave it at that and trust them to do what President Hadi pays them for."

Amir smirked. "All it took was money to build it. And all this for profit while our nation hungers, thirsts, and burns."

"Don't blame the mercenaries. They're trying to help."

Staring straight down at the water, Amir ignored his boss and sought a status of his ship's safety. "Tactical center, bridge. Mark the list!"

Over the loudspeaker, the *Tarantul's* executive officer replied. "Thirty-two degrees, sir."

"Very well, tactical center." Half-hoping to keep the corvette from toppling by shifting his weight to its far side, he stepped to the port windows. Walking uphill, he labored.

When he reached the bridge's far side and stuck his head through the open portal, his ship's skin masked the transport vessel's semi-submerged port hull.

The executive officer gave an update. "The *Xerses* reports complete surfacing. It holds four hundred and twelve tons, or approximately eighty-two percent of our weight in its cargo bed, according to its pressure sensors. It's going to try rotating us and moving us side to side in all directions as a test."

The *Tarantul's* commander wondered if his corvette had ever been weighed on a scale. "Very well, tactical center."

During thirty minutes of subtle maneuvers at imperceptible speed, the *Xerses* held the *Tarantul* in place with gravity. Shaped for holding rounded submarine hulls, the hydraulic presses remained retracted–those on the starboard side bearing the weight of the list, with those on the port side remaining unused.

Amir's global phone vibrated in his pocket, and he answered the video call from a junior officer on the fantail.

Looking into the small screen, Amir saw streaming video of

the *Tarantul's* stern. His corvette's twin propellers rested three-quarters out of the water, with the port side's blades higher than those of the starboard. "Thank you."

He hung up and put his phone away.

"Bridge, tactical center. The *Xerses* is complete with testing. The boarding team awaits your command to rehearse the boarding."

"Tactical center, bridge. Verify that all hands are clear of the weather decks."

"Bridge, tactical center. Topside watches are secured. All hands are clear of the weather decks."

"Very well, tactical center. Announce the drill to the crew and order the boarding team to rehearse the drill."

The executive officer's voice rang from loudspeakers. "Commencing boarding drill. All hands remain clear of doorways and hatches to the weather decks. Commencing boarding drill."

After an eerie moment of silence, Amir heard clicking and clunking of grapnels clamping his hull, and taut ropes appeared beside the port windows. Then four raiders in black wetsuits appeared outside the bridge.

Each commando held a line in one hand and a weapon in the other. The leader's weapon of choice was a megaphone, and he used his words convincingly. "We're retaking the ship for the legitimate Yemeni government. Open a window or we'll shoot our way in."

Obeying the soldier, Amir crossed the deck. As he scanned his full view, he saw a hovercraft flying in front of the bridge, aiming cameras at him.

He reached the window, opened it, and greeted a junior officer from the army's Special Security Forces. "What if they're waiting with firearms?"

The commando's leader was gruff. "Then we'll turn the bridge into a tomb."

"Understood. Where are your other men?"

"Four more on the forecastle. Six more on the fantail. The rest in reserve."

Amir glanced downward and saw a dozen commandoes standing knee-deep upon the *Xerses'* tilted port hull. They aimed rifles upward, seeking human targets. "Got it. And you're not worried about any resistance?"

"Worried?" The young commando tossed his megaphone to a comrade awaiting on the *Xerses*. Then he grabbed a rifle from his back. "If they try to stop me, they'll be doing me a favor. I'd enjoy shooting those thieves."

Amir stepped back. "Come on in, then."

The commandoes entered the bridge and made concise steps towards relevant stations. One took over a communications suite while one guarded the door. The others watched over the crew, whom they ushered into a corner.

After the soldiers established control of the engine room, tactical center, and bridge, they secured from the drill. Reversing of the feigned hostilities brought the exercise to an end, and as slowly as it had risen, the transport ship sank again.

When the *Tarantul's* mass was returned to the water, Amir waited until the *Xerses* repositioned and surfaced a mile away.

His executive officer prodded him. "Bridge, tactical center. The *Xerses* is surfaced and ready to answer all bells. I recommend tying up the fishing vessel for towing and getting started."

Two hours later, Amir ushered his ancient Russian-built *Tarantul* corvette warship forward at full speed.

He restricted his propulsion below an all-out flank-speed sprint so the *Xerses* could keep pace. He also wanted to avoid swamping the fishing boat he towed carrying MICA missiles to use as defenses against the Houthi's Styx missiles.

The propulsion restriction, the towing, and the dependencies upon two other ships weighed on Amir. To finish what the *Wraith* had started by hobbling the Houthi corvette with slow-kill torpedo bomblets required intricate planning.

Sinking the *Tarantul's* sister ship would have been easy. The *Xerses* could handle the task with railguns or torpedoes, or the two Styx missiles remaining aboard his corvette could do it.

However, with a return to Aden as his goal, he needed cannon power to support ground troops. Since the mercenaries' rented railguns were temporary assets, he wanted the three-inch gun from the Houthi warship to permanently double the firepower of his *Tarantul* and his navy.

Having considered a ship's capture the stuff of centuries past, of wooden ships and iron men, Amir had failed to conceive the idea. But his commodore and the crafty commanders of the Frenchman's fleet had pounced upon and started planning the opportunity as the first humanitarian crates had landed on Nishtun's pier.

Since his crew had trained for defeating Somali pirates–with his older veterans having boarded the hostile speedboats of maritime bandits–he knew the dangers of taking an enemy ship. But seizing a five-hundred-ton corvette was a higher echelon of brashness than he'd ever attempted.

Pirates came in small groups–not corvette crews of fifty trained in repelling borders.

Therefore, he needed the army.

After rapid negotiations, his boss had convinced the ground forces to put a squadron of commandos on the *Xerses*.

Alone with Captain Damari in a corner of the *Tarantul's* bridge, he shared his thoughts. "We're chasing a wounded bird with every naval asset we've got."

"If you approached it alone, it would be a suicide mission."

"A one-for-one exchange?"

"It still has four Styx missiles to our two. Despite its flooding and propulsion limits, which we're only guessing about, it has a firepower advantage over this ship."

Thinking of the two Styx missiles aboard the *Osa*, which drove off the *Tarantul's* beam, Amir saw parity in anti-ship missiles, and a complete advantage over the Houthi vessel when considering the *Xerses*, its MICA missile control, its torpedoes, and its railguns.

For four hours, Amir chased the wounded Houthi corvette,

which a friendly drone tracked as it lumbered towards distant Aden at a six-knot crawl.

When his first lookout called out the target's masts over the horizon, Amir glanced at Damari. "Sir, I request permission to order the *Xerses* to submerge."

"Order the *Xerses* to submerge."

"Order the *Xerses* to submerge, aye, sir." Amir raised his voice. "Tactical center, bridge, order the *Xerses* to submerge."

Moments later, the executive officer's voice issued from the loudspeaker. "Bridge, tactical center. The *Xerses* acknowledges the order to submerge. The *Xerses* is submerging."

"Very well, tactical center. To all ships in the task force except the *Xerses*, come to all-stop."

While his ship, the *Osa*, and the fishing vessel behind him glided to a dead stop, he waited two hours for the *Xerses* to slide unseen underneath the Houthi.

Although the transport ship remained beyond his horizon, Amir oozed anticipation when he heard the Australian crew's translator through an overhead speaker. "We're surfacing under the target now. We're matching its speed of six-point-two knots over ground."

The *Tarantul's* executive officer affirmed the communication. "Bridge, tactical center, I've confirmed that the *Xerses* has established radio contact on our encrypted net. You heard the rest."

"Very well, tactical center. Do you have a video feed yet?"

"Not yet, sir. Just voice and data with the *Xerses*. Give it about thirty seconds."

"Very well, tactical center." During a long half minute, Amir glared through binoculars at the masts of the Houthi warship. Then a video feed appeared on a display.

"Bridge, tactical center. I'm streaming the video to you now."

"I see it, tactical center." Amir recognized the perspective of a hovercraft in front of the Houthi corvette's bridge. As with the rehearsal, the target listed hard to starboard atop the *Xerses*, hidden from view below.

But unlike the rehearsal, the men on the tilted bridge were

terrified, desperate, and willing to fight back. Some of them lifted firearms and then collapsed as rifle rounds broke through the windows and cut down the resistance.

After the first men fell, the remaining Houthi crew threw up their arms, went to their knees, and let the commandos board. Controlled pandemonium overtook the bridge, but within tens of seconds, the Yemeni commandos had the Houthi rebels assembled in a corner, kneeling, and with their arms bound.

Then minutes ticked away with little visible action. Status reports trickled in, updating Amir of the boarding party's incremental successes.

They secured the bridge.

They secured the radio room.

They secured the propulsion spaces.

They detained the Houthi rebels in the crew's mess.

Finally, the report came explaining the corvette's readiness for its new crew.

Amir recommended to Damari to have the *Tarantul*, the towed fishing vessel, and the *Osa* to approach the captured ship.

Half an hour later, the *Tarantul* corvette drifted beside its twin, which bobbed after the *Xerses* had released it.

Unsure when to silently declare victory, Amir gazed through the window at his prize.

Captain Damari disrupted his peace. "That's a bloody bridge."

Amir had avoided tallying the carnage. "Probably."

"I'm not letting you command it."

Amir questioned the change in plans. "Sir?"

"I'll take command. You don't need to see the gore."

Amir scoffed. "Neither do you."

"True. But I outrank you, and rank has its responsibilities."

"Sir, I can't ask you."

"It's not a request."

To prove himself worthy of warriorship, Amir wanted to test his mettle by absorbing the aftermath of a slaughter. "Then I'll go with you. My exec can handle this ship."

"As you wish."

Twenty minutes later, Amir road a skiff between corvettes.

Seated beside him, Damari reached into his windbreaker's breast pocket and withdrew his phone. "This will be interesting."

"Why?"

"It's Commander Hussein."

Amir checked his memory to align the name to a rebel *Osa* patrol craft's commanding officer. Unless Hussein intended to threaten, warn, or negotiate, his call to their commodore suggested teamwork.

Within half a minute, Damari slid his phone into his pocket. "We have another *Osa* in our ranks."

"Hussein's decided to join us?"

Damari nodded.

"Did he say why?"

"He didn't have to. Best to leave it unspoken."

Amir found his commodore's instant forgiveness moving. "He found his courage."

"Yes. He found his courage."

"And in a single day, we've doubled our fleet's firepower."

"Assuming we can salvage this corvette. Let's see what we have."

Another twenty minutes later, Amir set foot aboard the captured corvette and followed his commodore to the bridge.

When he entered the rapid battle's untouched scene, he smelled the sweetish coppery scent of blood mingled with the stench of feces from the dead.

Remaining where they'd died, the corpses showed bullet holes, lifeless eyes, and expressions of surprise and horror. Window shards covered portions of the deck, as did patterns of red splatter.

Standing in a pool of crimson, Amir gagged and coughed.

Beside him, Captain Damari looked pale. "Are you regretting

your decision to join me?"

Honest, Amir nodded. "But there's no turning back now."

"Very well, then. Grab the deck log."

Obeying, Amir left bloody boot prints as he walked to the book.

"Annotate in the deck log that I take control of this ship, the *Khalid*, for the legitimate Yemeni Navy, loyal to President Hadi. I take command of this vessel."

Amir finished writing. "You have command of this vessel."

"Very well. Let's reform the task force and get back to Socotra."

Fighting nausea, Amir accepted war's horrors and understood why men called it hell. He wanted to take his family home to Aden and live out his quiet years free of violence.

But to accomplish that, he needed to create more corpses.

CHAPTER 4

Captain Radwan Fayed tasted his pepper-flavored *shammah* smokeless tobacco and spat saliva into a gray plastic bottle. He then sealed the lid, wiped his lips, and strode across the bridge of his flagship, the *La Fayette*-class frigate, *Makkah*.

Shorter in stature, capable, but lacking the network for further advancement, his chief of staff, Commander Omar Hijazi, squinted at the makeshift spittoon. "On the bridge, sir?"

Fayed knew that chewing tobacco was illegal in the Royal Saudi Navy and in every square meter of his homeland kingdom. "I appreciate your candor, as always. When you become the commodore, you can enjoy a few indulgences. Until then, I suggest you don't mention it. Get me a helmet."

Obliging, Hijazi stepped to a cubby and grabbed the requested equipment. He returned to the commodore and extended the Kevlar protection.

Fayed slipped the inseam band around his skull and then adjusted the chin strap. After several steps, he checked a display showing his task force's formation.

Trailed by the replenishment ship, *Boraida*, and the patrol boat, *Faisal*, preceded by the old but capable *Badr*-class corvettes, *Hitteen* and *Tabuk*, and surrounded by three airborne anti-submarine helicopters, the Saudi Arabian frigate knifed through the Persian Gulf.

The unwelcomed presence on the tactical display was the presumed Iranian submarine that had exposed a periscope while lurking ahead of a Saudi natural gas tanker moving westerly through the Strait of Hormuz.

Hormuz.

It weighed upon the commodore's shoulders.

A stifling chokepoint twenty-one nautical miles wide at its tightest, watched by Oman, policed by Iran, and monitored by countless stakeholders to protect a third of the world's natural gas and a quarter of the world's oil while passing through its risky confines.

The bane of all maritime enemies of the Persians.

Fayed both hated and loved passing through the strait. It invited the dangerous Iranians, slowing his trek but offering him a chance to outsmart his enemies.

Foregoing further indulgence in his dirty habit, he emptied his mouth of tobacco and dropped the wad into a trashcan. "If we were at war with the Persians, what would you recommend?"

Hijazi cleared his throat. "I'd send the *Makkah* towards the datum of the sighted periscope to provide anti-air missile defense. And I'd send a helicopter from the *Boraida* to prosecute the submarine, protected by the *Makkah* from being shot down by shore-based Iranian anti-air missiles."

"Is that all?"

"I'd also move the *Hitteen* to *Tabuk* into a triangular formation around the *Makkah*, with their sonar systems active, to harass the submarine. But I'd keep the corvettes four miles away, to avoid making them easy targets. I'd keep the *Makkah's* sonar silent to listen for a torpedo launch."

"Anything else?"

In thought, the short commander stared through the windows at Oman's isolated village of one thousand people, Kumzar, backed by the low mountains of the Musandam Peninsula. "I'd dedicate a second helicopter to the task, which would require launching a third to provide protection to the *Boraida*."

"But we're not at war. So, given current events and our normal animosity with those Persian bastards, does your answer change?"

"Agreed, we're not at war, though sometimes I wish we'd declare it and get on with it."

"If only diplomacy were so simple."

"Given our high-tension relations with Iran, I'd offer the same recommendation except with weapons tight. I would not authorize an attack unless the Persians launch a weapon at our civilian tanker or one of our naval assets."

Fayed grunted. "Aggressive. Too much so, unfortunately."

Dismayed, the chief of staff protested. "How so? Crossing the channel? Violating the international laws allowing safe passage? The Iranians demand that all submarines be surfaced in transit, yet they keep theirs submerged in the strait liberally."

Prone to enjoy teachable moments highlighting his vaulted wisdom, the commodore formulated his thoughts. "One of the hardest challenges we face is outlining our rules of engagement. Your answer would have been perfect a week ago. But after the mercenary Fleet surprised the Persians with heavyweight torpedoes, their submarines are still staggering from the blow. Although misguided in their doctrine, the Iranians are human, and they're suffering basic human emotions–pain, grief, fear..."

Trying to protect his pride, the chief of staff crossed his arms and scowled. "I get that, sir, but they're professionals. They have sound standard operating procedures, and they follow them. I don't hold them susceptible to the whims of emotion."

The comment disappointed Fayed. A self-proclaimed excellent judge of character, he thought he could improve Hijazi's perspective. "You're judging hastily. Emotions are powerful, and they alter human behavior. At the moment, every commander of an Iranian submarine feels a deep sting. A prudent warrior avoids agitating a wounded enemy unless he's ready to engage in unrestricted warfare."

"I see where you're going... you will do something more reserved, I assume, sir?"

"The Iranians are disciplined. Don't you think the gift of an exposed periscope is reason to suspect a trap?"

"I'd considered it, but..."

"But what?"

"Like you noted, we're not at war. So, I wanted the training opportunity. Our fleet needs the practice against Iranian submarines, and I thought that shooing this one away from our tanker would improve our readiness and remind Iran of our willingness to challenge them."

As he listened, Fayed sought chinks in his subordinate's argument. "They've just lost submarines, they're doing everything possible to avoid visible military involvement on the Arabian Peninsula, and they won't be starting a war now."

"So, what will you do, sir?"

"I'll order all commanders to adhere to normal operating procedures. We pass through the strait, pretending not to notice."

"You'll do nothing?"

"Yes. Doing nothing is an option often dismissed too hastily. In this case, I suspect a trap. Perhaps they have another submarine nearby, or some shore-based surprise. I think a wise admiral among their ranks realized they needed a success–no matter how small–to regain his fleet's composure. Toying with us, even if at the cost of only our embarrassment, would suffice."

"So, nothing it is, then."

"Yes. Pass the order."

Hijazi turned and walked across the bridge.

Fayed watched his chief of staff meander through the white-shirted people staffing the combatant.

A quarter of the men stooped over a table verifying the *Makkah's* accurate position within the tight channel while another quarter aimed their naked eyes in all directions around the frigate's surroundings. The remaining sailors stood at the consoles and controls of their stations.

When Hijazi reached the ship's commander, a husky man with shoulders as large as his ego, he held a hushed but rapid conversation. Frowning, the big man shook his head and led the chief of staff across the deck and back to his boss.

Fayed greeted the *Makkah's* commander. "I assumed you wish to discuss my order?"

The husky commander's voice was gritty. "Do nothing, sir?"

Careful to coddle the man's ego, the commodore considered himself skilled in handling arrogant but incompetent underlings. The husky officer had earned his rank through political connections, and Fayed would set him to pasture at his first opportunity. "I respect your desire for action. It's the right instinct, but I believe they're trying to trick us into starting hostilities."

"You'd risk an entire tanker on that, sir? Maybe more?"

"It's a stunt. They're fishing for us to make a mistake and embarrass ourselves. The responsibility is on my shoulders, commander."

"So be it, then. The *Makkah* will comply with the task force commander's direction." The husky officer walked away.

The chief of staff leaned into his boss. "You're going to let him have the last word, sir?"

Fayed snorted. "Yes. "

"It's disrespectful, the way he talks to you."

"He's incapable of respecting anyone. That's his curse to bear. I'll have none of it, and I know how to manage him."

"I don't know how you stay so calm. I would have... well, I'm not entirely sure how I'd treat an underling with that attitude."

"It's very simple. It's a matter of compartmentalizing emotions. I don't care about his respect because he'll never give it. All I want is his compliance, which I have and will keep."

"We're back to emotions, sir."

Fayed sensed the apparent disconnect. "You're comparing the warranted emotions of a defeated Iranian submarine fleet to the unwarranted emotions I may be tempted to feel in a conversation. You have to express the former and suppress the latter. Make sure you know the difference."

"You're a wise man, sir."

The commodore let the compliment linger.

Ten minutes later, the tanker passed the periscope sighting's datum. Another fifteen minutes elapsed, and the massive ship carrying natural gas passed abeam the *Makkah*. After an hour had passed since Fayed's decision of restraint, the tanker drifted into the western horizon.

As he watched the huge vessel escape potential danger, the

commodore heard a report from the frigate's tactical center over the loudspeaker. "Hostile speedboats! Three sighted. Tracking as targets Master forty-nine, fifty, and fifty-one in our datalink."

Preferring to stand far from his commodore, the *Makkah's* husky commander issued his order from across the bridge. "All ahead full. I authorize the violation of local speed limits."

Fayed raised his voice. "This is the task force commander. I authorize the violation of local speed limits for all ships."

The husky officer crossed the bridge. Keeping his eyes on the closest speedboat, he queried his commodore. "It looks like we agree on getting out of here as quickly as possible."

"Indeed."

"What about weapons?"

"You've staffed each small and medium caliber weapon, have small arms shooters ready, and hoses prepared, do you not?"

The *Makkah's* husky commander seemed annoyed. "Like all ships in the task force, yes I do, sir."

"The weapons teams have standing orders to withhold fire until an enemy would shoot at us, correct?"

"That's what I'm challenging."

"You didn't challenge when we briefed this possibility earlier."

"I didn't think they'd really have the audacity to attack us, sir. Now that they are, if you're going to keep weapons tight on the other ships, may I at least defend my own frigate?"

"By shooting first? No. Stick to my orders."

Through a deep anger and haughtiness, the husky officer failed to hide his feelings. "But sir, those ships will be in rocket-propelled grenade range soon. I don't want one landing on my bridge because I was too afraid to shoot first."

Fayed squashed the one-man rebellion. "Do I look afraid?"

The husky officer gave a sideways glance. "No, sir."

"I would say that I look like the former commanding officer of a frigate half this one's size who withstood a three-speedboat attack by Houthi rebels in the Red Sea."

"Sir, I don't pretend to know your history–"

The commodore recalled lessons from an older frigate in the kingdom's western fleet. "Let me educate you. When I defeated a Houthi rebel gunboat attack in the Red Sea, I sank two of them but lost three men to the third as it exploded by my stern."

"I studied that scenario. Pardon my critique, sir, but I remember that you opened fire immediately. It sounds like you're proving my point for our present situation."

"Except that I was fighting Houthi suicide bombers. Put those binoculars to your face and tell me what you see about the crew on the nearest speedboat."

Sighing, the husky officer obeyed. "They're Iranian."

"How do you know?"

"Their uniforms are Iranian. Their flag's Iranian. Their ships are Iranian. I recognize them from the Revolutionary Guards Navy."

"Have you ever heard of an Iranian naval suicide attack?"

"No, but I have heard of their grenade attacks."

Fayed doubted the commander cared about anything more than his own hide and personal advancement. The *Makkah's* foolish commander would do nothing to shape the world. "A grenade attack against a four-thousand-ton warship? If it comes to it, and anyone from your crew is hurt, it will be on my conscience."

"That doesn't rest well with me, sir. There are many ways to nurse a troubled conscience And if it doesn't come to violence, you'll look brilliant for having guessed that it's a bluff."

Fayed judged that he'd given enough leeway. "You can obey me, or I can give command of your ship to my chief of staff. It's your decision. He's more than capable."

The shortish chief of staff blushed with the compliment while the
husky officer replied. "No, sir. I've said my peace and will obey your orders."

Fayed overheard reports from the corvettes and from the frigate upon which he stood. Also watching through the windows, he saw the speedboats spread out, one each gunning their engines towards each of the three Saudi combatants.

One of the boats traced a slow circle around the *Makkah*, but its crew trained no weapons against the frigate.

Yielding to curiosity, Fayed grabbed binoculars and lifted the optics to his face. As he watched the speedboat, he saw men with cameras taking pictures and videos–a minor success in reconnaissance, but a win nonetheless–for the downtrodden Iranian fleet.

Sensing the tension waning among the *Makkah's* bridge team, Fayed took his victory lap across the deck plates and stopped beside the husky officer. "Looks like they're just gathering intelligence. That was their game all along."

"My accusation of hedging your bet still stands, sir. You risked lives unnecessarily so that you could look brilliant after winning a coin toss."

Fayed considered relieving the man of command, but then he backed off. Though annoying, the *Makkah's* commander was controllable. "I assure you, commander. When the time comes, I will know when to attack."

The haughty officer remained silent, yielding the last word.

Fayed returned to his chief of staff's side. "There's no way they'd risk hostilities now. It's the worst time for them."

"I'm glad you knew the difference, sir. I admit I was unsure."

"Be sure the next time. Study this encounter. I'll be available for questions if you wish to learn more."

"Yes, sir. Thank you."

Fayed prepared to brag to his Yemeni counterpart about his successful passage of Hormuz. "Raise Captain Damari on a satellite phone. I'd like to inform him that we're safely through Hormuz and on schedule to join him in Socotra."

CHAPTER 5

Standing under the *Goliath's* dome, with half the red emergency lighting bulbs pulled to reduce the chance of an Iranian drone's camera seeing her, Danielle absorbed her newest revelation.

Britain's Royal Navy had provided her an invisible layer of protection she'd never appreciated.

Six months ago, when she'd commanded the *Westminster*, the Crown had served as a brand name with shielding. Any actor who would have threatened her, threatened a mighty nation and faced the deterring promise of retribution.

Working for Renard, she feared that his branding as the world's first and only mercenary submarine fleet left her exposed. Instead of offering a shield, the reputation surrounding the Frenchman's fleet placed a target on her back.

And the Persians stood first in line to attack.

The commanding officer of the Iranian *Kilo*-class submarine which pinned her atop an underwater mountain was proving his relentlessness. During a tense six hours, the Persian submarine had cut a slow perimeter around the submerged peak.

Six long hours.

Crawling within scant miles of the *Specter* and *Goliath* in a death-standoff, the Iranian submarine held the mercenary vessels hostage.

Danielle struggled to match the patience of the career submarine officers around her. She sighed. "Shit, Mike. Do you submariners always test each other's stamina like this?"

The balding executive officer smirked. "The first one to flinch loses." His demeanor downshifted to match the situation's gravity. "But I've never been through anything quite like this."

"Have you been through anything even remotely like this?"

He released a sad laugh. "No."

She recalled her standoff against a Turkish submarine. "I have. But everything I learned from that encounter is useless here."

"Agreed. Against the Turks, everything was exposed. You knew exactly where each other was. Bloody hell, you were talking to each other. Now, both parties know we're within one-for-one exchange range, but neither party can generate targeting data."

She showed off her growing undersea knowledge. "And the Iranians can maneuver freely. If we make a peep, we'll give away targeting data. We'd give a bearing with a pretty good idea of range and speed, since they know we're dead in the water on this mountain."

"You're talking like a submariner now."

She wanted to declare herself a submariner, and she had the right. But she opted instead to seek wisdom from the veterans. "At what point do we tell ourselves the *Kilo's* given up?"

Answering through a display, Jake exhaled a weary sigh. "Good question. Pierre suggested twelve hours, but I'm already losing my patience. We haven't heard a peep from it in almost two hours."

Danielle recognized Jake's allusion to an active sonar emission both their ships had intercepted. "You said you weren't sure if that transmission came from the *Kilo* or one of its drones."

"No, but either way, it meant they were still looking for us. Now, I'm not so–"

A deep boom hammered Danielle's skull, and the deck shook. As she staggered backwards, she half expected the dome to collapse on her. "What the hell?"

Taylor pressed his palm between her shoulder blades to balance her. "Shit! That was loud."

"No kidding. They just command-detonated a torpedo!" His voice tense, Jake added the burning question. "But how close was it? Was it a guess, or was it targeted?"

Taylor replied. "No idea, but that's a damned good way to pry us off this mountain. They've got enough torpedoes to do this all day."

Jake sounded calmer than the moments after the detonation. "But they can only do it five more times before having to back off and reload."

Taylor drew Jake deeper into their submariner banter. "Reloading isn't a noise farm like in the old days, but we'd still be able to hear them reloading unless they withdraw. Hydraulic valves clicking. Pneumatic drivers."

"Yeah, and I think this commander would be smart enough to open range to do it."

"You think he'll take five more shots and then back off to reload?"

"It's possible."

Inherent in the men's talk was the assumption of staying hidden. Danielle refused to accept the assumption without a challenge. "Both of you are ignoring the chance that they'll actually hit us."

A surface wave reached down and pushed the hovering tandem downward. Fearing a keel would scrape the mountain, Danielle held her breath, but seconds of silence proved that nothing metallic had hit anything rocky.

Jake protested her prior comment. "I admit they don't have to get terribly close to damage us, but it's like looking for a needle..."

A second explosion erupted, more deafening than the first. Danielle's tailbone smacked the deck, and she sprained her wrist softening her backwards landing. With the dome seeming to quiver with aftershocks, she stayed seated to assess her world.

Jake's howl echoed in her head. "Oh shit!"

As she regained her awareness, she saw the balding man's legs sprawled next to her.

Her executive officer groaned. "Dani?"

After he'd used her ancient nickname from their days at the Britannia Royal Naval College, she wondered how hard his head had hit the deck. "Yeah?"

"Making sure you're alive."

Other than cooling fans and the background bustle of sailors recovering on the *Specter*, the dome fell silent. The shock shook loose a memory of stock training footage with a warhead detonating five-hundred yards abeam a mothballed submarine.

In her memory of the film, she saw equipment the size of automobiles rising and falling with the deck plates as cameras recorded the blast shaking the engine room. The uninhabited vessel had survived, but the point was riveted in her mind.

No human could withstand such a shock without shattered legs–or worse.

She wondered how close the latest Iranian warhead had come to breaking her bones. "I'm alive. How about you?"

"Nothing broken or bleeding. You?"

"Same here. Nothing broken or bleeding." As a matter of pride, Danielle outpaced Taylor in rolling to her feet. She grabbed a railing for support and extended her other hand to him.

He accepted the assistance and stood. "That was close."

Before Danielle could answer, Jake's venom coursed through the speakers. "Assholes! That's it. We're fighting our way out of this."

She'd heard about Jake's anger, but this was her first witnessing of it. She hoped it wouldn't get her killed. "That's a great thought, but how?"

Jake scaled back on his emotions, and his voice was ice. "I've been considering something, and now I want to do it. We're about six and half miles from Vlak Bank. You let me go, surface, and make a run for the bank. Then you crash dive onto that bank and hide again."

"Just like I did here, only without you?"

"Yes. I'll be busy hunting."

She saw flaws. "I'd be an easy target, and you'd be hunting from a disadvantage."

"Unless I can force a mistake."

She doubted he could. If it were possible, she believed he already should have tried it. "How so?"

"I'll use a drone as bait."

Wondering why he'd withheld his idea until now, she folded her arms. "That's a new tactic for me."

"I'll launch a drone in swim mode, real quiet. Then I'll send it out in a circle around us like it's me hunting for the *Kilo*. It'll broadcast sounds like a *Scorpène*-class submarine. If the *Kilo* goes after it, runs from it, or shoots it, I'll get the info to shoot. And then I'll use a slow-kill."

She was suspicious of his confidence. "If it were that easy, we would've done that already."

"I didn't say it would be easy. I omitted the part where they'll probably hear me shooting and send a well-aimed torpedo at us. For me, that would suck. For you, you've got the speed to surface and run."

Exercising mental muscles she'd honed in the British fleet, she ran numbers through her head. "I'd be facing a sixteen-knot speed disadvantage against a U-SET 80 until it acquires me. Then life would get ugly, fast. That's about ten minutes to live if I'm three miles from the launch, and that *Kilo* could be closer than that."

Another explosion rattled the *Goliath's* dome, but Danielle held her balance. Farther than the prior torpedo attacks, the latest warhead gave the weakest jolt.

Jake shared his conclusion. "That one landed far away. That means it's random targeting. They have no idea where we are."

Danielle wanted her answer. "And we should keep it that way unless you can contradict my point about the *Goliath* blowing up."

Calming from his anger, Jake waved his palm. "Hear me out. I'd never put you in danger. As long as you can get to flank speed and then crash dive, you'll make it. I know the math doesn't work yet, but it will if you change the assumptions."

Although she recognized the American as senior, she considered herself his equal in a planning debate. She reverted to the terse ways which had served her in the Royal Navy. "Such as?"

Jake seemed receptive to her defiance. "Such as giving you a head start. I'll detach from you, you slip away on the outboards, and I'll deploy my drone. That's could take a couple hours, since I need to slip the drone away real quietly while you slip away real quietly."

She understood. "You didn't suggest this earlier because we weren't being torpedoed, but now you think it's worth the risk?"

"That's right."

Unfolding her arms, she agreed. "Okay. Let's do it."

Jake challenged himself. "You're sure? Part of the reason I never mentioned this was that you bear most of the risk. It's easy for me to plan a getaway where someone else is the bait. Are you sure you're up to it?"

She caught the multiple nuances of his tone, and she suspected he was provoking her to a decision. Tempted to roar back with strength, she recalled her leadership training and stayed cool. "Me? Yeah. But give me a moment to consider my crew."

Her reaction caught him off guard. "Uh... sure."

Without asking permission, she muted and darkened the senior commander.

The balding executive officer opined. "I see you've still got that audacity I remember from Dartmouth."

"Now's not the time for pandering. If we screw this up, we're dead. All of us."

Taylor's face darkened. "I understand the stakes."

She sighed but withheld the apology she thought she might owe. "I know. What do you think?"

"I think he's testing us."

The comment stirred her ire and curiosity. "How so? Our courage? My courage?"

"That, and our brainpower." He paused, glanced upward in thought, and then softened his tone. "But not in a nasty way. I think he wants to make sure that we're thinking this through before we sign up for it."

Her frustration growing, she snapped. "If you see something I don't, spit it out."

"Okay. While he was talking, he left out an important detail. If we slip away quietly, and then he does the hunting, what's to make the *Kilo* shoot at us?"

In her old world, ships didn't slip away undetected without an effort. Under the surface, submarines were invisible until heard. She saw the problem. "We'll need to make noise intentionally."

"Correct."

She mulled over the implications. "He assumed we'd surface and sprint to the closest reef, which would provide the noise, but he didn't mention the option where we stay quiet and keep slipping away unheard."

"Correct again."

"Why didn't he mention that?"

Taylor scratched the back of his neck. "Good question."

"We don't have time for games." She spun back to the monitor and invoked the *Specter's* commander. "Jake?"

"I'm here."

"You didn't mention that if I can slip away, I'll have to make noise intentionally to draw the *Kilo* to me. If I don't surface and sprint but instead decide to slip away quietly, I could get away, but I'd be abandoning you to a one-on-one standoff."

Jake smirked. "You wouldn't do that."

"Of course not. But if I can slip away, you certainly can too, in the quieter ship."

"I assumed that if you try to slip away, there's a low but significant probability that you'll be heard. The *Goliath* has too many jagged edges and moving parts to reposition itself in complete stealth."

"Like opening my hydraulic rams to let you go? If only one of the twenty-four are in a squeaky mood, we're screwed."

He nodded.

"Then why risk it at all? If I need to get away quietly, I may as well do it with you on my cargo bed."

"I was planning to draw the *Kilo* to me right here while you escaped."

She narrowed her eyes and folded her arms. "By making noise intentionally?"

Blushing, Jake looked downward and then back to Danielle. "You caught me. If the drone didn't get its attention, I was going to risk it myself. Guilty as charged."

"I'm not a bloody child, Jake. I'm a warrior, just like you. I won't place a colleague in unnecessary danger to save my own skin, and I demand that you show me the same respect!"

With gentle tremors and a distant boom, another Persian warhead detonated against the bank.

"Okay. Done. We'll do it your way."

Surprised she'd won a debate she wasn't aware of having entered, she lowered her arms. "My way? Slipping away together?"

"Sure. I've run the risks in my head a hundred times for both scenarios, and I can't make either one look better than the other. If you want to share the risk with me, so be it."

"Thanks?"

"No. I'll thank you if it works. Let's get moving now while that *Kilo's* still pounding the mountain."

"On my outboards?"

"Yes. Let's get rolling."

She turned her head. "Mike, go ahead. Maneuver us on the outboards straight towards Vlak Bank."

An hour later, the *Goliath's* commander dared to hope she'd escape without further conflict.

Jake interrupted her reflecting. "Let's risk using your main engines at four knots."

"You're sure?"

"If that *Kilo's* making laps around Twelve Mile Bank, it'll come back this way soon and hear us unless we get farther away. Let's open the distance while we can."

Knowing it was a gamble to stay slow and allow the *Kilo's* proximity or to increase speed and allow the greater noise, she considered the decision a coin toss. For lack of better intuition, she agreed with the *Specter's* commander. "I'll shift propulsion to my main engines and come to four knots."

Another forty minutes later, Jake ruined her hope. "Torpedo in the water!"

Danielle shouted. "Send me the data!"

"It's coming. Antoine's entering it into the system. We don't have a bearing drift, but it could be a good shot. It's too soon to tell."

She barked over her shoulder. "Why don't we hear it?"

Taylor deadpanned. "We don't have Antoine."

Facing the balding man, she frowned. "Have our sonar team listen down the bearing."

Holding a sound-powered phone to his cheek, he nodded. "I'm talking to the tactical center now. They're listening to our talk with Jake and are trying to hear the weapon."

Jake interjected his command. "Bring us to eight knots."

"Eight knots, aye, sir." She maneuvered her digits over a console. "I'll handle it, Mike. I'm coming to eight knots." She tapped keys, and the huge transport ship indicated its obedience.

After a minute of walking from the danger and driving geometry, Danielle saw in the display the answer she'd feared. The shot was accurate. She expected the *Specter's* commander to order a surfaced sprint.

But Jake ordered a different escape. "Keep us submerged and bring us to twenty knots."

Remembering the hated and foreign undersea limits of anaerobic propulsion, she eyed the *Specter's* commander. "I can only sustain that for a few minutes before my battery dies."

"I'll help with the *Specter*. I'm coming to twenty-one knots now to give you a boost. Watch your presses and make sure we're not ripping them off."

Tapping the keys to order the unsustainable submerged speed, she grimaced as an alarm highlighted excessive current from her ship's battery cells. "I'm making turns for twenty knots on the MESMA units and the ship's battery."

"I'm matching your turns plus one knot on the *Specter*."

Her nerves got the better of her. "Why not surface and sprint? That's what I'm built for."

Jake shook his head. "The waves. God only knows if it's better or worse up there than when we got driven below. And we can make it to Vlak Bank at twenty knots. This was a longer shot than the one that put us on Twelve Mile Bank. The weapon should run out of fuel."

She checked the icons and noticed their best estimate of a U-SET 80 torpedo's fuel capacity having the weapon fall short of catching them–barely. "By a whisker."

"I know. We'll double-check the solution in a few minutes. That's one reason I want to stay submerged–so we can slow for a minute and hear it."

"Slow? I don't like the sound of that."

"Okay, for half a minute. It won't take long, and it'll be worth the peace of mind. Remember, we can always surface and run if we have to. We'll do this in six minutes."

Danielle envisioned a dozen ways she could lose some or all of her propulsion and die, but she trusted the designers and builders of the battle-tested vessel.

Six minutes later Jake barked the order. "Okay, prepare to slow and turn to the right. We'll drive a little geometry on this."

"We're ready."

"On my mark, we both slow to eight knots. Three... two... one... mark!"

She tapped keys, and the *Goliath* obeyed.

"Bring us right sixty degrees. Use full rudder."

Announcing her actions, she angled her ship to the right and slowed it with the turn's water friction. "My rudder's right-full, slowing to eight knots. Coming to course one-zero-six."

"Antoine hears the weapon again. Hold on. Give him a minute."

As if her voice's volume could distract the French sonar guru, or if it might rupture her neck's pounding veins, she half-whispered. "You said half a minute."

"It was a figure of speech. He'll figure it out faster than–"

The French ace's voice echoed throughout the *Specter's* control room and into the *Goliath's* bridge. "I've resolved the incoming weapon's solution. I'm updating the system. You can accelerate again, please."

Turning his face from the *Goliath's* commander, Jake yelled over his shoulder. "Are we going to live, Antoine?"

"Yeah, yeah. I would've told you otherwise."

Jake faced his monitor. "You heard him. Come back to base course at twenty knots. I'll come to twenty-one again."

As the hostile torpedo's updated solution appeared on Danielle's display, she sighed in relief. The data showed they'd outpace the weapon's fuel reserves with a comfortable margin.

Four minutes later, her battery neared depletion, and her fathometer generated an alarm over the rising seafloor. "Jake, I–"

"Right. We're starting to cross over Vlak Bank. Bring us up to twenty-five meters. Use five-degrees up-angle."

Danielle worked her display. "Coming to twenty-five meters with a five-degree up-angle."

Jake sounded confident. "That weapon's about out of steam. We'll be safely on the other side of the bank–"

An explosion shook the deck plates under Danielle's feet, and she collapsed to her hip. Thankful her tailbone had escaped a second impact, she checked on her executive officer. "Mike?"

The balding officer was still standing, but his voice carried pain. "I'm alive. I was leaning forward when... I guess that was a command-detonation of the incoming weapon."

Concerned he wasn't helping her, she forced herself up and saw her executive officer curled forward coddling his midsection. "You okay, Mike?"

"Maybe I bruised my ribs. I don't know. But I'll be fine. I'll get on the phone and check on the crew."

She faced the *Specter's* commander. "How's your crew?"

His forehead bleeding from a fresh gash, Jake looked like he'd lost a boxing match. "Better than me, I hope. Damn." He turned his head and yelled. "Antoine, was that the incoming torpedo?"

"Yes. We've escaped."

Jake kept looking away. "Henri, you okay?"

"I've had worse... I think."

"Check on the crew."

Danielle glared at Jake's wound. "You're bleeding pretty bad. You might need stitches."

A young man appeared next to the *Specter's* commander and pressed a rag against his forehead.

"I've had worse." Jake reached for the cloth and dismissed his crewman. "Thank you, Julien."

Danielle sought her next move. "We need to surface and charge both our batteries, Jake. It's going to be rough up there."

"We'll be fine. That was a tail chase shot because we were opening distance from that *Kilo*. It won't catch us again after you surface us and drive us away."

"I'll take care of it. I'm surfacing us now." She lowered her gaze to her console.

Jake chuckled.

As the seas rocked her bridge and then translucent light broke through her windows, Danielle couldn't resist asking. "What's so funny?"

"If I ever meet the bastard commanding that *Kilo*, I'm shaking his hand. He set up a perfect ambush against us and did everything right. Shit, if I'm ever ready to retire, I'll ask Pierre to recruit him as my replacement."

Danielle wasn't as forgiving. "Can you picture an Iranian submarine commander taking orders from a woman? I'd be senior to him."

Jake chuckled. "No."

"Good. Hold off on those plans for now."

CHAPTER 6

Alone in his stateroom, Jake rolled onto his rack. As a passenger aboard the surfaced *Goliath*, he enjoyed minimal managerial duties over his submarine.

This mission included more quiet moments than any campaign he'd undergone with the mercenary fleet, and when relaxing, he explored topics to satiate his philosophical curiosity.

From his work on his Master of Divinity degree, he'd generated a lengthy reading list about mankind's existence. He picked up his phone and thumbed to his furthest location in NT Wright's *Simply Christian*. As he probed the book's treatment of humanity's origins, some of the arguments resonated with him, but the book was leaving him wanting more knowledge.

Unsure how to judge the text, he was pushing through one of its final chapters when he heard a knock on his door.

Henri's muffled voice carried a playful tone. "Hey, boss?"

"Yeah? Come in."

The French mechanic entered and closed the door. "A few of the guys and I wish to play a joke on Danielle."

Smelling a lengthy conversation, Jake set aside his book. "Really? Nothing could possibly go wrong with one warship's crew playing a joke on another's. Do tell."

Henri scooted the guest chair next to his commander and sat. "Not that type of joke."

"Not what type?"

Searching for a word, the Frenchman gestured. "I don't recall the term in English." He studied the deck plates while accessing his long-term memory. "Ah. Not a prank! A joke, but not a prank."

Jake was dubious. "You mean, we're going to call her up and

tell her a joke? All the fun will be in the words… not in anyone's deeds–deeds that could go awry?"

"More or less, within poetic license."

Between deadly encounters with rogue waves and Iranian submarines, boredom was the greatest enemy. Jake was willing to hear any option to break the monotony. "Just tell me what you have planned."

Fifteen minutes later, Jake was giddier than Henri and hoping to win a bet against three Frenchman. "I think she'll fall for it." At his captain's seat on the elevated conning platform, he glanced to either side.

To the right, the conniving Henri. "For the pride of America, you must do this impeccably, lest you be mocked by Frenchmen forevermore."

To the left, Remy's toad head, blushing with a bitten lip, remained silent.

Jake also smelled his wiry engineer's nicotine-soaked frame behind him. "You're sure it'll look real, Claude?"

"Trust me, Jake. But why should I be the expert?"

"I don't know. Because you're always smoking something."

"Bah. Call her. Let's go."

The *Wraith's* commander was unsure if his team were ready, but he succumbed to peer pressure. "Fine. Here goes." He tapped a key to hail the *Goliath's* commander.

Danielle answered. "*Goliath*."

Jake replied. "Well, hi there, *Goliath*. This is *Wraith*, as long as we're speaking about ourselves by ship titles in the third person."

She shrugged. "Just keeping it professional."

Jake saw his opening. "There's nothing wrong with relaxing the formality a bit, don't you think?"

She folded her arms. "Like how?"

"I don't know. After that close brush with the Iranians, I thought we could all use a break."

"We're on a tight schedule."

Jake recalled the team's location. Passing between Mozambique and Madagascar, they faced a significant distance to Socotra. "It won't slow us down a bit."

"What do you have in mind?"

"While the waves are gentle, I thought I'd head outside for an exchange and share some of our stash with your crew."

"What stash?"

Tucked against consoles offscreen, a giggling gaggle of Frenchmen hunched over a ceramic pipe. They needed three and a half hands to light the ground and pressed buds, and wiry Claude LaFontaine extended the smoking bowl to the *Wraith's* commander.

Jake lifted the lit smoking instrument to his face. "Thought we'd all enjoy a little hemp. You know, some ganga, weed, pot, marijuana, cannabis, herb.... What have you."

Expecting the scent of Claude's tobacco as a prop in the ruse, Jake slid ceramics into his mouth. The smell was odd, more earthy than he'd anticipated, but within the joke he was committed to the gesture. He drew in a mouthful of smoke.

Her eyes big, Danielle gasped.

Although Jake tried to avoid inhaling, the combusted particles caught in his throat, and he coughed. "What the hell?"

The three Frenchmen busted out laughing and waggled fingers at their commander as they abandoned him to his shame.

Between hacks, Jake voiced his burning question. "Is this weed for real?"

Smirking, Danielle answered. "So, a joke on the new girl gets turned around on the veteran."

Bending over to clear his airways, Jake hacked violently.

"Are you okay?"

He sat again and faced her. "Yeah. I think so."

Her smile grew, and her face blushed like a confession.

"Oh, no! You were in on this?"

She raised her arms. "Guilty. You got me. Or technically, I got you, though it was your team's idea."

He hated being the brunt, but he appreciated her newfound

camaraderie with the Frenchmen. "Shit. You and the boys got me. Whose idea was it?"

"Claude's, supposedly. And from what I know about him, that shouldn't surprise you."

"Not at all." As Jake recovered his breathing and his dignity, he realized he'd ingested cannabis. Although his HIV medicine functioned without interference from marijuana, his military mindset prevented him from using the drug. "Claude couldn't have planned out having weed just for a joke. This means he's had a personal stash, at least since Ascension."

She shrugged.

"I think we have fleet rules against this."

"Hey, not my ship, not my problem. Try to keep your crew from floating away in a puff of smoke." As she tried to withhold her laughing, she tapped her console, and the display went dark.

After recovering from the humiliation, Jake cornered Henri in the mess deck as the Frenchman refilled his coffee cup. "Well played, all of you."

"I was hoping you'd be a good sport. And if you're wondering about where we got the weed..."

"The question had crossed my mind."

"Claude uses it for low back pain."

"I didn't know he had problems."

"He hides it well, but you know how fidgety he is."

"Well, yeah."

"That's from the pain. I think he blew out a disk or two in his low back in a football game long ago... soccer game, rather."

"And that's why he has weed?"

Henri shrugged. "We all keep an eye on him, and he seems to keep his dosages to a minimum. I wouldn't worry about it. Weed is hardly the monster people try to make it out to be."

Jake raised a quieting palm. "I know. It's a growing industry in America. And I believe it can replace a lot of synthetic drugs, but I prefer to leave it off my ship."

"He could have kept it hidden from you indefinitely. You

know, there are edibles which are practically undetectable. Instead, he chose to expose his habit to you."

"How long..."

"I'd say, he's been using it for five years or so."

Jake accepted the outcome. "Shit. What's done is done. When you see him, let him know that I don't mind. Just keep doing his job the way he always has, and you guys keep watching him."

The next day, Jake propped his palms against the control room's central plotting table, and the chart showed his position between Kenya and the Seychelles.

He then toggled to a view of Yemen. Icons of surface combatants, submarines, aircraft, and shore-based missile and gun sites from half a dozen fighting factions dotted his chart.

The Houthi's salvaged and stolen vessels patrolled Yemen's largest port, al Hudaydah, the rebel-controlled city. To the southeast, on the other side of the Bab al-Mandab choke point issuing from the Red Sea, the Houthis had joined with the Southern Separatists in holding the port of Aden.

That was the mission's next phase–his phase–to return the proper Yemeni Navy to Aden.

Iranian submarines had retreated near Bandar Abbas for repairs and maintenance and for private ceremonies for the dead. Since the Persians weren't supposed to be fighting, they lacked the option for a public relations retaliation against the mercenary fleet.

But the most disturbing movements concerned a new actor.

Saudi Arabia.

Renard's fear of Riyadh and the Red Sea's longest coastline had prevented Jake from using the Suez Canal, although the Saudis were allied–in spirit–with the mercenaries as they fought the Iranians, the UAE, and the Houthis. They'd even led the coalition to back Yemen's recognized government against all rebel factions.

But with the United Arab Emirates recoiling from Cahill and Volkov's humanitarian missions, the Saudi admiralty sought to fill the void and extend its power around the entire Arabian Peninsula.

The Saudis were filling the vacuum.

Restricted to the Red Sea to the west and the Persian Gulf to the east, the Saudi kingdom was trapped. To achieve global shipping, their merchant marine force had to pass one of two choke points, either of which a bad actor could shut down.

Taking control of war-torn Yemen allowed the Saudis to extend their maritime reach without the risks and costs of passing through Bab al-Mandab or Hormuz. Fighting the Houthi provided the excuse for Riyadh to control Yemen's land, air, sea, and economy.

Cahill and Volkov had benefited from the Saudis' quiet observation of the mercenaries battling against the Emirates and their allies. With the former Saudi allies sidelined, Jake wasn't sure what to expect next.

But he knew that warships from varied factions with unstable alliances belonged far apart.

His chart showed the opposite.

A Saudi task force was about to arrive in Socotra, and despite his myriad speculations about it, the Saudi agenda was murky.

Of the four faces looking back at him from a segmented section of his screen, he expected only one of them to clarify the confusion. "We're all here, Pierre. Would you like to address the Royal Saudi Navy elephant in the room?"

Renard cleared his throat. "It's not entirely unplanned, but the Saudis have pushed their way into this, despite my hopes."

Jake pressed for insights. "What were you hoping for?"

"I'd hoped the Saudis would remain observers until we departed. In fact, I was hoping to educate them on our tactics against the Emiratis and Iranians as a gesture of goodwill for future business."

Jake chuckled. "And since they have no submarines, you'd hope to sell them automated Caesaron submarines, probably with a large commission from our Israeli friends?"

The Frenchman frowned. "We have no Israeli friends whom

I trust, other than Terry's wife. And you give me far too much credit for my foresight, although I won't begrudge you this pedestal you've propped me upon."

Jake folded his arms. "And I won't begrudge you your narcissistic fantasy that I hold you in high regard."

"You're far too kind. Now, as for this elephant, I urged President Hadi to hold off the Saudis until our departure from the region, but he has no other option."

"What the hell, Pierre? The Saudis are taking over, and we just got ambushed by the Iranians. That's a lot of chess pieces moving around the board."

The Frenchman seemed uncomfortable and adjusted his blazer. "Let me be candid. I owe you and Danielle an apology. I knew an Iranian *Kilo* submarine was unaccounted for, but I misread the evidence of its agenda. I never thought they'd send a submarine so far from home, but in hindsight, it was a perfect ambush point. I should've seen it coming. It's on my shoulders."

The confession surprised Jake and invoked conflicting emotions. "I don't mean to be difficult. It's just that I'm wondering about this mission. We almost died before even getting here. And now you're saying the Saudis want to take over for us."

"That's not exactly...

Jake expected an interruption while his team's boss gathered his thoughts mid-sentence, but the collective silence from Danielle, Volkov, and Cahill spoke a thousand words. The hard looks they wore hid deep concerns they feared to voice.

The Frenchman changed his tone. "To be transparent, Jake sent this conversation in a warranted direction but one I did not expect. I should recommence at the appropriate beginning, which is, in my opinion, my latest conversation with President Hadi."

Again, the *Specter's* commander examined the faces of his colleagues. Silent hardness.

Renard continued. "President Hadi is fighting for his people, his pride, his legacy, and his life. Since I started exploring the possibility of a Yemeni operation, this mission has been a maelstrom of politics, diplomacy, war crimes, and human suffering. The unforeseen shock to the system, so to speak, was this forsaken Wuhan COVID virus."

Having spent the global quarantine aboard a naval vessel, with his only port call an isolated British island, Jake had experienced little of the world's response to the outbreak. His concept of closing down the global economy remained abstract. "A virus did this?"

"A virus turned the world's eye away from the humanitarian efforts we're attempting to publicize, and the timing was impeccably bad for us but good for the Saudis."

Jake suspected the Frenchman's failure in foreseeing an event among the half dozen nations and factions vying for control of Yemen, and he saw Renard's blaming of the virus as a potential excuse. But he held his tongue and let his boss continue.

"Now that the international media won't come to Hadi's rescue, his only ally will be the Saudis. Riyadh, of course, recognizes this and will use this opportunity to tighten its grip around the peninsula."

Jake had to speak. "Then why aren't the Saudis just steamrolling their way across the land?"

"You're thinking like a warrior. A diplomat, however, recognizes that long-term acceptance by the populace requires winning hearts and minds. There must be an enduring military presence to hold the peace once achieved. It takes time to establish. Terry and Dmitry saw this at Socotra."

Cahill said his first words. "Yeah. It was all Emirati military around the airbase and harbor. They used to have a garrison on the island, too, and lucky for us they decommissioned it."

Renard reasserted himself as the voice of wisdom. "Not luck, entirely. It was a failed experiment. It was the right idea tactically from the UAE perspective, but the Socotrans ended up protesting such a blatant presence of boots on the ground."

"Right, mate. The local population matters. And I think that's your point. Our entire operation would never have gotten off the ground without support in Socotra, and from what I understand, the hardest part was keeping the goods flowing in that the UAE had been providing."

"Therein was my opportunity for profit and for sneaking extra weapons to you. While the Socotrans are happy with us, they'll let us stay. That has been the plan all along, and it's going to hold Socotra. However, things will be different as we approach the mainland. The first wrinkle in the plan that I must address is the humanitarian escorts to Nishtun."

Cahill protested. "If we let the Saudis get involved, they'll go back to skimming profits and all that other nasty stuff, like jacking up prices. That's the first thing we were trying to undo with this mission."

Renard raised a defensive palm. "Agreed, but I am in no position to argue it. President Hadi will be left to deal with the Saudis long after we're gone. He must make concessions to Riyadh, and the escorts is one of them."

"Will Dmitry and I still be escorting the humanitarian convoys?"

"Yes. The Saudis don't really want to help. They want credit and bragging rights for helping, and they want control of the goods when they arrive in Nishtun. I don't see a way to stop those outcomes. We can only mitigate the effects."

The Australian crossed his arms. "Mitigate how?"

"You and Dmitry will always hold the ultimate trump card, so to speak. As long as the *Wraith* is submerged and undetected, the Saudis will know they can't act against you with impunity."

"So, we keep Dmitry submerged all the time?"

"Correct."

"The rendezvous point for escorting each convoy is too far away for the *Wraith* to keep pace all the way to Nisthun. His battery can't hack it."

"It can if we pull the rendezvous point in one hundred and fifty nautical miles closer to Nishtun."

Cahill paused in thought and then replied. "That'll create easy pickings for any Iranian submarine that wants to attack convoys, and long before we'd get there to defend them. And if what happened to Jake and Danielle is any indication, the Iranians aren't sitting back licking their wounds."

"But they are indeed scared, at least as their less capable *Ghadirs* are concerned, and that's enough. In fact, with the Saudis visibly joining us, the Iranians would be fools to attack. They may attempt reconnaissance, but the last thing they need is an excuse for Riyadh to get violent."

The Australian seemed placated. "So, we move the rendezvous point closer to land. Yeah, I suppose Dmitry can keep up."

Since his translator lagged the conversation, Volkov added his approval late. "Yes. I will keep up. I assume you want slow-kills only against Saudis?"

During an extended silence, Jake admired the simplicity with which the Russian had pushed the entire group to the hardest question. By broaching the subject of weapons employment, he'd forced the Frenchman's hand.

Renard outlined the team's revised goals. "Unless the Saudis threaten us directly, we will not attack them."

Jake changed the discussion's direction. "Then tell us about our new allies and their agenda."

The Frenchman's tone became perky. "I've done the research."

"I'm sure you have."

"The task force is led by a Captain Radwan Fayed. He's a rising political star and a capable tactician. What that means to us, I'm not entirely sure. If he's there because he's a rising star, then this could all be for show, a political win for Riyadh. But if he's there because he's their best tactician, we must keep awareness of him turning against us."

Jake cringed. "Shit, Pierre. Are you trying to kill us?"

"Not at all. The Saudi task force will arrive in Socotra tomorrow. Captain Damari will handle the diplomacy with Nuhah Shaman. President Hadi has assured me that Shaman will be receptive of the Saudis, though the Socotran populace is actually dubious of their presence. It's more a necessary tolerance from her end."

Cahill frowned. "And from our end? What should I say? I can

look pretty in the audience, but I expect this mongrel to corner me at some point and ask difficult questions."

"The rendezvous point and Dmitry's constant submergence without the Saudis knowing his position. That's all you need to assure for the ongoing convoy escorts. If he challenges you, I need you to make sure Captain Fayed realizes that representing the largest local navy isn't enough to deviate from agreements between governments."

The Australian scoffed. "In this environment, it's a valid concern. I'll do what it takes."

"Excellent. That will consume most of tomorrow. Then, you'll escort the convoy the next day and then return to Socotra. Then the following day Jake and Danielle are scheduled to arrive. However, I want them to delay an additional forty-eight hours."

Jake snapped. "What? I'm going crazy out here."

"Hear me out. If you and Danielle show up on time, the Saudis will carry out whatever they've planned for such arrival. However, if you're late, they'll have to adjust. While they adjust, they may be forced to show aspects of their agenda they don't wish to share, and making them wait is a power play. It may seem silly, but it's prudent statesmanship."

Hating the extra sea time, Jake agreed. "A show of power."

"And by exercising it, it gets stronger. Terry, be ready to deflect if Fayed makes accusations about intentional delays or incompetence. The Saudis know we faced a *Kilo* near South Africa, but they don't know how long the encounter endured. Just add two days to it, and never admit out loud how long it took. You'll be speaking in a mix of candor and operational security."

"Shit, mate. That's a bloody fine line."

"Agreed, and it goes for all of you when you're with anyone who's not part of our fleet–including our Yemeni clients. We need to beware of their loyalties pivoting from us as mercenaries to the Saudis as neighbors."

Jake drew an alarming conclusion. "If the Yemenis turn against us, and the Saudis want to replace us, why are we even bothering? Shouldn't we just leave?"

Renard smirked. "You see things clearly, my friend. I was concerned about the same issue. However, there's another angle you're forgetting."

Given the moment to consider it, Jake drew a blank. "I can't see it, whatever it is."

"The Saudis are friends of Hadi now, but what's to keep them from annexing Yemen, or the portions of it they want? Given the turmoil in the world, I see little to stop them."

Jake sensed a battle brewing. "Except us? You want us to stop them? Four ships to stop a kingdom from taking over a failed nation, and with rules of engagement precluding all but our non-lethal weapons?"

"Not quite. While supporting his navy in reacquiring Aden, President Hadi wants us to protect it from the Saudis."

"So, we'll play along like we're all sharing duties in escorting convoys to Nishtun and helping retake Aden, but in reality, we're the secret police force between neighbors?"

"In a way, yes."

Jake was perplexed. "I don't know how to plan for that."

"Don't worry, my friend. Those two days of delay aren't just a power play. I need the extra time to finalize my planning adjustments."

CHAPTER 7

Captain Fayed spat pepper-flavored *shammah* into his gray bottle. He sealed the lid, wiped his lips, and then stuffed the container in his pants pocket.

The oldest of his siblings, he pulled out his phone and called his younger brother. For the first time in years, Fayed felt privileged in his role as a naval officer. More privileged than the playboy millionaire, Jabbar.

A lion in the oil industry, his brother roared. "Director Fayed."

The naval officer snorted. "Director Fayed? Is that how you greet your family?"

The brother's voice softened. "Radwan." After a pause during which Fayed assumed his sibling sought privacy, the director's tone became meek. "Everything's going as planned."

With the lion reverted to the lamb of their boyhoods, the naval officer asserted his firstborn authority. "Give me the details."

"Sure, Radwan. The package..." He lowered his volume. "The package is secure, but..."

Since their father had died of lung cancer, Fayed had taken care of his younger siblings, starting with fulfilling their dying father's wish of one son pursuing a military career. By taking the naval burden, Fayed had pleased his father before his passing, and he'd freed his brother to make the big money that their family connections allowed.

The younger man had joined Saudi Aramco and was growing wealthy from the lofty paychecks, bonuses, and bribes.

Although he'd foregone the pursuit of money for the hardship of naval service, Fayed was unafraid to take money and favors from his sibling, using an unspoken burden of guilt as leverage.

"But you don't have it yet, do you?"

"I will."

Fayed knew that Jabbar faced hardship in acquiring the assets they collectively called "the package". He checked his brother's commitment. "Are you sure?"

Jabbar became haughty. "When I say I'm going to do something, you can count on it."

"Spoken like a man with a track record in business and politics. But what about doing something dangerous for your brother, your king, and your nation? How confident are you under those circumstances?"

The brother sighed. "As confident as I can be about such a thing."

Fayed knew he was putting his brother in danger, but the reward–shaping the balance of power in the region, with himself at the helm–was too great to ignore.

If the commodore succeeded, a future-king-prince would make him an admiral with the career momentum to take charge of the entire navy–a navy that would reverse its recent embarrassments around Yemen and dominate the Arabian Peninsula.

Craving for success drove Fayed, and he reminded his brother about how the highest echelon of royalty supported that craving. "Mohammad bin Salman himself recognizes this opportunity."

With international attention on the coronavirus and its economic impact, the world ignored Riyadh's complex internal politics. Two months earlier, Saudi Arabia's de-facto ruler, Crown Prince Mohammad bin Salman had imprisoned his rivals with complete freedom.

During the imprisonments, the untouched Saudi King had said nothing, echoing the global silence about the prince's power grab.

As Bin Salman sought the throne and a ten-year plan to revitalize Saudi Arabia's strength and economy, the enduring crisis in Yemen remained unresolved.

The would-be future king wanted a decisive end to the conflict, and he wanted it before he took over the kingdom. His eye fixed on the kingship, Bin Salman moved while the world ignored him.

That movement had allowed Fayed to approach his future king's underlings to approve and provide covert resources for the delivery of his special package–as long as the operation stayed untraceable to the royal family.

Financing and enactment fell onto the shoulders of the millionaire brother, Jabbar. "I said I'd get it to you."

The naval officer believed his brother's resolve. "Good." The rocking deck unbalanced Fayed. Standing alone in the *Makkah's* wardroom–emptied by the frigate's officers tending to berthing duties, he moved his face to a porthole. "I can see Socotrans on the pier from here."

"So what?"

"They look like pawns... they are pawns, pawns to be commanded by a king, like all of Yemen. I can't believe we let the Emiratis have this island. I can't believe we shared this stage with such a little country."

"We were allies at the time."

"And that misconception is one reason we need a new king–and a new vision for dominating the entire Arabian Peninsula."

Jabbar scoffed. "You sound like you'd be the new king. I hate to remind you that our family connections fall a bit short of that."

"The new king will know my name and my deeds after this campaign. When he names his top military leaders, I will be among them. I expect to soon thereafter rise to the highest naval spot."

Jabbar sounded annoyed. "Can I get back to work? I have a department to run when I'm not subsidizing your rise to power."

"Deliver the package." Fayed slid the phone into his windbreaker.

After walking forward through austere passageways, he opened the door to the *Makkah's* bridge and yelled to his short chief of staff. "Do we have permission to dock yet?"

Commander Hijazi's tone was defensive. "The port authority says they're having trouble finding Captain Damari. We don't yet have the Yemeni Navy's formal permission."

Fayed recognized the gamesmanship. In a matter of weeks, Damari had quadrupled the Yemeni Navy's firepower, secured ports at both Socotra and Nishtun, and had established regular escorts of humanitarian shipments.

The Yemeni commodore didn't need Saudi help.

Not yet.

Not until the mercenaries departed.

Seeing no naval vessels ahead of him, Fayed had hoped the Yemenis were nearby conducting exercises. But as the snub grew obvious, he lifted his phone and called Damari to remind him of the intertwined fates of their navies.

After reaching voicemail, the Saudi officer hung up and gave his order to the task force. "Forget protocol. Tell Port Authority which berths and anchorages we'll take, and let them know it's only out of courtesy that we're informing them."

Hijazi scowled. "You want retaliate against Damari for a petty power play? Being unavailable and making us wait is–"

"A textbook power play, yes, but it's also wildly unacceptable for the circumstances. And if Damari wants to rebuke me, he'll find little patience. Park my task force on this forsaken island."

Two hours later, Fayed led a gaggle of his ships' senior officers into the waterfront building. Expecting a welcoming party, he instead met a lone mid-level officer with a skeletal staff of Yemeni enlisted sailors.

Although the Yemeni officer ranked as a lieutenant commander, he appeared a decade older than the early thirties of his peer group, marking him as a prior-enlisted veteran. He offered a fake grin as he shouted. "Attention on deck!"

The handful of staff members manning the waterfront building stopped and stood at attention.

Familiar with the protocol, Fayed responded with a strong voice. "At ease, everyone."

Scowling, Fayed marched towards the lieutenant commander and stopped at his desk. Although he seethed inwardly for the absence of senior Yemeni officers, he composed himself. "I am Captain Fayed, commanding officer of the Royal Saudi Navy task force that just overwhelmed your berthing areas. I'm sure someone told you we were coming."

Unflappable, the old Yemeni officer remained seated and stared back with hard eyes. "Yes, of course. Welcome to Socotra, captain."

Although Fayed knew nobody liked having help forced upon them, the Yemeni Navy needed it, and he expected some gratitude from his weak neighbors. "I was hoping to meet with Captain Damari. He's expecting... he should have been expecting all four hundred of us. I have five warships parked outside."

"Oh yes, I know."

Fayed realized the old officer was playing the role of a stoic antagonist. "Oh, you do. Do you know if he'll be gone long?"

As if speaking to an impertinent child, the lieutenant commander corrected the Saudi captain's assumption. "He won't be back tonight, sir. He's aboard one of our ships escorting a convoy to Nishtun."

Fayed's inner rage grew. "Excuse me?"

"Didn't he tell you?"

"He told me we would jointly escort the next humanitarian aid convoy after my arrival. That was in a phone conversation only yesterday."

"Ah. One of the convoy ships reported a propulsion plant casualty and called for assistance. Everything's fine now, but they called upon the Navy's services earlier than expected. I'm sure you understand."

Fayed suspected the convoy ship's propulsion plant was fine and always had been. The call for help was Damari's fabrication to make the Saudi Navy wait for his navy–'the Navy'–as the Yemeni officer had emphasized. Recognizing the game, the Saudi captain calmed himself and played along. "I see. Yet he didn't have time to call me? Or to answer the phone when I called him?"

"I can't speak about his phone habits, sir. I can only tell you that things got hectic as they raced out of here this morning."

Fayed suspected that any detail he would challenge about the supposed distressed ship would be deflected. He accepted the impasse and moved around it. "I understand. Safety at sea is paramount. So, when can I expect Captain Damari?"

"He left me instructions to welcome you and asked me to show you every courtesy. I've called the local hotels and have reserved almost forty rooms, which could allow your senior staff to–"

Seeing himself as the senior leader of the only relevant navy in the vicinity, Fayed interrupted the stooge. "That's thoughtful but unnecessary. All my sailors will spend the night on our ships."

"As you wish, sir. I've also got stores, oil, and fuel ready for any of your ships that need it."

"That will also be unnecessary." Fayed reflected upon the gesture. "But if I were to accept the offer, you don't have enough berthing for all my ships."

"I'd provide for whatever ships need provisions. I assume after a journey of only several days that you don't need much."

Fayed dropped the argument. "Very well. What are the new plans?"

"Meet here tomorrow morning at seven o'clock, and Captain Damari will lead a planning session for a joint escort."

Knowing the Yemeni officer would report back every detail to Captain Damari, Fayed refused to give the satisfaction of displaying dissatisfaction. He pasted a politician's smile on his face. "So be it, then. I'll be here tomorrow morning. Good day."

"Good day, sir."

The captain turned, ushered his underlings to follow him, and marched out of the building.

The next morning, Fayed saw Yemeni sailors scattered about the pier, walking between fuel trucks and food pallets, or puffing cigarettes while loitering between their tasks.

Their presence signaled hope in finding their commodore, Captain Damari, inside the waterfront building.

Leading his tactical team, Fayed escorted his commanding officers and staff members into the Port Authority structure.

This time, through the windows of a conference room, he saw the people he wanted. In the conference room, several commanders stood around a tall, thin, homely man in a captain's uniform.

Damari looked up, found the senior Saudi guest, and locked eyes with him. "Captain Fayed, I'm Captain Damari, commodore of the Yemeni fleet. On behalf of our navy, I welcome you to our joint operation."

The Saudi captain inhaled while noticing the lack of recognition of the prior evening's snub. And he considered the cordial greeting for a 'joint operation' an attempt to reduce the Saudi naval influence to a temporary task.

As Fayed walked the long way around the table, behind Yemeni underlings' backs, he recognized another subtle power play.

Damari made him approach the head chair like one bowing before a king in his court.

When Fayed reached him, he extended his hand.

Damari accepted the greeting with a firm grip and met the Saudi captain's stare.

Although disliking his weaker position in the room, Fayed had expected it. He knew to be unthreatening in the lion's den, withholding his strength until he could face Damari elsewhere.

Later, he'd prove himself the stronger lion.

Now, an illusion of humility.

His presence in Socotra was a right–not to support Damari and his sailors but the government above them. "It's our pleasure to be here, and it's our honor to carry out your president's desires."

Damari pivoted the discussion to military action. "Please sit, Captain Fayed. I've reserved seats for you and your staff."

The Saudi officer noticed five open chairs. "What about the

rest of my team?"

Shadows formed above Damari's hawkish nose. "This planning is a mere formality. Our governments agreed that you'll manage the air defenses, we'll manage the anti-surface and anti-submarine defenses. Let's keep it simple, stay out of each other's way, and let the politicians celebrate when it's done."

"I'm not arguing any of that. This is a veiled training exercise serving as a veiled public relations exercise. I won't belabor the details." Fayed paused for effect. "The real battle will be in Aden."

"You noticed that? I was afraid your king missed that little detail while planning our navy's future."

"Our king trusts me to assess such dangers, and I believe we will meet heavy resistance at Aden. I was hoping we could hurry through the humanitarian aid escort planning and get to planning the Siege of Aden."

"At least we agree on that."

"What do we disagree upon?"

With a clink, Damari lowered his stylus to the table and then buried a glare into the Saudi captain. "Your presence here."

Fayed nodded. "I appreciate your candor. You've accomplished great victories with a ragtag fleet, and I commend you. But now, I'm here as your neighbor and ally. Why not share the load in bringing peace to the region?"

"Because, as you noted, I'm doing fine on my own."

Seated by Damari's side, the only non-Arab in the room matched the image in Terrance Cahill's dossier. He uttered something in English, which a man beside him translated. "Commander Cahill says that he and I will excuse ourselves if the officers representing sovereign nations wish to speak without his presence."

Damari shook his head. "That won't be necessary. Captain Fayed, will you join me in my office?"

Private time with his future victim served Fayed's intent. "Yes."

The tall Yemeni captain stood to his full length. "Everyone, take a break. I'll send for you when I need you."

Entering the Yemeni captain's office, Fayed examined the clean desk and empty shelves. The room was bare with few personal effects, reflecting the occupant's life of constant motion.

Damari lowered himself to his seat. "Please, sit."

Fayed complied. "What can I do for you?"

"Turn around and go home."

"You know I can't do that–for good reasons."

"Name one."

"When the mercenaries leave, you'll stand alone against the Emiratis and the Iranians. Each navy unilaterally could smash your ancient fleet, and both of them hunger for revenge."

"Then sign a treaty with us, waive it at their noses, and go home."

"Why are you protesting the inevitable? You may as well move past your resistance and start working with me."

Damari sighed. "Perhaps I'm testing your resolve."

"I considered showing up here with a task force resolve enough."

The Yemeni captain opened a drawer, withdrew a pen and a pad, and then slid them across the desk. "Draw your plan."

"For the next aid escort?"

"No. That's a political stunt, like you said. I want your plan for the 'Siege of Aden', as you called it."

"So be it. The Siege of Aden. But you want me to draft a plan for it on a pad of paper?"

"I'm sure you've already drafted it in your mind a dozen times. Show me your latest iteration."

Fayed admitted his desires. "You're quite correct. I want to succeed in Aden, and I've thought of this much in recent days. I'll draw a formation I've been considering for offering naval gunfire support." He accepted the pad and doodled a geometry.

Damari took the paper and examined it. "You've split the positioning by nations. You've got our ships closest to land, and danger. Then your ships. Then the *Goliath*."

"Correct."

"I like it. I was considering the same thing. Men fight more bravely for their own countrymen."

Fayed sensed the common ground forming between himself and Damari–the ground he needed a footing upon to outmaneuver the Yemeni commodore. "Yes, they do. That's why I suggest it."

"Very well. We'll use one of your ships in an escort mission tomorrow for a photo opportunity. You can steam with us and then turn around when you have your footage. After that, we'll use your drawing here as a basis for designing the Siege of Aden."

Aden.

Fayed's glory awaited him there, and the first lynchpin of his plan, creating the illusion of an alliance with Damari, was complete.

CHAPTER 8

Commander Amir looked through the *Tarantul's* bridge window at the drone banking over the *Makkah*. The setting sun painted a rosy hue over the Saudi frigate as its rakish bow cut the Arabian Sea abeam of an escorted container ship. "That's a gorgeous photo opportunity."

Behind him, his commodore offered an unexpected response. "I'm sure the UAE is enjoying the view, too."

Amir recalled the current state of his enemy. The Emiratis had retreated, but a military of such caliber recovers and regroups. Though withdrawn into an unspoken ceasefire, the UAE had ramped up its airborne reconnaissance. "Any footage they're catching won't show up on the Internet."

"I suppose not, sir."

"But this pretty footage as captured by our new so-called Saudi friends will probably be on Al-Jazeera tonight."

Damari sighed. "We must give credit to them for protecting our country. They've fought and bled for us."

Amir let the sentiment settle. Yes, the Saudis had protected the Yemeni populace from Houthi destruction, but a side effect thereof was a de facto occupation. Like many of his countrymen, the *Tarantul's* commander wanted the foreigners to leave. "Good point. The Saudis have bled for us, but it doesn't mean I have to like them."

"They'll turn back to Socotra soon."

"Already?"

"I agreed that Captain Fayed could sail with us for his public relations footage and turn back whenever he wants."

"Footage of him giving us help we don't want, delivering humanitarian aid to a region crippled by his kingdom's informal occupation?"

Damari grunted. "Such is our lot."

Amir pressed further. "Where will he go?"

"The wildlife park on the south side of Socotra for gunnery exercises. I'm having targets set up that mimic some of those in Aden."

"At least that part I understand–tactics, shooting an enemy. Not politics."

Damari's tone turned solemn. "I hear the consternation in your voice. I wish I could say that you're worried about nothing, but I can't convince myself of that."

The *Tarantul's* commander was comforted that his commodore shared his concern about the Saudi presence. "Then you dislike this as much as I do."

Damari folded his arms. "I don't like it at all, but I understand President Hadi's concession to let them join us."

"Join us, sir? I fear they've come to colonize us."

The commodore snorted. "That's a slight exaggeration."

Amir allowed himself a moment of familiarity. "Are you joking? After all we've been through... fleeing for our lives, uprooting our families, overthrowing our naval hierarchy, combat against the UAE and Iran. After all that, you're comfortable with this?"

Damari firmed up his tone to a reprimand, but he restricted the volume to avoid embarrassing the *Tarantul's* commander in front of his bridge staff. "Watch your bearing."

Amir swallowed his anger. "I apologize, sir."

"Accepted. Let's move on."

As the emotions drained from his forgiven frame, Amir slouched and saw Damari inch closer to his shoulder.

The commodore lowered his voice. "We're strong men in a weak position. We'd be fools to feel comfort with this, but we're stuck with the Saudis for the indefinite future."

His mind buzzing with speculation, Amir remained restless. "Why did we hear nothing about them joining us until now?"

"I didn't know, but I've suspected for months."

"How?"

"My predecessor."

Remembering the naval coup that had uprooted the Yemeni admiral, Amir frowned. "That joker?"

Damari nodded. "I'd heard rumor of him taking conference calls with Saudi officers."

The reach of those pulling the political strings made Amir consider himself a pawn. "Per my understanding, we exchanged selected information with the Saudis as a courtesy to prevent running into each other."

"I'm sure that's how it started. But while our navy was shriveling, the Saudis saw an opportunity to take over our maritime regions."

Amir sensed an unfinished thought. "And?"

"And it's become obvious that my predecessor was setting up agreements with the Saudis to be unofficially but effectively absorbed into their navy."

"Then we're heading right where he aimed us–under Saudi control." The *Tarantul's* commander risked additional candor. "They're a modern fleet with big money and nice ships but they've been stymied by Houthi rebels on patrol boats. They can hardly pass the Bab al-Mandab Strait without being harassed by amateurs, and you want me to take orders from them?"

"It hasn't gone that far yet."

"Yet?"

Although his navy's senior officer, Damari became defensive. "I understand. I had considered warning you–the commanders–about this earlier, but I let you stay focused on the Emiratis. I'm unsure if it was the correct decision, but it's done."

"You did the right thing, sir. It would've been a distraction. In fact, that's all I hope these Saudi invaders are–a distraction."

Damari grunted. "Unfortunately, they're probably saying the same thing about us."

The realization hit Amir. "They expected us to fail against the UAE."

"Correct."

"They wanted us to fail?"

"Sort of. They wanted us to destroy ourselves while crippling their enemies."

"But we surprised them. Us and our mercenaries."

"Correct again. We rekindled our fleet into something from nothing. They didn't expect that."

"And now we're what to them? A nuisance?"

"At best, and the Saudis want us to become their puppet navy, an informal division within their regime. But they couldn't act upon that while their rivals wanted the same."

Additional realization struck. "And we've done them a favor by pushing out the UAE and the Iranians."

"Correct. But it's only a temporary opening until their enemies regroup. So, whatever the Saudis intend, they must act quickly."

Amir checked the flying camera's position as it crossed the *Makkah's* bow. "They're getting video showing how humane they are. At Aden, they'll get video showing how brave they are. What's after that?"

"That's my concern. They'll help us retake Aden, but I can only wonder what's next on their agenda."

Amir flipped the conversation towards the Saudi task force commander. "Captain Fayed strikes me as overly ambitious."

Taking the bait, Damari concurred. "He's the type who might interpret orders from Riyadh to suit himself."

"Agreed. I'm wary of his agenda." Amir reflected upon the smug arrogance he'd seen pasted on the Saudi officer's face. "I'm wary of him."

Damari stirred. "Damn it."

"What?"

"The drone. I told him to keep it two miles from the *Xerses*. He doesn't get free looks at the mercenary fleet. Warn it off."

Through the window, Amir checked the flying camera's trajectory. It veered away from the Saudi frigate and towards the group's southern flank and the mercenary vessel. He shouted upward. "Tactical center, bridge, the Saudi drone's too close to the *Xerses*. Warn it away."

From the *Tarantul's* innards, the executive officer replied. "Bridge, tactical center, I'm warning away the Saudi drone." Fifteen seconds ticked away. "Bridge, tactical center, no answer from the *Makkah*."

"I'm not playing games." Damari snapped a cold order. "Have the *Xerses* illuminate the Saudi drone with Goalkeeper fire control."

Impressed with his commodore's decisiveness, Amir relayed the order through his executive officer to the transport ship.

Half a minute after the mercenary close-in-weapon-system energized its radar, the drone darted from the *Xerses*.

"Bridge, tactical center, the *Makkah* acknowledges the order and is bringing its drone back to the ship. The Saudis also inform us they're heading back to Socotra."

Damari grumbled as he turned from the *Tarantul's* commander. "That jackass is testing my limits. God help us if I give him an opening."

After mooring in Nishtun, Amir glanced at a bright blue rectangular container dangling from a crane. The small but busy pier reminded him he was trying to feed starving people despite the world's attempts to thwart him.

Across the pier, his ship's twin presented a mirror image of the *Tarantul*-class corvette. Despite its half century of life, the corvette *Khalid* appeared regal in its new berthing, after Yemeni soldiers had swept it for boobytraps, replaced worn parts in the engine room, and had used the *Xerses* as a dry dock to weld patches over the small holes of a slow-kill torpedo's bomblets.

With the ship returned to the water, several sailors hung over its sides paining the hull a fresh gray.

After the *Khalid's* recapture, Amir had called upon veteran members of its prior crew. Most of them had agreed to return to fight for their country, their pride, and–most importantly–a paycheck. With varied uniform pieces missing, two dozen men stood in a platoon formation beside the *Khalid's* brow.

The prior commanding officer, now returned, saluted. "Commander Amir."

Amir returned the salute. "Commander Halabi. I don't suppose you remember how to drive this thing?"

"Better than you ever could." Halabi extended his hand.

Amir accepted the handshake. "After three years, I'd feared you'd forgotten everything."

"I can remember much for a paycheck. So can they." He nodded to the crew standing behind him.

"Some of them couldn't find their old ballcaps or uniform shirts."

Halabi snickered. "A few of them don't fit anymore."

"Do you need to borrow uniform items from my crew?"

As Halabi shook his head, his oversized nose swung side-to-side. "Nothing serious. It depends how formal Captain Damari wants to make this."

Amir considered their boss. "He's a hard man. Tough to read."

"Unless he fusses over it, we'll manage with the uniforms we have. All I need are the spare parts on the list I sent you."

"I've got about half of them."

"I'll take what I can, especially the damage control equipment."

"Done. I'll have some shoring sent over, too."

Clopping heels grew louder behind Amir's shoulder.

Halabi aimed his bulbous nose at the sound. "Captain Damari's coming. He came out of nowhere..."

"Don't worry. You'll like him. He's the only guy from the old guard who made rank for competence."

"Good to know."

"Bring your crew to attention."

Halabi looked over his shoulder. "*Khalid*, attention!"

Amir stepped aside and let his commodore face the new ship's old commander.

Halabi saluted. "Commander Rami Halabi, presenting the *Khalid* and its crew for service to Yemeni Navy."

Damari returned the salute and ratcheted up the formality,

ignoring any mention of ancient ships masquerading as modern, a corvette being stolen and recaptured, and a crew who'd lost its ship years ago returning to it. "Very well, Commander Halabi. Follow me."

Acting as a scribe, Amir took notes on his phone as Damari walked Halabi through an inspection of his people.

The commodore stood at attention in front of the first sailor. With the officers forming a line in front, he started with a young lieutenant.

"What's your job on the *Khalid*?"

"Navigator, sir."

"Have you plotted a course to Aden yet?"

"I have, sir. Two of them based upon my captain's orders. One from here, and one from Socotra."

"Good. Did you plot firing arcs for all known shore-based enemy weapon systems around Aden?"

"Uh… not yet, sir. I'm planning to overlay that data this evening."

"Make sure you do, before our gunnery practice."

"Yes, sir."

"What have you been doing for the past three years?"

"Refinery work, sir. My degree's in chemical engineering."

"That pays well, doesn't it?"

"Yes, sir!"

"Yet you came back when we recaptured your old ship."

"There's still work to be done, sir. The money can wait."

After hearing similar stories of exodus and return from the remaining officers, some abandoning paychecks and others not, Damari moved to the first row of enlisted sailors. "What's your job on the *Khalid*?"

"I'm an electrician, sir."

"What did you do for the past three years?"

"I repaired appliances for my cousin in his shop, sir."

"Was there anything you couldn't fix?"

"No, sir! I can fix anything! Well, except for the stuff that's really broken and needs to be thrown away."

"That describes half the equipment in this fleet."

"Then I'll find a way to fix it all, sir."

"That's a good attitude. Did you promulgate a list of equipment discrepancies to your division chief petty officer?"

"I don't have a division chief, sir."

Damari eyed Halabi. "You told me on the phone last night you had all billets staffed."

"I do, sir. His division officer is quite experienced and is capable for covering for lacking a chief."

"So be it." Damari stepped to the next man, who wore khaki pants below his uniform shirt. "You lost your trousers?"

"No, sir. My wife threw out my uniforms. I kept my boots and cap, and I borrowed a shirt. But I'm too tall and skinny for anyone to lend me pants."

Damari faced the *Tarantul's* commander. "Commander Amir, note the discrepancy of missing pants. Get the man's measurements after the inspection and find him some trousers."

Amir snapped. "Yes, sir."

Damari faced the other commander. "Commander Halabi, I notice you have several men with uniform discrepancies. Have you considered the repercussions for those who fail to meet uniform requirements?"

Amir prayed his colleague would avoid the obvious excuse of having resurrected a financially strained crew from its remnants.

Though caught off guard, Halabi avoided the excuse. "I... have not, sir."

"What do you think is an appropriate repercussion?"

Amir cringed as Damari cornered his colleague.

Halabi muddled through an answer. "Well, sir. There's nonjudicial punishment called out in our personnel manual. I'd work through that on an individual basis."

"No need. I'll make it easy for you. The funds for this crew's next paychecks are available now, awaiting my release. If your crew and ship stand up to my test, I'll release the funds today. However, those with uniform discrepancies will have to wait until the discrepancies are cleared to receive their pay."

Halabi smirked. "I understand, sir. I'll take care of it."

A murmur rose and fell with the crew.

Damari raised his voice. "Your ship was stolen from its berthing years ago, but now you're back while it's being resurrected. I don't care what you did in the past. You're in my navy now, and you'll carry out your duties, including looking like a legitimate fighting force. Is that clear?"

The crew's response was mediocre. "Yes, sir."

Halabi interjected. "Your commodore asked you a question. Is that clear, gentlemen?"

"Yes, sir!"

"Good." Damari faced Halabi. "Where's your battle stations gunner?"

"He's in the next row, sir. He's excited to show you what he can do on the range."

"Take me to him. I want to look him in the eye."

After inspecting the *Khalid's* crew, Damari dismissed the sailors and pulled Amir into a private conversation. "They're not ready. Tell me I'm wrong."

"You're wrong."

"No. Tell me why you think they're ready."

"I can't, sir. I was just following orders."

Political stress compounding his tactical considerations, the commodore released a rare nervous laugh. "I don't know whether to commend you or reprimand you."

"How about you let me just tell you what I think?"

"Sure. Go ahead."

Amir connected the consequences of current events. "I helped Halabi find most of his old crew, but they're more thinly staffed than I'd feared."

"They're skeletal."

"That's not my biggest concern. It's the need. We no longer need them in Aden. When the Saudis arrived, we increased our inventory of three-inch cannons from two to six. We can leave the *Khalid* behind and do it with five."

Damari crossed his arms and looked upward in thought. "One under our control and four under Saudi control."

"And the *Goliath's* railguns."

"Right. What else would you consider?"

Amir launched the counterargument to his original point. "We need to let the *Khalid* fight with us. They'll remember their training, and they only need to manage propulsion, ship handling, and guns."

Damari grunted. "Correct. They're not ready, but I didn't bring them back to spectate."

"So, you'll let them help us retake Aden?"

"I'll decide after the gunnery exercises. I'll ride them, and if they perform to my satisfaction, we'll include them."

On the return trip to Socotra, Amir stood as the ranking officer aboard his *Tarantul*. He assumed that Captain Damari, who'd posted himself aboard the *Khalid*, was living in Commander Halabi's hip pocket reminding how to command a warship.

The first test–marksmanship.

His executive officer's voice marked the test's commencement. "Bridge, tactical center. From the commodore, hold course and speed. Commencing live fire exercises."

"Very well, tactical center. We'll hold course and speed." Through an external camera, Amir watched the orange target his ship towed cut a small wake a mile behind his stern.

A distant boom thumped the windows, and five seconds later, white spray shot up behind the orange target.

Over the loudspeaker, the executive officer announced the verdict. "Round one from the *Khalid* is two meters right and three meters long."

Another boom, and seconds later, arcs of whitewater spray formed in front of the target.

"Round two from the *Khalid* is four meters left and five meters short."

As Amir feared the reformed crew of the *Tarantul's* twin

would fail their first test, the third round enveloped the target in falling cascades.

"Round three from the *Khalid* is a hit!"

The *Tarantul's* commander admired the skillful adjustment to the targeting. "Very well, tactical center."

The next seven rounds proved accurate, and then to test the *Khalid's* propulsion plant, the corvettes raced the last twenty-five miles to Socotra.

Having won the sprint to the Socotra by half a mile over the recaptured corvette, Amir saw a dark submarine riding high in its berthing area. As he slowed the *Tarantul,* he saw a mercenary transport ship underneath its cargo.

Message traffic had revealed an hour earlier the arrival of the *Goliath* with the *Specter*, and Amir thought he was seeing twins of the *Xerses* and *Wraith*.

An absence of Saudi vessels suggested his de facto allies had already transited to the island's far side shooting range.

The executive officer's voice rang from the loudspeaker. "Bridge, tactical center. From the commodore, proceed to the starting point for gunnery exercises."

Amir appreciated his commodore's efficiency. A political man might have delayed real work for ceremonies, and the freedom to move forward was a pleasure. "Very well, tactical center. Take us there using the best allowable speeds."

As Socotra's Hajhir mountains slid to his starboard beam, Amir wondered when he'd meet the new mercenaries.

The peaks blotted the sun and the executive officer called to his boss. "Bridge, tactical center. I'm starting a conference call with Captain Damari, the *Specter*, and the *Goliath*. I can send it up there if you're interested."

Amir had lost track of the wires and screens with which he'd updated his ship. "Can I spy on them without them seeing me?"

"Of course, sir. I'll send it now."

The *Tarantul's* commander spun towards a large display mounted against the bulkhead and selected the video stream from the tactical center. In squarish quadrants appeared his commodore's hawkish nose, the rugged lines of the handsome American, and the subtly alluring visage of the female Brit.

Beside each Anglophone stood a translator, who spoke for each commander.

Damari greeted his mercenaries. "Commanders Slate and Sutton, I am Captain Damari, commodore and ranking officer of the Yemeni Navy. Welcome to Yemen's tourist paradise of Socotra."

The muscular American answered through his translator. "I'm Jacob Slate, commanding officer of the naval submarine *Specter*, and my colleague is Danielle Sutton, commanding officer of the naval transport ship *Goliath*. We're honored to join you."

Damari replied. "I don't know if we'll meet in person, but we can conduct our briefings with video conferences. I won't delay our mission further for the COVID crisis."

Through a two-way translation, the American replied. "Have your ground and air forces confirmed their commitment?"

"Yes. These are young, healthy men. Colonel Muhammed has assured me of the commitment."

"Good. We're fortunate to be protected from the virus within our ships. I agree to avoid face-to-face meetings and to continue as planned."

"Excellent. I appreciate your flexibility, Commander Slate. I propose to pre-brief our gunnery exercises while we transit to the range. Our Saudi colleagues are already there."

"We saw the Saudis shooting as we approached. I won't participate from the *Specter*, but Commander Sutton on the *Goliath* has been looking forward to the exercise."

Observing the conversation, Amir felt a renewed sense of hope.

"And I welcome your arrival. Having the full mercenary team here will let us do what we must."

"I'm glad to help, Captain Damari."

"I'll send you coordinates to begin gunnery exercises. Enjoy the training. The next time we do this, we'll be fighting our way home."

CHAPTER 9

As the exploding warhead rumbled through Socotra's foundation, along the African continental shelf, and to the *Specter's* shallow hydrophones, Jake discerned a deep drone.

His toad-head swiveling, Remy confirmed it. "The first round of the live-fire exercises has landed."

Jake joked. "Did it hit the target?"

"I'm good but not that good. How about you? Can you tell through the periscope?"

Looking at the screen showing the view through his exposed and auto-rotating optics, the *Specter's* commander saw a panorama of the world above his bobbing submarine. To the north, he saw the upper mast lights of a Saudi corvette and one *Tarantul*, and in all other directions he saw stars dotting a black canvass. "I'm not that good either. I guess we'll have to wait for the reports."

Remy's head rotated back towards his monitor. "No, thank you. Since there's nothing I can do about their accuracy, there's nothing I care to know about it."

Jake digested the sonar technician's wisdom and then muted his link to the Arabian task force, which had formed south of the island. He looked at the screen showing the four faces of his team–Renard, Cahill, Volkov, and Danielle–as he queried his boss. "Pierre, how's this lining up with your plan?"

Another distant boom caressed Jake's ear, and he glanced at his sonar ace.

Shortening his report in anticipation of many booms, Remy bounced his voice off his panel. "The second round landed."

"Very well. Belay your reports on exercise rounds."

Through cynicism, Remy revealed the waning patience that

pervaded the *Specter's* crew. "Not another word."

Jake returned his attention to his leadership. "Sorry, Pierre. Go ahead."

Renard shook his head. "It's no problem. To your question, other than having the *Goliath* stolen in Oman…" The Frenchman looked away to grab an aging memory. "I also lost some valuable cargo in Russia long ago, although I'm not sure I truly ever possessed it. But compared to those two disasters, this mission ranks in my top three ass aches."

Recalling the mercenary fleet's collective worst day when an unexpected enemy had stolen their flagship, Jake scowled. "You planned on having the *Goliath* stolen?"

Renard waved a dismissive palm. "No, you fool. You asked me about my worst missions, and that technically evolved into a mission as we recaptured our property."

Wondering if a linguistic nuance had crossed wires in the Frenchman's brain, the *Specter's* commander corrected him. "I didn't mention anything about missions. I asked about how this campaign compared to your plan."

Blushing, the Frenchman fell silent and gathered his composure. "*Touché, mon ami*. I had internally translated your question into one about my worst missions."

Jake snorted. "And this made your top three?"

"Unfortunately. I'm seeking a silver lining in this blasted COVID virus, but it ruined my effort to place Yemen in the international spotlight. Now, instead of leading an economic stimulus, we'll be serving the Saudis."

With his brethren silent, Jake continued speaking for the commanders. "You mean the Yemenis, right?"

Renard sighed and then replied. "On paper, yes. But the reality is that the Saudis are filling a vacuum, one we created by pushing back the Emiratis and Iranians."

Jake assessed the situation from a global perspective. Even after taking the long way around Africa, he was willing to detach from his desires for excitement. "Why don't we say goodbye and move on? Let's get out of the Saudis' way. Maybe this is

'Mission Accomplished'."

"As I said earlier, President Hadi entrusts us to protect him from the Saudis."

Jake was still unsure whom to fight, if anyone. "Does that include protecting the Saudis from the Iranians? You're turning our operations theater into a tinderbox."

His comfort zone threshold apparently crossed, the Frenchman withdrew a Marlboro and flicked flint into flame underneath it.

"I thought you quit."

After blowing smoke and letting his facial muscles relax under nicotine's cruel grasp, Renard scowled. "You're not letting your encounter with the *Kilo* sully your judgment, are you?"

"Bite me. You didn't answer my question."

Renard doubled down. "We're making a show to Hadi of watching the Saudis while our real work is protecting all our clients, including the Saudis by association, from the Iranians."

Anger rose within Jake, threating to assume its old flare, but age and wisdom curtailed it. "The Iranians wouldn't even be here if the Saudis weren't crashing the party. They muscled their way in, and all they did was become a fishing lure for *Ghadirs*."

"They're not in the way–"

The *Specter's* commander interrupted his boss' interruption. "We had them beat before the Saudis arrived. Now, the task force is too interesting for the Iranians to ignore."

"If you still consider yourself American, the Saudis are your countryman's allies."

Jake recognized an alliance with evil. "That's a political necessity. But seriously, why should I care if every Iranian and every Saudi kill each other out here?"

Renard chuckled.

Jake lowered his voice's volume. "What's so funny?"

"The divinity student wants everyone to die."

As the other commanders chuckled, humility gripped Jake.

"Okay. Okay. We're all sinners."

During quietness, the Volkov whispered with his translator and then faced Jake. "You are hypocrite!"

The words came as a partial joke but stung. Right or wrong, he felt himself leaning towards faith in a creator God. And his God taught him to value life, which posed a possible contradiction to a career that demanded killing.

Going the long way around Africa had let him ponder his seemingly growing contradiction, but it remained unresolved. He stuffed down his frustration and set the concepts aside for future thought. "Okay, Dmitry. I'll stop preaching. But let's see how pissed off you'd be after going the long way around Africa!"

Cahill rescued his fellow anglophone. "Don't worry, mate. That was a long trip. I'd be testy, too."

Remembering his colleagues' heavyweight torpedo attacks on *Ghadir* submarines, Jake convinced himself that joining the mission late had its upsides. "Yeah. I thought I'd envy you and Dmitry, but after you had to throw big punches, I'm not so sure."

Dmitry droned a dirge in Russian for his translator to relay. "It was one of the hardest decisions of my life. Fortunately, I had made it prior to deploying. But it was still hard."

"Yeah, mate. Me too. This whole region stinks of death."

Renard reasserted his control. "And it will get worse. We must adapt to the rapidly changing circumstances. The Saudis are too interesting a target, and they're attracting all the attention we've worked to eradicate from the area."

Jake sensed a shift in the campaign's momentum. "Attention such as?"

"Such as, the UAE has ramped up reconnaissance and combat air patrol flights–over the water and at their Saudi borders. Emirati troop movement towards the UAE-Saudi borders is being noticed, too. Make no mistake that the Emiratis have noticed the Saudis usurping the role we denied them."

Cahill characterized the team's disappointment. "All that work pushing them back... the MICAs... the deception... the death. For nothing?"

Ignoring the question, the Frenchman piled on. "And the *Ghadirs* may come back. Intelligence reports already show three of them making preparations to deploy."

Delayed echoes of mortal fear played through Jake's memory. "The Iranian *Kilo* that ambushed me and Danielle... it's got a stud for a commander, and he could be chasing us."

"He's at least four days behind you. I wouldn't worry."

Jake recognized the Frenchman's dismissal of the Iranian submarine as a conversational tactic. They could deal with that submarine later, when its threat window opened, and he allowed the team to address more immediate concerns. "Okay, Pierre. Let's ignore the *Kilo* for now."

"Thank you, *mon ami*. One thing I appreciate about COVID–"

After a quick reflection upon the conversation, Jake interrupted. "You said you couldn't find any silver linings!"

"Dear God, man. You're both charmed and anal retentive."

"Sorry."

"May I continue?"

"Please."

"As I was saying, COVID isn't all negative. It will keep the Yemenis and Saudis separated. Though they are lukewarm allies now, I fear they'll become bedfellows as they rediscover their Arabic heritage. The COVID quarantine prevents them fostering the relationships that could lead to that."

The *Specter's* commander appreciated his boss' worldview. He hadn't considered the upside of quarantine, and he shifted his energies from talking to listening.

Renard continued. "But our original plan is no longer valid. We've been forced into a supporting role. Based upon our discussions to this point, I've identified two options to take Aden–one with a distraction for the Iranians, and one without."

Jake chewed on the inferred riddle and guessed. "You would use one of us as bait for the *Ghadirs*?"

"Not exactly. We'll use the next humanitarian convoy. I'll put MICA anti-air missiles on a container ship and have it leaked as a poorly guarded secret. Spies will notice, and those whom we've defeated will have to consider a mission of harassment."

Knowing his boss, the *Specter's* commander dissected meaning from his words. "Harassment from those whom we've defeated? Submarines don't harass. They hunt and hit, but they don't harass. So, you expect the Emiratis to come back?"

"Correct, *mon ami*. I can't imagine them retreating forever. They'll be as interested in Saudi activities as the Iranians. Possibly more so, and their air and naval forces are too proud to recoil in defeat. But perhaps we can use them to dislodge the Saudi grip enough."

Jake's head spun. "Enough for what?"

"Enough to break away from this region with our reputation and with hopes of acquiring new business after this blasted pandemic ends."

In a sullen moment, Jake recalled his weakened immune system.

Much as he feared incoming torpedoes, he also feared leaving the *Specter's* isolated environment and facing the virus.

Accustomed to managing medical dangers, he sought facts about the pandemic from Wuhan, but the information was inconsistent. Perceiving himself within the high-risk population, he needed to learn everything about it for his survival. But after months of data, conservative sources downplayed the dangers while mainstream media screamed terror.

Unsure what to believe, he mumbled his reply. "If this pandemic ever ends." To avoid emotional ruin, he tucked away his frustrations and returned the conversation to tactics. "The UAE might work to our advantage if they come. You got any intel on them?"

"Nothing damning beyond what I've already shared, but the UAE's leadership is becoming increasingly vocal about Aden."

Breaking her silence, Danielle interjected her immediate needs. "I've got to run, guys. It's my turn to shoot, and I'm going to oversee my gunners."

Renard held her back. "Humor me a moment. Tell me, what sort of rounds are you shooting?"

"Guided non-splintering for starters. Then unguided non-splintering if there's time."

"Good luck and shoot straight, *mon amie*."

"I will." She lifted her chin. "Mute channel three."

Renard frowned. "What's a 'mute channel' command?"

Jake remembered having approved Danielle's modifications. "She wrote some software to let the *Goliath* respond to her voice."

Cahill protested. "She did what to me ship?"

"It's just a convenience. She can roll it back if you don't like it."

Reddening, Renard seemed flustered. "I told you to make no modifications to any weapons or communications systems."

"She didn't."

"Then explain yourself. That sounds like a communications system."

Jake recognized his boss' consumer marketing ignorance. "It's not. That's a separate module, a bunch of them, really. Everyone's using voice commands now. There's even a voice recognition module. That's all she changed."

"I don't like it."

Cahill piled on. "Me neither. What if she breaks something?"

Having seen and approved the software changes, Jake knew his colleagues' fears were unfounded. "She didn't. She made only a few mods, and the module's insulated from the major systems. Worst case, it can be disabled with the touch of a button."

Seeming cool to the idea, Renard scowled. "She wrote the code by herself?"

"She had someone check it, but yeah, she minored in computer science in her undergraduate work and likes to tinker."

Renard's eyes narrowed. "Dare I ask who checked her work?"

Jake smirked. "Yours truly."

The Frenchman's features hardened. "Terry, get a copy of her code and have some of your boys look at it, just to be sure my two commanders didn't break the *Goliath*."

"Bloody right, I will."

Sighing, Jake acquiesced. "Just to keep you guys from having aneurisms, I'll have her roll back the changes." He heard Danielle's railgun round's sonic boom cutting through the *Specter's* hull.

Remy confirmed the first shot. "The first railgun round from the *Goliath* has passed overhead."

Jake lifted his face towards the sonar ace. "Did you hear it hit?"

"No. It's too small. No warhead. No seismic footprint."

"Fine. Belay your reports on the *Goliath's* exercise rounds." As he looked to the table, Jake saw his inquisitive boss' lips moving.

"How far away is she?"

"Twenty-four miles. She dropped me off and then turned back the way she came to practice a little long-range work. Damari wanted her to shoot over us so they'd get used to railgun rounds flying overhead."

Renard nodded. "Damari impresses me the more I know him."

The same sentiment rolled through Jake's head as he examined the communications window of the newly formed Saudi-Yemeni-Mercenary task force.

With a simple and legible design, a scorecard with Arabic characters hovered over the images that cameras showed of their host vessel's innards. A laminated index card was taped to the table's side, revealing the translation of Arabic numerals to those Jake understood. After a few mental translations, he tallied the scores.

Left of the *Tarantul's* bridge, which Jake recognized from its ancient electronics gear, azure pixels formed cells proclaiming five of six shots fired from the Saudi corvette *Hitteen* hitting, the Yemeni corvette *Khalid* revealing its veterans' rustiness with three hits out of six, and the *Goliath's* first shot landing square on target.

Impressing the *Specter's* commander further, an aerial perspective from an Arab drone framed real-time infrared views of the range, the targets, and the bright blasts.

After a sonic blast cracked above Jake's head, a flashing object traced a white streak across the screen and then stopped dead in Socotra's nature reserve. "Hey, guys. This is actually kind of cool. Are you watching the–"

Seated behind him, listening to the task force, the *Specter's* translator stirred. "Jake!"

"Yeah?"

"Unknown submerged contact bearing three-four-two, range approximately seven nautical miles from our ship. The task force commander orders you to investigate."

Adrenaline flooded Jake's bloodstream as he watched an icon appear on the tactical map. A Saudi helicopter flew over the location, begetting myriad questions.

But first, based upon military instinct and commitment to his team's client, Jake obeyed. "All-ahead two thirds, make turns for eight knots. Right ten-degrees rudder, steady on course three-four-two." As hands grasped yokes and levers, the deck tilted below his feet. "Let the task force commander know that we're investigating."

"I'll let him know." The translator rattled off the confirmation with Arabic's guttural and throaty vowels.

Jake looked to his ace. "Antoine?"

Understanding the one-word question, Remy replied. "Nothing on bearing three-four-two, but seven miles is too far to hear a loitering submarine."

A suspicion nagged Jake. "Where's our Caesaron robot?"

Remy tapped his screen. "It's guarding the western approach. Per its prescribed pattern and positional update twelve minutes ago, it's at least four and a half miles northeast of the submerged contact."

Unsure how to judge the Israeli robot's efficacy in anti-submarine warfare, Jake considered the Caesaron a distraction. "Very well, Antoine." He cast his voice over his shoulder to the translator. "Confirm with the task force commander that his helicopter is leaving the area so he doesn't drop a torpedo on me."

His eyes growing large in recognition of the risk, the translator relayed the message.

While driving towards the discovered danger, Jake formed a mental checklist of actions. He started with a mercenary team conference and glared at their faces. "Did you guys hear that? A Saudi helo found an unidentified submerged contact."

Renard reasoned aloud. "If it's a *Ghadir*, it had to surface and snorkel frequently to have arrived there from Bandar Abbas. It also would've had to sprint by Dmitry, Terry, and the Caesaron without being heard. Quite dubious."

"Right, mate. We're alert, watching to the north and east. Getting by me would have been unlikely–really hard for a sprinting *Ghadir*. The *Xerses* is a second-rate hunter, sure, but getting by Dmitry would've been almost impossible. But I can't say impossible for sure. Sorry."

Jake's recent brush with death offered a different option. "It could be that *Kilo* coming to finish its ambush."

Renard shook his head. "No. I had my calculations triple checked from your encounter in South African waters. Even with your two-day delay, that *Kilo* is days behind."

"Did you account for it sprinting and refueling?"

The Frenchman flicked the air and then stabbed his cigarette butt into an offscreen tray. "Bah. Of course, not. Submarines don't have such luxuries."

"Yeah, I know. But anything's possible. Sneaky refueling at sea is the sort of thing we'd do. Maybe the Iranians are doing it without us knowing." Jake judged himself paranoid as his words circled within his memory.

"Whatever it is, you'd best get deep to find out. Standard rules of engagement apply, and count the Saudis among our clients until I tell you otherwise."

"Will do. I'm going deep. And keep everyone out of my way, especially the helos. I don't want to die from so-called-friendly fire."

"Indeed!"

"Make your depth thirty meters!" As the deck angled downward, the faces on Jake's communications screens froze. Freed from political concerns, he welcomed the solitude of his submarine and his crew. At depth, the bobbing and slanted deck leveled and steadied. "Anything yet, Antoine?"

"No!"

Jake had expected an unfettered gunnery practice, and the unidentified submarine's interference surprised him. "Got any theories?"

The sonar ace's spoke with palpable cynicism. "Plenty. Would you like to hear them all, or should I enjoy relative silence so that I may listen for the bad guy?"

"Understood." Straightening his back, the *Specter's* commander accepted his predicament. He raised his voice. "Whether it's a figment of Saudi imagination or not, I assume we have an unwanted visitor. Henri!"

Seated at his forward console, the silver-haired Frenchman glanced upward. "Sir?"

"Pass the word. Rig the ship for ultra-quiet."

"I'm rigging the ship for ultra-quiet."

"Very well." Jake looked back at his sonar team. "Antoine, have your team assign tube four to this new contact."

With the gravitas of an assigned weapon, Remy twisted his torso and faced his commander. "Tube four, a limpet weapon?"

"Yes, tube four. Anyone watching us knows that our fleet is willing to kill. A limpet's a fine warning for whoever's out there watching us now."

CHAPTER 10

Danielle snapped orders into an overhead microphone. "Secure port and starboard cannons. Secure from gunnery exercises. Remain at battle stations."

Her mind churned for the next step a destroyer commander would take, and that inspired her desire to vector in an anti-submarine helicopter.

But she had no helicopter, and the one discovering the suspected submerged contact was a Saudi asset under a Yemeni command she didn't yet trust.

She stabbed her finger into an icon to accelerate the *Goliath*. "Coming to all-ahead flank." As confusion wrestled awareness within her, she glanced at the former submarine commander.

She wanted to ask him, *"is this the bloodiest mess you've ever seen*?" Instead, she filtered her anxiety. "Any recommendations?"

Mike Taylor raised his eyebrows. "That depends what you're doing, ma'am."

"I'm not sure yet. But..." She wanted to add a golden nugget of tactical insight, but submarine-versus-submarine combat remained her weakness. Tired, unsure of her standing within the fleet, and starting her sophomore mission with a potential undersea ambush, she was flustered.

Instead of reasoning her way through it, she applied her intuition. "I'm sprinting ahead of the surface combatants to sweep for a second submarine."

The balding man checked his tactical display. "Good thinking, in case it's a trap. But the surface combatants are accelerating to flank speed. We won't catch them."

She studied the geometry and agreed the Arabic surface combatants would outrun her. "We will if they let us."

"To submerge and search ahead of their escape route?"

After nodding her affirmation, she spoke over her shoulder to the translator. "Hail the Task Force Commander. Tell him I recommend that all ships maintain twenty knots. I intend to position myself to the east and sweep ahead for other submarines."

After a quick verbal exchange, the translator relayed Captain Damari's agreement. "The Task Force Commander agrees to twenty-knot on all ships fleeing east. However, two ships have turned south and will continue to evade at flank speed."

"Very well." Danielle watched the Arabic ships' velocity vectors shift across her iconic chart and fan away from the island's southern waters. Then she looked at sea spray shooting over the cargo ship's twin bows.

In a daydream, she recalled having borrowed her sister ship's executive officer, Liam Walker, during her first undersea encounter against a Turkish submarine. She'd lacked a submarine officer of command caliber during that mission, but now she had Mike Taylor.

And she considered herself wise enough to use him.

But as she prepared to defer him for undersea, anti-submarine tactics, an icy chill consumed her. Steadying her voice against her unnerving feeling, she hoped it was a false internal alarm. "I'm not sure what I'm doing. This is your game."

His voice was strong. "I've got your back."

"Here goes." Finding his confidence assuring, Danielle projected her voice to an overhead microphone. "Attention, crew of the *Goliath*, the Saudi helo has found a submerged contact to the west. The helo is retreating to let the *Specter* investigate. We're sprinting to the northeast to search for a possible second submarine. Mister Taylor has the deck and the conn. I retain weapons launch authority." She looked at Taylor.

Taking the hint, the submarine officer announced his intent. "This is the executive officer, I have the deck and the conn. The commanding officer retains weapons launch authority." He then hardened his voice. "Until we know otherwise, this is as real as the *Kilo* at Cape Agulhas. We're looking for Iranians, and we're shifting from defense to offense, team. Vacation's over. Begin Sonar Search Plan Alpha. Carry on."

His courage calmed her. As she stabbed an icon to close the circuit, she admired her choice in executive officers. "Vacation?"

He shrugged. "Got to talk tough once in a while."

"You don't think this is real, do you?"

He scowled. "The unknown submerged contact?"

She nodded.

With the transport ship reaching its top speed, sea spray speckled the windows behind Taylor. "I signed up for the excitement. I'm just getting what I asked for."

She snorted and folded her arms. "I wouldn't put it beyond them to claim a false target."

Taylor seemed more trustful. "Seriously?"

"Why not? Who are we to them?"

"Huh. Good point. But which navy? I trust the Yemenis far more than the Saudis."

"Because Dmitry and Terry have already earned their trust, and vice versa?"

He shrugged. "Yeah. That's about all I've got for a warm fuzzy, but I trust the home team over the team that pushed its way in."

"You think the Saudis forced Hadi to accept them?" She seeded his answer with her own thoughts. "I thought it happened rather fast and with a lot of doubletalk."

"I agree. And bad things are going to happen because of it. I hope we get in and out before there's any Arab infighting."

As she sped towards them, the Arabian combatants grew larger and looked like toys. Her doubts grew. "They accepted my twenty-knot speed limit rather quickly."

Taylor raised an eyebrow. "You doubt they believe their own report?"

Danielle glanced over her shoulder at the translator. "You didn't hear any fear in Damari's voice, did you?"

"No, ma'am."

She faced the submarine officer again. "He doesn't seem too concerned."

"You think he's testing us? With a false claim?"

"I don't know what to think. He may think the Saudis are testing him, or all of us."

Taylor frowned. "It's an ugly game, but we've got to play it. Until we prove otherwise, we're facing Iranian submarines."

She glanced ahead and judged the distance to the fleeing ships. "When will you submerge?"

"About another two minutes."

"Crash dive?"

He smirked. "Sure. If the Saudis are really testing us, let's give them a show."

Having been uncharacteristically passive, Renard interrupted. "Danielle?"

Surprised by the Frenchman, she squeaked. "Pierre?"

"I've been listening to your debate. Such trickery is well within the Saudis' grasp. But keep your wits about you. Fight the enemy until you're sure there's no enemy to fight."

In a moment of doubt, she wished she'd never set foot on a submarine. The exhausting journey around Africa, a task force of dubious clients, and a new fleet of strangers in sterile khaki-and-white uniforms formed her bizarre new world.

She hid her discomfort. "Roger that, Pierre."

"This is one of the few hunts where I hope you find nothing."

She looked for Jake's face in the *Specter's* communication window but saw only darkness. "Have you heard from Jake?"

"He sent a communications buoy about five minutes ago. No news, other than he was slowing to search." Looking offscreen, Renard scowled. "*Merde.* That Saudi corvette is too close to you."

Glancing at a display, Danielle disagreed. "The closest ship is still twelve miles away."

The Frenchman faced her. "Your closest point of approach will be five and a half miles, unless those clowns change their evasion course. Five and half miles would put you within range of a friendly-fire torpedo."

Danielle's skin tingled with heightened awareness.

She knew that any respectable surface combatant commander would keep the ship's torpedoes tight with friendly submarines nearby. Only an idiot would try to identify, target, and attack an enemy submarine with a friendly nearby.

An idiot, or an enemy.

"Understood, Pierre."

"Don't worry. I'll take care of it. I'm in communication with Captain Damari directly."

Before she could withhold blurting her answer, fear forced her response. "But not the Saudis? Not Fayed?"

He paused in thought. "No. Just Damari. And this brings us to the point. To negotiate favorable outcomes, I will need your promise to sink Saudi vessels upon my order, Jake's order, or if fired upon."

Unsure whom to trust in a quagmire of deception, she shut down.

Renard noticed her hesitance. "Danielle?"

"Yeah?"

Dark shadows carved harsh lines on his face. "Your answer."

"I'm ready, Pierre. I'm a professional."

"Good." The screen went dark.

Minutes later, the *Goliath* moved at ten knots, and the submarine officer sounded eager to hunt. "I request permission to submerge the ship."

Studying icons, Danielle examined and trusted the geometry that would keep her transport vessel clear of the fleeing Arabs. "Submerge the ship."

Taylor's voice carried excitement as he addressed the *Goliath's* crew. "Prepare for crash dive."

Instead of being terrified as with her first such maneuver, she anticipated the roller coaster ride.

Taylor tapped a screen. "I'm shifting propulsion to the MESMA units... propulsion is shifted to the MESMA units."

As the rumbling subsided, Danielle's world became quiet, and the rhythmic sloshing of waves against the *Goliath's* starboard hull soothed her ears. She stared in admiration at the port hull's bow wake, which held firm as the vessel maintained ten knots. Machinery the *Goliath's* size was supposed to make louder noise at ten knots, but the MESMA systems were quiet.

Taylor announced the obvious. "The gas turbines are secured, ma'am." He prompted her next order. "The ship is ready to dive."

"Very well. Submerge the ship."

"I am submerging the ship."

After he hit icons, the deck dipped downward, the seas raced up the ship's sides, and Danielle's hands became vice grips on the railing while water engulfed the dome.

Translucent fluid filtered the sunlight above, turned into blue, and then yielded to blackness. As the sun became a memory, the bridge's artificial lights illuminated the room.

As the deck leveled, Danielle's stomach settled. "Wow. That's almost worth doing just for the fun."

"With the windows and the view... yeah. Wow."

Danielle had once found this silent world paralyzing, but now it was somehow invigorating–like a hidden realm welcoming her to a secret sisterhood below the waves.

She respected the deep's numinous awe, for the fear and respect it demanded, and for the dangers and glories of the submerged.

Taylor pulled her from her daydreaming. "The ship is submerged, passing ten meters."

"Very well."

"Fifteen meters."

Danielle found the silence calming. "Very well."

"Steady on thirty meters, ma'am. Commencing Sonar Search Plan Alpha."

"Very well."

He aimed his voice at the open microphone. "Commence Sonar Search Plan Alpha."

From the control room, the sonar supervisor replied. "Commence Sonar Search Plan Alpha, aye sir. We are commencing Sonar Search Plan Alpha."

Danielle wondered if Plan Alpha included phantoms of Saudi fantasies. "At least it's quiet down here."

"Let's hope it stays that way." As the ship's hydrophones endured slower flow friction underneath the noise of surface swells, Taylor's gaze shifted to the dancing lines representing raw sounds. "Either that, or we find whoever's out here fast."

Accepting the unknowns of false targets and dubious alliances, Danielle steeled herself for battle. "What do we hear?"

His eyes on a display, Taylor grimaced. "Nothing useful yet... a ton of broadband noise from the combatants... they're correlating–"

From speakers, the sonar supervisor's voice filled the bridge. "Bridge, control room. We've got a couple dozen sounds to correlate. We hear new surface ships. We're sorting it out, but we have no new submerged contacts."

After acknowledging the supervisor, Taylor turned to his boss. "We're still too far away too fast. I'll bring us to five knots and turn to course zero-four-zero."

"Very well." She watched lines of sound appear and grow brighter as the noise around the *Goliath's* hydrophones receded. But nothing resembling evidence of an Iranian submarine appeared. "Talk to me, Mike. Tell me what you're doing."

Nodding, he extended a finger towards a display of icons. "I'm slowing and turning our hydrophones broadside to the threat. If this ship were quieter, I'd maybe get more aggressive, but we're so loud that I need to be cautious."

She agreed with the assessment, a simple conclusion. But she realized she would've struggled to generate the tactic herself. "Very well."

She looked at empty textual fields where she expected data from the low-bandwidth communications that penetrated deep water. But the gunnery exercise included no such transmissions, and her ship was incommunicado.

Accidentally mocking her sense of isolation, Taylor shifted his gaze to his commander. "It's good be alone again. Nobody can bother us."

The comment revealed her discomfort with the sensory isolation. Her dismissive grunt required effort. "Whatever."

"I'll get some communications buoys ready for–"

The sonar supervisor's voice cut the air. "Active sonar! Bearing two-nine-one."

Fearing herself within minutes of death, Danielle's guts twisted.

Taylor managed the question. "Whose is it?"

The supervisor's voice was tense. "Analyzing."

"Analyze faster."

Hearing the men's trepidation sent Danielle to a corner of her soul. In stark terror, she locked eyes with the submarine officer and spoke with her face. "*Have we been betrayed into a deathtrap?*"

Reading her fear, Taylor clenched his jaw but said nothing.

And saying nothing told her everything. He inwardly agreed the deadly deception was possible.

For countless seconds, she froze and sensed her awareness leaving her body.

Then, the supervisor's enthusiasm flushed her with relief's warmth. "It's Jake's torpedo. It's going away from us."

His body softening from the report, Taylor replied. "Very well, control room. Get a message ready for Pierre with data about Jake's torpedo..." he glanced at his boss.

Danielle answered his gesture. "How long will this take? I don't want to make noise near an enemy submarine."

"Three minutes. Five tops." The submarine officer explained himself. "If Jake's in a fight, Pierre may not know about it yet."

Recovering from her fright and confused about Jake's actions, she offered a curt response. "Right. Good idea. You may launch a communications buoy in the next five minutes. If it takes any longer, inform me."

Taylor nodded to his boss. While setting a five-minute timer on his screen, he raised his voice. "Launch the buoy when the message is drafted."

"Bridge, control room, aye, sir."

Taylor returned his attention to the sonic data coming from the *Goliath's* hydrophones.

As she regained her awareness, Danielle voiced her concern. "Any idea what Jake's shooting at?"

The submarine officer snorted. "Anything but a friendly, a neutral, or himself is fine for now."

She revealed her doubts. "Mike, I'm not sure who I count as a 'friendly' in this."

He digested her statement in silence and then replied with her old nickname from their officer formation. "That's warfare, Dani. You have to consider the agenda of all actors."

A drawback of mercenary life smacked her. Losing the British fleet's protective umbrella had hurt, and her newfound awareness of toggling loyalties compounded her despair. "Fair enough."

After another hour of searching, Jake's torpedo proved itself an errant shot intended to roust a phantom.

The phantom never appeared.

Nor did a second phantom reveal itself to the *Goliath's* commander.

Two hours of searching degraded into a groping for ghosts, sullied by the triple nightmare of searching for Iranians, avoiding fratricide with the Arabic ships, and learning to communicate from the deep with their new clients.

After exposing a periscope and receiving an order to stand down, she had her executive officer surface the *Goliath*.

As the Arab-Mercenary task force slinked back to its homeport, Danielle wondered if she'd joined the mercenary fleet to flee historic pains only to land chaos.

CHAPTER 11

With the *Makkah* docked, Captain Fayed watched his steward lower a dish of red snapper onto the tablecloth. "Thank you."

The young petty officer backed away. "My pleasure, sir."

Fayed admired the courtesy he showed his underlings. Like a magnanimous master, he wrapped a gentleness around the force of his commands.

Biting into his dinner's firm meat, he enjoyed the sweetness and wondered what the working pawns were doing outside. Through the private cabin's window, he glanced at sailors on the pier without COVID masks.

The masks had appeared on the Internet, but the island's isolation allowed the Socotrans to avoid the virus by shutting down commercial travel.

Fayed wondered how long that would last.

Panic would reach the island, and he pondered ways he might use it to manipulate the hearts and minds of the Socotrans. But that was a different fight for another day.

First, there were military battles.

And, if he had his way, there would be more than just Aden.

Seated to his right, Commander Hijazi washed down his first bite with sparkling water. "The gunnery exercises went very well."

Looking through the distant bulkhead towards a destiny he shaped, Fayed agreed. "Yes... Perfectly."

"Our ships scored respectably while the Yemenis struggled."

"Only the new crew on the stolen *Tarantul* struggled."

"Oh yes, the... what do they call it, again?"

Fayed smirked at the ancient Yemeni naval weaponry. "The *Khalid*. They call it the *Khalid*, and they gave it to the command of some washed up commander named Halabi"

"Right, sir. Anyway, they were laughable."

Fayed sensed overconfidence in his underling. "Careful. They struggled, but they might have improved if given time."

Displaying a sly comfort with his boss, the short chief of staff queried him. "But they didn't have time, did they?"

Accepting the change in subject, Fayed jabbed his fork into a baked potato. "They did not. The submarine detection kept them off balance."

Animated, the Commander Hijazi relished the Yemeni embarrassment like a giddy child. "Did you hear how frustrated Damari was when he sent the mercenaries on the hunt?"

Fayed savored the memory. "I'm sure he realized how asinine he sounded. Him, an Arabic commodore, reminding me, to avoid so-called friendly fire against Western hirelings. And then threatening me with the Frenchman's resolve to consider even accidental weapons launch an act of aggression? Damari's in bed with the devil."

"You'll correct his errors, sir."

Eying Hijazi, Fayed sensed a curiosity approaching suspicion.

The short chief of staff seemed to examine his boss for a sign, any gesture of indignation or remorse revealing that he'd ordered the fake submarine detection. But for a lack of evidence, Hijazi held his tongue.

As did the Yemeni commodore, who'd withheld any accusations.

Knowing he'd made Captain Damari wonder about a false detection report without a basis for challenge made Fayed smile. He then reflected upon the 'package', which his brother had acquired. The timing was right. The package would be ready for Aden.

Yemen's commodore off balance, the package ready, the mercenaries undermined... everything was perfect. "Damari will correct his errors himself, or I will condemn him."

The chief of staff nodded a gracious smirk and then changed the subject. "I'm sure you will, sir. Just think of all the successes you've enjoyed thus far. You'll have quite a career ahead of you, after you take control of Yemen's waters."

After reminiscing with Hijazi over dinner about transiting Hormuz, gaining humanitarian convoy footage, and witnessing growing doubts among the Yemenis and mercenaries, Fayed sat alone chewing his pepper-flavored *shammah*.

As a distraction, he thumbed through screens on his phone.

While he'd operated at sea free from pandemics, he'd marveled at how fear consumed humanity. Economies were shuttered, poverty destroyed lives, and political lies overshadowed the virus itself.

Powerbrokers ran global affairs, giving whatever answers suited themselves at the sheep's expense. He chuckled as he silently promoted himself into the ranks of the elite.

Fayed spat into his gray bottle, sealed the lid, and then stuffed the container in his pants pocket.

Three loud knocks and a strong voice issued from the cabin's door. "Lieutenant Mahmood, sir. I request permission to enter."

The commodore spat and then barked. "Come!"

Wearing a flight jacket, the young helicopter pilot entered, closed the door, and stood at attention. "Lieutenant Mahmood reporting as ordered, sir."

"Were you seen entering my quarters?"

"No, sir."

"Very well. Sit." Fayed nodded to seat at his left.

Under the thin veneer of formalized respect, the young pilot wore a smug smile. "I did what you wanted."

Donning a politician's smile, Fayed sensed the foolish youngster examining him for a weakness, possibility with the interest of blackmailing him for extra payment. He made the pilot watch him chew a slow mouthful before responding. "Yes, you did."

The pilot pressed. "I had to bribe my crew."

Fayed remained silent.

Squirming, the lieutenant pleaded. "I paid from my own

pockets."

"I knew you'd find a way."

Leaning forward and lowering his voice, the pilot seemed fearful of making his accusation. "You promised a reward."

The commodore glared at the underling. "Never speak of it again. When I tell you to keep something secret, that means keep it secret. Even in perceived privacy. Is that clear, lieutenant?"

"Yes, sir."

The first use of the word 'sir' inside the cabin told Fayed that his pawn had remembered his place–for the moment. "Good. What did you tell your aircrew?"

"Nothing, sir! I told them nothing beyond the ruse itself."

Fayed rejected the claim. "But they asked who was behind it, didn't they?"

"Well, yes."

"And what did you tell them?"

"I said exactly what you told me to say."

The commodore screamed. "Damn it!"

"What?"

"Don't implicate me, whether you think you remember my actions or not. I'm too valuable a target to those who would oppose us. You'd put the whole campaign at risk."

"I won't do it again."

Disappointed that the pilot's retort fell short of an apology, Fayed was gruff. "Tell me what you told them. Verbatim."

The pilot looked upward in recollection. "Men loyal to Mohammed bin Salman are rebuilding the glory of our past and extending our influence around the Arabian Peninsula. The westerners will be evicted, and the Yemenis will be brought back into the fold of the righteous."

The delivery quelled the commodore. "Those were the proper words. However, you apparently told them with insufficient fervor, since you still had to bribe them."

"Perhaps. I was nervous at the time. I'm doing high-risk work for you, as you know."

Fayed satiated his minion's greed by reaching into his breast pocket for a wad of cash.

The young man accepted his bribe and then seemed to probe the commodore's face for a gesture liberating him from the room.

Fayed denied him the gesture and chewed a sweet, nutty bite of snapper before his next offer. "I have another assignment for you."

Suddenly greedy again, the pilot leaned forward. "I'm listening."

"In Aden, you'll be doing similar work, perhaps a bit more complex, and with the same... arrangements." To clarify, Fayed eyed the cash in the young man's hand.

"More complex? That sounds quite risky."

"The reward will be commensurate."

The pilot grinned while vocalizing his response. "So be it."

Hating the underling's smugness, the Saudi commodore decided to have him killed after his usefulness. Leaders had to use and sacrifice lesser beings for the common good, he knew. "Good. Dismissed."

The young officer departed.

Alone again, Fayed shifted his thoughts to warfare.

He called up a chart showing combative forces along Yemen's southwestern coast. Where the conflagration for Aden appeared as multicolored icons of military units scattered like a kaleidoscope, he shifted his gaze to something he better understood.

Farther east, the city of Zinjibar promised an opportunity.

Saudi military intelligence told him that friendly ground forces were breaking the Separatists' hold on Zinjibar, and the city was returning to President Hadi's loyalists.

But Fayed saw an opportunity to soften the Separatists' air defenses and facilitate the city's retaking.

He stood, walked to a porthole, lifted his cell phone, and dialed the Yemeni commodore.

Cold, his counterpart's voice revealed fatigue. "Damari here."

Fayed jumped to his point. "We must hit Zinjibar before moving on to Aden."

"That's not part of the agreement."

Silently, the Saudi commodore mocked his victim. To Fayed, agreements between diplomats were works of fiction. Once signed, they were to be discarded. "No plan survives contact with the enemy. You know that. We need to adjust."

"Who needs to adjust and why?"

Fayed resisted the urge to sound patronizing. "We, our task force, need to adjust to the Separatists in Zinjibar who've established rooftop control over urban fields of fire. We, your Saudi allies, are clearing the city of Separatists. But we need helicopter support."

"My latest intelligence report says the Separatists are all but defeated in Zinjibar.

Enjoying the gray area of unproveable claims, Fayed countered with another generalization. "But we can't let friendly ground forces be sacrificed for lack of air cover. We can take down the anti-air defenses and save dozens of lives."

The loud sigh confirmed Damari's inability to challenge the logic, or else it was his lack of interest in arguing. "If we do this, how long's it going to take?"

To reduce the attack to a foregone conclusion, Fayed mentioned it in the present tense. "Less than a day. It's just a quick strike. Consider it unfinished target practice."

Damari snapped. "What's the target?"

Fayed let his counterpart's frustration linger before responding. "There's an anti-air battery that's well entrenched atop the Aman Insurance Building. The army can't take it out without grave risk of collateral damage. But once it's gone, we can rule the city with helicopter support."

"That city's been shelled before."

Recognizing the comment as the end of his counterpart's resistance, Fayed sought capitulation. "You, of all people, can't dismiss your countrymen's welfare."

A pause. Then the admission. "No. Damn you, what do you want from me?"

"The *Goliath* can handle this readily with railguns, can it not?"

"I'm sure it can. It's the collateral damage I'm worried about."

Fayed leapt upon his prey. "Precisely! You said it yourself that the city's been shelled before. Spare the city and take out this air battery with a few rounds from the *Goliath*. Stray rounds, if any, won't hit civilians and might even land well beyond the city."

"I can't argue that."

The Saudi commodore attacked with an irrelevant platitude. "You have to protect your people."

A display of vulnerability. "I'm doing the best I can."

Fayed appealed to his counterpart's frustration. "I know you are, but there's only so much one man can do."

Damari recovered his composure. "I don't need your pampering."

Fayed appealed to his counterpart's pride. "I'm acknowledging the gravity of your burden. While we're rallying troops and civilians around Aden, we don't need this neighboring city becoming a distraction."

"Agreed."

"We can do this. We must. It will be a minor effort well worth the trouble. And the littoral threat is only–"

Damari interrupted. "I know the threat in my own littorals."

"Of course, you do. Shall we have our staff members draw up a joint plan?"

"After I verify your intelligence on my end."

The Saudi commodore grinned. "That's understandable. But please hurry, for your people."

Damari sounded like he wrestled himself. "Yes. I should hurry. But, no. There's no time. The ground units at Aden are waiting."

"Ah, but Aden is a hot battle zone. Not so in Zinjibar–not yet. You have a chance to quell that fire before it erupts. Let me help you douse it, and then we can focus on Aden."

Over the phone. Damari released a long sigh. "Fine. But I'm not committing the entire Aden task force to this."

"Of course, not. I wouldn't dare ask for something so inappropriate. I was thinking you could send the bulk of the force ahead to search for submarines around Aden."

"Good. I'll do that."

"The attack on Zinjibar will be a simple and effective plan. Trust me."

CHAPTER 12

The next morning, Commander Andi Amir reached for a microphone. "Secure from the small-boat defense drill."

He stepped to a window, leaned through it, and watched a column of water from a firehose die. Echoing off the choppy sea, the final training rounds from the ship's smaller guns and personal firearms subsided.

Amir faced the bridge and walked to Damari. "The small-boat defense drill is completed, sir."

The commodore nodded. "The *Osa* has completed its drill as well. Very smooth. Your crews are capable."

Proud, Amir affirmed it. "We've fought enough pirates over the years to do this in our sleep."

Seeming to draw confidence from his underling, Damari enjoyed some gloating. "Yes. We do small boat combat well."

Amir risked voicing his curiosity. "Did the Saudis report completion of their small-boat defense drills?"

Damari shrugged. "Yeah."

"Well?"

The commodore snorted. "You think I care? They're terrible at it because they think it's beneath them. That's why the Houthi have been pummeling them in the Red Sea. It's why I'm almost tempted to trust them... to trust him"

"Sir?"

"True, he's an ass, but aren't most men of high rank? I can't deny that we complement each other, our fleets."

Emotions and speculations ran wild through Amir's mind amid the impossible possibility of his commodore welcoming ongoing work with Saudis. But he clamped shut his jaw and gazed at the sea.

Gentle waves formed whitecaps, dotting the panorama his ship's windows framed.

Politics behind the *Tarantul's* commander, he pushed his corvette towards his next battle, which his commodore had announced the prior evening.

Zinjibar.

Amir saw the Saudi focus on Zinjibar for what it was–a ruse. Something ugly would happen, he suspected, and it would come from a foggy event like a dubious submarine detection.

He noticed unusual motion beside him.

It was his leader's rare gesture of weakness, with Damari slumping his shoulders and rubbing his forehead.

"Sir?"

After a drawn sign, all bravado evaporated, leaving a man's soul exposed. Damari confessed. "I hate this."

The comment spawned fluctuating emotions within the *Tarantul's* commander. He realized his commodore trusted him, placing him in elite company, and possibly in a unique role of confidant. He questioned his ability to strengthen his boss in his moment of weakness. "What do you hate, specifically, sir?"

Damari jumped three steps deep into his answer. "I'd challenge him but..."

"Him? Fayed?"

Damari grunted his affirmation.

"But you're... concerned?

The commodore remained stone.

Amir prodded. "Concerned that we're... underequipped?"

The sigh from Damari was like life's final breath. "Yes."

Listening to soothing waves hugging his ship's hull, Amir drew inspiration as he encouraged his boss. "Weak in number and technology, yes. But strong in heart."

The Yemeni commodore seemed to draw encouragement from his underling. "Indeed. If only that could save our people."

"It will, sir. We must trust in ourselves."

As the conversation lulled, Amir excused himself. "If I may, sir, I'd like to check our formation."

Damari nodded his approval.

After stepping to a tactical display, Amir saw icons representing the small, ad hoc Zinjibar task force.

With the *Goliath's* railguns trailing the formation, the *Tarantul* led an *Osa* along with the Saudi combatants *Makkah* and *Tabuk* into Amir's homeland's waters.

The *Tarantul's* commander recalled that the remaining ships scouted waters near Aden, where the major battle loomed.

Hoping for a quick strike on Zinjibar, Amir sought insights about the waters before him.

Ahead of the small formation, one Saudi helicopter hunted hostile submarines while another aircraft offered an aerial perspective. From video feeds and sensor information, the *Tarantul's* commander examined the threat ahead.

Nothing.

And Amir believed it, having patrolled Zinjibar's waters for years and knowing that its shallow, smooth contour gave little place for submarines to hide.

Noticing Damari beside him, he worried that his boss was following him like a wounded puppy.

But the Yemeni commodore had recovered his resolve. "This attack favors our strengths. Let's help liberate Zinjibar."

Perhaps, Amir hoped, his listening ear had placated his boss' doubts. "Of course, sir. We're an hour from the *Goliath's* launch point. God willing, this will soon be a memory of a successful intervention."

An hour later, Amir slowed his ship from transit speed to a slower twelve-knot patrol. Dotting an arrow's tip around the *Goliath*, the *Tarantul* sliced water within sight of the small city.

With his naked eyes, he scanned the bobbing horizon and saw the small city's tallest structure, the twelve-story rectangular Aman Insurance Building.

Lifting binoculars to his face, he steadied the targeted rooftop in his field of view. He saw climate control equipment and elevator shafts above the roof's ramparts.

Rooftop walls concealed the enemy's anti-air battery. Aircraft dare not overfly it, and the combined Saudi-led ground forces retaking the city claimed a credible inability to thwart it with shelling or from attacking the building from within.

Lowering his optics, Amir stepped to a screen showing an aerial vantage from a Saudi helicopter.

Through the lens, three twin-rail surface-to-air launchers aimed skyward under grayish camouflaged netting.

Manning the weaponry, a team of six enemy soldiers stood ready to knock Saudi and Yemeni aircraft from the sky.

Amir marched to the bridge's port side, stuck his head out the window, and scanned the waters around the *Tarantul's* wake. Six miles behind him, the twin-hull catamaran presented two dark, bobbing specs.

As he crossed the bridge towards the far side, Amir slowed behind his commodore and eavesdropped.

Damari spoke into a handset. "... have my permission to fire six rounds, and six rounds only. Commence fire."

Unable to see hypersonic railgun rounds, Amir heard the *Goliath's* fury whiz overhead. As seconds elapsed and the *Tarantul's* commander craned his neck after the streaking rounds, another pair of fires erupted from the *Goliath*, and then a third salvo.

He yanked his head back into the bridge and found himself lacking for words. "Impressive."

Wide-eyed, Damari's face revealed astonishment as he stepped towards the forward windows for spotting rounds. "Wow."

Seconds later, Amir watched through binoculars as tiny clouds of dust rose from the bank's roof.

Aerial video showed the beauty of kinetic energy.

Having splintered into buckshot, the *Goliath's* first two rounds were invisible shards peppering the roof. Conical clouds of dust, stucco, and mortar revealed the trajectories of supersonic metal.

Enthusiastically, Amir faced his boss. "Those rounds were still on the way up. From ten miles away!"

Damari nodded his silent awe but then verbalized it through a hoarse, tightening throat. "Mach seven."

Amir looked back the display and watched the next four rounds strike. The blistering buckshot cast hazy clouds of dust over smoke, atomized mists of hydraulic oil, and avulsed metal. He replayed the attack in slow motion, this time noticing the human carnage. Cringing, he watched men squirm in horror and agony with their final thoughts and breaths.

Of the fallen men, half were in death's merciful bosom while the others writhed from searing puncture wounds. One by one, the living fell limp until the last young man reached for an indifferent sky and then collapsed in hateful spite of his mortality.

As a numinous silence enveloped the *Tarantul's* bridge, Amir realized others were watching the video–notably, his boss.

Damari grimaced. "War is hell."

Fighting his rising nausea, Amir redirected the conversation. "That was excellent targeting."

"Against a building, guided by satellites? Yes. That's expected."

Amir shamed himself for having stated the obvious. "Right, sir."

"Let's be sure about this damage assessment. I'm sending in twelve more rounds."

Minutes later, the anti-air battery's transformation into a weapons junkyard provided testimony to the *Goliath's* attack.

Stress rising from his shoulders, Damari straightened his back and announced into a handset. "Secure from Zinjibar attack. Set task force base course of two-five-five, speed fifteen knots. Carry on. Good job to all who–"

A young officer called out. "Sir, a fishing ship has approached within four miles and is on an intercept course."

Amir barked. "Hail it. Waive it off."

The young officer reached for a radio handset. "Aye, aye, sir."

A dark feeling overcame Amir as he yelled into an overhead

microphone. "Tactical center, bridge. What's that fisherman to the northeast doing?"

The executive officer's voice filled the compartment. "It's been sitting dead in the water, fishing and watching our attack, I assumed. The propulsion plant kicked in half a minute ago, but the officer of the deck announced the four-mile tripwire before I could analyze an evasion course."

"Evasion?"

"Yes, sir. I thought we'd get out of here without any trouble."

Overhearing, Damari interjected. "Do we want to look like cowards, running from a fishing ship?"

Amir mulled over his options. "Good point, sir. But I also don't want to kill them if they get too curious." He raised his voice and glanced at the young officer on the radio. "Did you hail them, yet?"

"Five times. No response, sir!"

Amir yelled into the overhead. "Tactical center, bridge. If that fisher to the northeast approaches within three miles, send one round from the main cannon across its bow."

"One round across the bow at three miles, aye, sir."

Outside the front windows, the three-inch muzzle swung to the right and arched upward.

Adding to the mounting confusion, the Saudi commodore interrupted, speaking for himself instead of through a phone-talker. His tone was dismissive, bordering on mockery. "*Tarantul*, this is Captain Fayed. I notice a fishing vessel attempting to intercept you. Do you require assistance?"

Damari replied. "Yes. Send a helicopter to usher it away. It's not responding to our hails."

"I'll send a helicopter right now."

"Very well." After seconds of digesting the offer, Damari frowned and leaned into Amir's ear. "He's lying. Break formation, come to twenty knots, and get us out of here."

Afraid of Saudi betrayal, Amir accelerated his ship. As the deck undulated with speed, his executive officer harkened from the ship's inner nerve. "Bridge, tactical center. The merchant ship to the south, bearing one-nine-one, range four miles just kicked on its engines and is heading on an intercept course."

Amir judged the civilian ships' movements a trap. He'd seen the tactic before where vessels carried and then launched, or concealed and then revealed, speedboats armed with improvised explosives. "All ahead flank! I have the deck and the conn."

His eyes glued to a display, Damari seemed to wrestle with an evasion course. Though not his duty to recommend it, survival compelled his analysis. "Roughly course two-eight-zero."

Amir glanced at the geometry, agreed, and turned his ship.

The executive officer announced the situation's worsening. "Bridge, tactical center. There's a third boat coming for us from the east. They've got us triangulated."

"Tactical center, bridge. Give me a recommended course."

"Keep the one we're on, sir. We'll have to outrun this third ship."

As the deck tilted, Amir noticed a tactical limit and shared his rising suspicions with Damari. "I can't evade them all, and I can't engage them all with the cannon, sir. I can only attack two of them, and I need to swing the barrel almost the full range to do it."

Damari scowled. "A coordinated attack. Fast boats will be coming. Motivate your men."

Amir grabbed a handset. "Crew of the *Tarantul*, we're under a small-boat attack. With the exception of the main cannon, all weapons are free on any target within range. I say again. With the exception of the main cannon, all weapons are free. Carry on."

Adding emphasis, the executive officer called out over the loudspeaker. "Shooting one warning round across the bow of the northern fisherman."

Amir shouted. "Belay my order on a warning round. Shoot to kill!"

"Shooting to kill, sir!"

Bridge windows shook within the shockwave.

Half a minute later, the shell exploded in the fisherman's

path.

Over the loudspeaker, the executive officer's voice was shrill. "Radar separation on two of the three incoming ships... now separation on all three! The ships have delivered two small boats each and are veering away. We have six incoming small boats!"

Amir sank deep within himself and tapped his knowledge and his courage. Like an exhausted boxer in the late rounds, he became a combination of instinct, adrenaline, and training.

He'd fought small boats before, but they'd been pirates–not a coordinated suicide attack.

Around him, the crew fell into the familiar but harried routine of self-preservation. Alarmed lookouts pointed rigid arms towards the incoming speedboats, and a flurry of reports filled the background chatter of several open circuits.

From overheard conversations, reports flying to and around him, and sensory data, Amir gleaned tactical awareness.

One sailor, who wore a sound-powered headset, gave the most anxious report. "They're loaded with explosives on the bows, sir."

Amir glared at the youngster. "Which one?"

"All of them!"

Shouting for all to hear, the *Tarantul's* commander tested the underling's situational awareness. "How many is 'all of them'?"

"I count six, sir. The tactical center says the same."

The information aligned with Amir's understanding. "I see six as well. We'll destroy or evade six fast small boats, then."

Exhaling a strained sigh beside him, Damari protested Amir's confidence with a hard look. The pain in the commodore's face revealed what the *Tarantul's* commander admitted silently.

The six boats had surrounded them, negating the corvette's advantage of breakneck speed.

Escape required good fortune.

Amir ran mental scenarios, picked the least damaging, and shared his intentions with his boss. "I'm going to mow down the one to the southwest. God willing, the cannon will take it out first."

Capturing the deeper meaning, Damari replied. "Then the one to the south will intercept us broadside, unless you face it head-on."

Amir gave his affirming grim. "Facing it head-on would let it explode at our bow."

"An explosion is inevitable."

The *Tarantul's* commander accepted his fate. "We'd be hurt bad, but with a bow impact, we'd still have the propulsion to evade."

"Move everyone to middle and after compartments and prepare damage control teams to fight flooding in the bow compartments."

With his crew fighting six incoming waterborne bombs, the *Tarantul's* commander grabbed the young officer of the deck's shoulder and whispered an order to prevent a fatal blow from becoming fatal.

Wide-eyed with defeat's acceptance, the young officer affirmed the order and left the bridge to coordinate the shifting of people to safer compartments.

Amir pointed his ship towards the southwestern boat. "Helm, left five-degrees rudder, steady on course two-four-four."

As a sailor rotated a wheel, the deck angled into the turn.

Outpacing all but two seaborne threats, the *Tarantul's* commander sought the destruction of the small boat two miles ahead. "Tactical center, bridge. Concentrate all fires on the boat the southwest. I mean to overrun it, and it had better be burning hulk when I do."

"Bridge, tactical center, aye."

Moments later, a phone talker extended a handset. "Sir! It's the executive officer."

Amir strode to the phone and lifted it. "Speak!"

"What about the boat to the south, sir? It's making twenty-six knots. I won't have time to get it with the main canon. Even if we can slow it with small arms, it's going to hit us."

Knowing it was a thin hope, Amir gave a wishful answer.

"We'll hope for really good shooting, then."

The executive officer's hoarse reply caressed Amir's ear. "You know the odds of hitting small crossing targets at high speeds."

Amir looked at the sailor who'd handed him the phone and raised his voice. "We'll either shoot them both out of the water, or we'll absorb explosions at the waterline. Do your job and pummel those boats!"

Outside the bridge windows, the cannon bobbed with the seas, dipping in a trough to reveal the threatening boat and then hiding it on the next crest.

Aiming forward, the cannon shot one round every half second.

As shells smacked the water, domes of turquoise and white billowed around the nimble, jerking boat.

Trusting his gunner to adjust his fire with feedback from radar, eyes, and video feeds, Amir checked his position.

Four attacking boats fell behind the speeding *Tarantul*, leaving them as afterthoughts–unless damage slowed the fleeing corvette to their speeds.

Less than a mile off the bow, a crack accompanied the exploding round's deep boom, and fire engulfed the target's small hull.

Sounding elated, relieved, but scared, the executive officer announced the success. "The southwestern target is destroyed. We're turning the cannon south now."

"Very well." Amir marched to the port bridge windows and leaned through an opening to scan the waters.

What he saw terrified him.

A shoulder launcher rested aside one boat assailant's cheek. It spat fire, and a rocket-propelled grenade raced across the water. Seconds later, the corvette's superstructure shook, and Amir flinched backwards into a charting table.

As he recovered, he heard a damage report.

One dead, one injured, and his Kashtan close-in weapon system down.

His only legitimate defense, the main cannon, sought the final assailant. But the distance, which the suicide boat and the corvette closed at highway speeds, was short.

In a mortal moment, Amir saw faces aboard the incoming vessel. Except for one man in his thirties–the apparent leader–they were teenagers.

One childish face reminded him of his eldest son. He locked eyes with the youngster and saw hatred.

Surprising himself, Amir pitied his enemy.

A young fool was cutting off his life in exchange for false gods and vapid promises. A waste!

Damari withdrew the *Tarantul's* commander from his meditation. "Dare we risk turning?"

Amir considered veering away, but the maneuver risked exposing his vulnerable broadside. Accepting the inevitable explosion at his bow, he lifted a microphone and steeled his voice. "All hands, brace for–"

Two sonic booms swept across the sea, and then two more traced an audible line across Amir's horizon.

The *Goliath*'s translator spoke over the radio circuit. "Commander Sutton has crippled the fast boat's engines and urgently recommends a hard steer to starboard. I say again, Commander Sutton recommends a hard steer to starboard–"

Amir obeyed his mercenary. "Right hard rudder! Starboard engine, stop!"

Reality flopped to the left, carrying Amir and two unbalanced sailors into the bulkhead.

Groaning from a bumped elbow, the *Tarantul's* commander forced himself to the window and sought his enemies.

Dead in the water, the harmless boat carried frustrated men and drifted beyond its explosives' blast range. Smoke rose from its engine room where hypersonic metallic shards had spoken.

A young face glared back at Amir with defiance, but also with relief. Somehow, the boy grasped that his escaped fate had been a fool's destiny.

His adrenaline ebbing, the *Tarantul's* commander recovered his sense of calm, slowed his ship, and sought repairs. "Tactical center, bridge. What's the status on the Kashtan?"

"Bridge, tactical center. The grenade took out the power, but we'll reroute around the damage within thirty to sixty minutes."

"Very well."

Damari, against Amir's wildest expectations, had returned to the perfect image of stoicism. "We expected Zinjibar to cost us little. Thanks to the *Goliath*, I have only one widow to console."

CHAPTER 13

In her mind, Danielle replayed the video.

Then she mentally watched it again.

And then, yet again in a never-ending loop.

A force beyond her drove the infinite cycle, tormenting her with the bloody horrors her cannons had wrought.

Her head spun with a repeated number.

Six.

That's how many young men she'd killed.

Six soldiers had been fighting for a cause they believed righteous until her uncaring tapping of computer icons had sent supersonic metal through their flesh.

Since her childhood, she'd steeled her will for killing–and for dying, if need be–to protect her beliefs. Serving the Crown had tested her mettle, but she'd never been responsible for another person's death.

Until today.

She tried to reduce her victims to nonhumans, like Nazi prison keepers or Socialist gulag guards who convinced themselves that German Jews, Russian Christians, or Chinese Uyghurs were animals. But her nature prevented the deception. Six men, some half her age, were lifeless corpses thanks to her.

Trying to shake memories of the fleshy carnage, she shut her eyes. But the enraged plea from the terrified face of a dying youngster spitting blood-soaked anger and grasping an indifferent sky petrified her.

"Dani?"

She found the distant voice familiar, but her memory crushed her under the slaughter's repeated replay. Human bodies burst like bags of blood as her imagination united with her recollection in mocking her conscience.

Taylor's harsh voice cut through her fog. "Dani!"

Recognizing the ancient nickname from her Dartmouth days, she uttered a whisper. "Yeah."

"Dani, can you hear me? It's Mike."

The hand falling on her shoulder was soft, but she recoiled. "No!"

"I'm sorry." Her executive officer withdrew his arm.

"It's… it's okay."

"You tuned out there for a bit."

"I'm fine."

His voice was soft. "It's okay. You did what you had to do. You did your job."

She interpreted his tone as an insult. "I said I'm fine. I don't need babying."

From the display below her nose, Renard's face was compassionate. "Danielle, please listen. You've just been through a lot."

She shut her eyes. "Why's everyone treating me like a child? I command a bloody warship!"

Lowering his eyes, Taylor exposed his shiny scalp. "Look at your hands, Dani."

Obeying, she raised and inspected her palms. They were trembling, and rivulets of blood rose from the puncture wounds of her fingernails. She balled her fists and crossed her arms. "I…"

Renard called out. "Danielle. Look at me. Danielle!"

She forced her eyes upon the pixelized version of his, but she could say nothing.

"Danielle, this is my doing. The responsibility rests squarely upon me. I agreed to this attack, and I issued the order. This is my burden to bear, not yours."

Her weak voice wavered. "It was horrible. How can you…"

Renard shook his head. "How can I be so callous?"

She nodded.

"I assure you, young lady, it's merely an illusion. After that scourging, I imagine I'll vomit when I get the opportunity. Nobody can witness this without disgust."

She glanced to her executive officer.

Taylor shrugged and nodded. "I'd be spitting out, too, if I had any food in my stomach. I won't be eating tonight, not after seeing that."

Gaining some solace from the shared trauma, she faced her boss again. "Okay. War is hell. I get it. So, we deal with it and move on."

"Right you are, Danielle, but a commanding officer also needs rest. Let Mike handle the aftermath with your tactical team. Take a few personal hours to rest and reflect."

Appreciating his advice as wisdom, she agreed. "Okay, Pierre. I can do that. But first, I want to know what the bloody hell went on with our supposed suicide boat screen."

The Frenchman's face darkened. "This is a delicate matter, and one for which I must take an unusual stance."

Unsure what 'unusual' meant, she asked. "What's that mean?"

"It means that I suspect a ruse of disinformation. Commander Fayed is the devil incarnate, and one does not fight a devil head-to-head."

Enjoying her relief from her replayed loop of mental torment, she delved deeper into the Frenchman's thoughts. "Then how does one fight a devil?"

"We trick him into thinking he's defeated us."

"I see what you mean by 'unusual'. How does that happen?"

"We and the Yemenis speak of nothing but the excellent skill with which the assailants assaulted the *Tarantul*. They seemed to predict our every move, as if we'd been betrayed by locals who knew the Yemeni anti-suicide-boat tactics."

"But that's not why we failed, is it? I mean, you have to at least suspect this was a trap by the Saudis, don't you?"

"Of course, I suspect them, and I'd wager my personal fortune on it. But what of it? Truth is subservient to power in this theater."

She saw his intent. "We're playing dumb?"

"Dumb enough to let them suspect we're playing dumb, but

not enough to accuse us."

Recalling a truism from an Ayn Rand novel, Danielle complemented the Frenchman's tactic. "The worst lie is the half-truth. It's believable, and just enough to deny the premise of a challenge. Exactly like Fayed is doing with is."

"Precisely. We'll act as if Saudi disloyalty is beyond conceiving. It will lurk in our minds, and it will govern our tactics, but it will never shape our speech."

She folded her arms tighter. "Makes sense, but you're still talking at a high level. This doesn't have many options that I can see, and if we take the wrong one, it's exposed and collapses."

"It's a gamble, indeed, but I believe Fayed will fall for it. He's arrogant and will credit himself for fooling us. That's our advantage, and we'll exploit it."

Having spent a career learning how to lead warriors, Danielle found herself untrained in diplomacy. "This is like playing poker, or being a lying politician. I suppose I can do my part, as long as it's just playing dumb. But how do we exploit it?"

"I'm sorry to disappoint you, young lady, but I must keep much of it secret. I can only ask you to trust me and let me prove myself when the moment arises. Hopefully within the next few hours, if I can arrange it."

Wanting to ask why the mercenary fleet should bother finishing its Yemeni assignment, she instead opted to obey. She considered herself a rookie among veterans, and if the other commanders wanted to support the Frenchman's decision, she'd accept it. "Okay. Do you have new orders for me?"

"Other than getting your rest right now, I do not."

Alone in her quarters, the *Goliath's* commander sat at a foldout desk and withdrew a hand-written letter from Dmitry Volkov.

Although her heartthrob's grammar was clunky, his penmanship was impeccable, like he'd conveyed esteem with each line and curve for his one-lady audience.

The Orthodox Russian confessed his love for her, but in the

same pen strokes proclaimed a love for his god.

She examined his writing, trying to separate his feelings for her from those he claimed for an invisible immortal. But the submarine commander's sentiments for a human woman and his distant deity seemed inseparable.

For any given moment during which her wildest imagination envisioned and allowed the existence of Hell, she believed that her affections for Volkov dragged her into it.

They loved each other, but he insisted upon her adopting his god if they were to possess each other as husband and wife.

But no god she could reckon would allow evil and suffering. So, she sought a path of logic to unravel his fantasies.

Centuries of scientific exploration had revealed nothing about a phantom deity's existence, but it had instead offered a multitude of rational explanations for the creation of the universe.

Unfortunately, she couldn't recall any of those explanations, having spent her free time since girlhood studying the practical arts of leadership, technology, and naval tactics.

Frustrated, she folded the qualified letter into a notepad, locked it inside her desk, and crawled into her rack.

She sighed. "Damn you, Dmitry."

She awoke with a start and willed herself free of a lingering dream. Visions of a wedding feast with herself as the bride and a rugged Russian groom spilled from her mind and fell beyond reach into an infinite abyss underneath the *Goliath*.

Forcing a yawn, she grasped her phone and checked the time. She'd slept six hours. "Damn it, Mike. You let me sleep too long."

After a quick refreshening at her sink, she marched through the crew's mess where a cook stirred a huge pot of stew. The smell of tomato paste spurred her hunger, but she had other issues on her mind.

When she reached the bridge, she gave her executive officer a hard look. "Why'd you let me sleep so long?"

"I figured you could use it."

Having not specified a waking time, she acquiesced. "Well, sure. But you really didn't need me all this time?"

"I'm a bit surprised myself, but after you went down, Pierre held a conference call with Fayed and Damari. At least on the face of it, everyone's getting along."

She respected the Frenchman's exquisite negotiating skills, but in her opinion, a renewed commitment to a joint operation with the Saudis and Yemenis required supernatural intervention. "Seriously?"

"He convinced Damari to play dumb and blame everyone and everything possible other than the Saudis for the suicide boat attack, and apparently, Fayed played along with it. He was even apologetic, according to Pierre."

She guffawed. "That's rich."

"Yeah, Pierre said he didn't buy it, but it was a great acting job. And as long as everyone acts like we're all getting along, we can fake it until we get out of here. I can replay the chat I had with Pierre about it, if you want."

She spoke while examining the tactical display. "Maybe later. What's going on?"

"We're in formation with the full task force, ready to begin the Siege of Aden, just waiting for Jake to give the go-ahead."

She'd expected more efficiency from a mercenary fleet submarine commander. "He hasn't cleared the area yet?"

"We're still waiting. Pierre said not to worry. Jake's not familiar with the waters and should move slowly, since there's a few good places for other submarines to hide. I'm sure it'll be fine, though."

"So, by the end of the night, we'll be lobbing shells on young kids again."

"Take heart. It's to prevent worse atrocities."

She wanted to talk about anything else. "Yeah. Tell me something I don't know."

Taylor shrugged. "Well, the elephant in the room is why we're marching along like nothing's wrong. Like the flipping Saudis were honest about the submarine detection during gunnery, and like they were honest about being unable to stop the suicide boats."

Danielle rethought watching the video, but she'd wait until Taylor was sleeping. "I guess we have to trust the boss."

Surprising her, he sighed his tension. "I suppose. I wish I could say I trust him outright, but I hardly know him."

His comment struck a nerve. "And you think I do? Hell, Mike, he recruited me in a whirlwind of promises. He had me convinced that I was a queen worthy of riches and adventure that only he could deliver."

Taylor smirked. "But her highness is a queen worthy of riches and adventure."

She punched his arm. "There's a 'no ass-kissing' rule on this ship."

"I'm just another silver-tongued devil, like Pierre."

"I think I know him less than I understand the commander of that Turkish submarine who nearly killed me."

The former submarine officer chuckled. "Yeah. Know your enemy, right? You get to know someone when you negotiate with each other at gunpoint."

She faced him. "And how well to we know Pierre?"

His tone shifted to doubt. "Fine enough, I suppose. Think back on how well we knew the Crown, or thought we did. Given the brazen lies in the news media today, I don't trust anything." He paused in thought and then continued. "Come to think of it, we may know Pierre a lot better than we think."

"How so?"

"His motivations are obvious. He can talk about doing the right thing and fighting good fights–and he makes good arguments about that, otherwise we wouldn't be here. But..."

She appreciated his candor and encouraged more. "Go on."

"But from what I can tell, that's so he can sleep at night, while he follows his greatest passion." Taylor paused for effect, seeming to imitate the subject of his talk.

"Okay. I'll bite. What's his greatest passion? Money? Winning?"

"No! Not quite. You're stopping short. His top passion is to play God. He wants to be a god. He wants to bend the world to his will."

She wondered if every power broker suffered a god complex. Desiring to be more than one is, she assumed, was a suffocating trap of narcissism. "Maybe. I hope it's not that bad."

An unexpected heaviness weighed down Taylor's tone. "For our sakes at Aden, I pray that it's not."

CHAPTER 14

Submerged, Jake read the report he'd received over the low-bandwidth feed. Happy with the Renard's opening sentences, he announced the verdict. "Zinjibar was a success."

Seated at the *Specter's* control station, Henri was enthused. "Ah, finally. We were due for a plan to unfold, well... per plan."

Jake returned his eyes to the screen and read further. "Damn it."

The silver-haired mechanic assumed his informal role as psychologist. "What news? You seem dismayed."

"Dismayed is an understatement. The *Tarantul* was attacked by suicide boats and grenade launchers. One dead, one injured, and the Kashtan close-in weapon system was temporarily knocked out of commission."

His face pale, Henri stood. "Seriously?"

"Yeah, and Danielle saved their asses from a suicide boat."

"I wasn't aware she bore any defensive responsibilities."

Holding his thunderous thoughts at bay, Jake answered. "She didn't. Apparently, there was some confusion between the Saudis and Yemenis, and the suicide boat slipped through the screens. She stepped up and took the initiative."

Henri gave a slow nod of respect. "I think I like her."

Admiring his female counterpart's impressive resume, Jake scowled. "You didn't used to?"

The Frenchman shrugged. "Well, I liked her enough, I guess. I respected her more than liking her, really, especially after she showed nerves of steel against the Turks. But she was pushed into that exchange, and the encounter was accidental."

Jake interrupted. "Your point?"

Henri sighed. "So young. So rash."

"Me? I'm forty-one."

"As I said. Young. Back to our subject. Mind you, this time, Danielle identified the need to act and embraced it willingly. That's crucial for our commanders."

Pursing his lips, Jake pondered his unofficial psychologist's insights. Finding them profound, he let the French mechanic's last word linger.

But Henri interrupted his commander's thoughts. "Any other news?"

His eyes flitting across the screen, Jake saw nothing else in the communique. But the absence of clarifying details–an artifact of undersea limits–crafted a message within a message.

Danielle had no earthly reason to intervene when the combined gunpower of the Saudi and Yemeni ships could have and should have stopped the assailants.

As the *Specter's* commander pondered her actions against the inaction of the ships around her, his silent verdict condemned Commodore Fayed and his unwelcomed Saudi ships.

Assuming a man guilty without evidence cast a cloud over Jake's soul. But his souring worldview made him suspect all but trusted friends.

Suspicion bred doubt, doubt bred fear, and he hated the slippery psychological slope. Avoiding further confusion and dissent, Jake kept his doubts unspoken. "No, nothing. That's it."

Then, the *Specter's* commander considered his teammates.

Five hundred miles to the east, Cahill and Volkov escorted the mission's largest humanitarian aid convoy towards Nisthun.

Renard had leaked to intelligence channels that his *Wraith*-and-*Xerses*-led convoy contained illegal weaponry inbound for the Yemeni resistance.

Jake recalled the sly Frenchman's intent of luring Iranian and UAE forces towards the humanitarian convoy to distract them from Aden. The *Specter's* commander disliked the plan, since it left the mercenary fleet's best anti-air platform, the MICA-armed *Xerses*, a day's journey away from the Aden task force.

He liked the plan less after the Saudi commodore had urged

the attack in Zinjibar, all but announcing the Yemeni naval forces' progression towards Aden. But Renard's insistence of Saudi air support's sufficiency trumped Jake's concerns.

His head spinning with tactics, politics, and an examination of his morality about his actions in Yemen, Jake plopped his tailbone on his captain's chair.

Growing in his faith, he said a quick prayer to clear his mind and his conscience.

Then he studied his tactical display.

Scouting the waters around the prized Yemeni port, the *Specter* cut holes below the Gulf of Aden's crowded maritime crossroads.

Jake expected to find nothing beyond fishing boats seeking food for Yemeni families and huge freighters and tankers crossing through the Bab al-Mandab Strait. The scattered icons and speed vectors on his screen verified the heavy traffic and suggested high levels of background noise to complicate his sonic search.

Safe from any hostile submarine that would challenge the retaking of Aden, a handful of Arabic combatant ships steamed behind Jake's detection range. But after reading of the Zinjibar debacle, he doubted his client's new partners.

He'd stay submerged, uncaring about surface or air battles.

Motion in front of him caught his attention, and he studied the curling torso of his sonar team's shift supervisor, the young Julien.

With stress levels high and endurance required for a prolonged siege, the *Specter's* commander insisted upon six hours of sleep for his guru, Antoine Remy.

Competent, but less than his mentor, the apprentice Julien slipped a muff behind his ear and queried a technician seated beside him who pointed at his sonar screen.

After a hurried exchange, the Frenchman shouted. "Submerged contact, bearing two-four-one. Fifty-hertz electric plant."

Jake uttered his fear. "Is it that Iranian *Kilo*?"

Julien shrugged. "Probably. I can't be sure. We'll need to get closer."

The *Specter's* commander eyeballed Henri. "Wake Antoine."

As the silver-haired mechanic obeyed, Jake stepped behind his sonar team and glared at the data. The fifty-hertz tone was the only sound within five degrees of either side of the submerged contact's bearing, suggesting a quiet ship.

Julien justified himself. "The sound propagation profile says a surfaced fifty-hertz tone can't reach us outside three miles. For this to be coming from farther away, it must be at least thirty meters deep, or else the sound wouldn't bend enough to reach us."

Jake's quick glance at pixels of graphical curves confirmed the Frenchman's claim. "Got it. Set the distance in the system at four miles and enter a speed of four knots, coming straight at us."

Julien tapped icons. "Four knots, four miles, straight at us."

The *Specter's* commander checked his ship's speed. Eight knots was aggressive. "Slow to five knots!"

After thirty seconds of deceleration, Julien leaned towards his sonar screen. "Active sonar, bearing two-four-one!"

Jake felt his body stiffen. "Probability of detection?"

"Less than fifty percent. It wasn't a strong ping. I barely heard it."

Selecting a slow-kill torpedo, the *Specter's* commander was decisive. "Then we take it out now. Designate the contact on two-four-one as the Iranian *Kilo*. Assign tube three to the *Kilo*. I'm shooting in sixty seconds."

In the flurry of activity, Henri prompted his commander. "Shall I send a note to Pierre?"

Jake had forgotten to inform his boss. "Yes. Shit. Get the targeting data into a communications buoy and launch it when I shoot, zero time delay."

"Zero time delay, when you shoot, aye, sir."

The *Specter's* commander scanned the room. "Where's Antoine?"

An answer echoed from the control room's rear. "I sprained my ankle."

Jake looked over his shoulder at the toad-headed sonar guru. Wanting to say something cavalier, the *Specter's* commander found his chest tight. An unusual fear rose within him, restricting his utterance to a growl. "Get to your station."

His face puffy, Remy gave a harsh look while limping to the sonar monitors. "I wish I never had to sleep."

"Just keep us from dying." The depressing words circled Jake's head, making him question his mental state.

For the first time, he knew he was scared–the wrong type of scared–the destructive brain-erasing kind, as opposed to that which brings adrenaline-heightened clarity. Something gnawed at him from inside. "Antoine, is my weapon ready?"

Another first–Remy snapped at the American. "Son of a whore! I just got here!"

His fingers flying over screens, Julien overcame the impasse. "I'll have it in ten seconds."

During a slow silence, Jake's pulse pounded.

Julien's tone was hopeful. "Tube three is ready."

Henri reported. "The ship is ready."

"Shoot tube three." As the pressure change of the pneumatic impulse launch popped Jake's ears, he examined the chart and realized he'd ignored his defense.

His de facto psychologist and executive officer assisted him from the ship's control station. "Perhaps an evasion course?"

"Right, Henri. Helm, come right, steer course three-three-zero."

After the deck tilted and then steadied, Remy, who'd taken management of the sonar team, shared bad news. "Our weapon has gone active, but no return yet."

Jake saw his torpedo's icon three miles from his target's expected location. "It should detect something by now."

Sleep falling from his face, Remy attempted optimism. "The target could have a narrow aspect. Give it another mile."

As the weapon reached two miles from the target, Jake glared at his sonar ace. "Well?"

The toad head shook. "Nothing."

Tension tightened Jake's jaw. "Shit. Any sign of counterfire?"

"Nothing."

"Are you sure we're shooting at the right thing?"

Twisting his torso towards his boss, Remy shrugged. "I hear fifty-hertz and nothing else. The active pings Julien heard have stopped."

As he turned towards a display, Jake shared his thoughts. "Maybe the solution is tracking off a bit? Push the *Kilo* out another mile?"

"I'll try it. Do you want a new speed?"

"The slowest you can, to make it fit."

Ten seconds later, Jake watched shifting lines of bearing to the target bracket the enemy submarine's minimum speed at seven knots. "You'd hear it at seven knots, right?"

"Of course! We're so close, I suspect the speed is zero."

"Show the speed of zero. Pull the range in."

Remy's fingertips flashed across a screen, and the display's shifting lines drew the Iranian submarine closer to the *Specter* and its torpedo. "Our torpedo's less than a mile and a half away."

"And it hasn't gotten a single return?"

The toad head shook. "I can't explain it. The fifty-hertz tone is still there, and our solution is solid."

"See if the torpedo can lock on the fifty-hertz tone."

"We'll give it a try." The sonar ace delegated the task to Julien, waited half a minute, and then sounded encouraged. "The torpedo has locked onto the fifty-hertz tonal. Time to impact, ninety-one seconds."

A minute and a half later, Jake's flimsy hope waned. "The weapon doesn't hear anything but fifty-hertz?"

"No."

"It's right on top of it."

Remy shrugged. "I know that, but it's not detecting a hull. Do you want a command detonation?"

Tempted to inflict his frustrations upon a random chunk of

the Gulf of Aden, Jake refrained. "No. I'm not sure we even have a submarine out there."

"I didn't want to say it. You woke me up for good reasons, but now I don't hear anything out there, other than the fifty hertz."

After letting his weapon run for another minute, Jake admitted the futility. "Shut it down."

"I am shutting down our weapon." Remy reached for his console. "Our weapon is shut down. Would you like the wire cut?"

"No. Let's use our weapon as a drone. This fifty-hertz crap without any other noises is bullshit. I'm heading back towards the *Kilo* to get some data."

Five minutes later, the fifty-hertz tone went silent, and the *Specter's* commander had no more data.

An hour later, after circling the phantom *Kilo's* location, Jake flopped back in his captain's chair. "It's gone. It got away."

At his sonar seat, Remy nodded his toad head. "I agree. If it was ever even out there. I don't know what we were tracking."

Sighing, Jake questioned his sanity and his effectiveness as a commanding officer. "Do you believe in ghosts, Antoine?"

"I guess so. But not ghost submarines, if that's what you mean."

"That's exactly what I mean." Jake raised his voice. "Henri, get a communications buoy ready for Pierre. Tell him we found a ghost, but we let it get away."

CHAPTER 15

Saudi Commodore Fayed chuckled. "Did you see the Frenchman and Damari's faces? They were so furious, I thought they were about to accuse me."

His short chief of staff, Commander Hijazi, frowned. "You're tempting me to ask, accusing you of what, specifically?"

Fayed snorted. "Do you really want me to spell it out for you?"

"No, sir. In fact, I like it better this way, where I have to infer everything from your craftily vague statements. And the less I truly know, the less I have to deny."

The Saudi commodore liked his underling's compliant wisdom. "You should thank me for not sharing everything with you."

"I do, sir."

Fayed reflected upon the intelligence he'd shared with the Separatist resistance at Zinjibar. The suicide boats had followed his plans, and only the lucky interaction of the harlot commanding the *Goliath* stopped him from crippling the *Tarantul*.

And while the Yemeni Navy had a corvette-sized warship, it had a spine. Unacceptable, per his desire to dominate.

He misled his underling. "But to your point, I half expected them to blame me for their failures with the small boat attack."

If Hijazi suspected his boss, he either hid his dissent or tacitly agreed. "What lunacy! I can't imagine any argument they'd dare mount about that."

The commodore feigned compassion. "Well, at least they didn't take their anger that far. I commend them for their restraint. After all, they did suffer casualties."

"Such is war, sir."

Ignoring his underling's platitude, Fayed glanced at a wall-mounted display. The flagship rolling underneath his feet, the *Makkah*, trailed an expendable Yemeni *Osa* patrol boat, which forged ahead of the formation towards Aden as a low-value sacrificial anode against any unforeseen attacks.

Content that everything unfolded per his will, he released his chief of staff. "That's all. Dismissed."

The short officer excused himself and left the commodore alone in his quarters.

Fayed withdrew a packet of *shammah* tabaco and jammed a wad into his mouth. As the tangy sweet flavor piqued his tastebuds, he looked out the porthole.

The sun painted the water blue, except for whitening crests atop each wave. Far offshore, the visible seas around the *Makkah* were empty, save for the Saudi corvette, *Tabuk*, off the frigate's quarter.

While gazing at the sea's hypnotic rhythms, he felt his phone buzz with an awaited call.

He lifted his phone and skipped pleasantries. "I've been expecting your call, Jabbar."

His younger, oil-rich playboy brother replied. "Come on, Radwan. Do you think this was easy?"

Ignoring the question, the commodore pushed. "Is it done?"

The relief in his sibling's sigh was palpable. "Yes."

"Tell me. Spare no details."

"I rented a private trawler and its crew. It's a good-sized, seaworthy ship, and it was up to the task."

Fayed envisioned a high, exposed masthead. "I told you to procure a small vessel! Did you want to arouse suspicion?"

"Why do you worry? Your forces control the sky!"

"They do, but you're risking detection by periscope, if the *Specter* gets close enough."

"It's not that big a ship. Only twenty-two meters."

"You should have procured a dinghy, you idiot."

"Hey, I need my personal space, and what's done is done."

Fayed sighed. "Where are you?"

"Drifting about a mile and a half from the... what do you call it again?"

"Datum. You're a mile and a half from the datum."

"Whatever. Anyway, I hired some muscle to get the package and the sonar suite aboard."

"Any... loose ends? Men suffering from overdoses of curiosity?"

"Not when I stuffed cash in their pockets."

"Good. And what about the sonar?"

"I had them lower the suite to fifty meters deep, and I broadcast those submarine sound recordings you sent me."

"And what about the evidence? Did you hear anything?"

"I think it was the high-speed propellor of a torpedo. Listen for yourself from the recording. Are you ready?"

"Yes. Play it."

The telltale sounds of an undersea weapon's propulsion rose from Fayed's phone. "Wonderful. You've done well, my brother."

The director at Saudi Aramco gained confidence. "I told you I can get things done."

"That was fooling one submarine into shooting at the ghost of another. Delivering the package is another task altogether."

"I'm on schedule with that too, brother. And before you ask, I've also made arrangements for those rebel combatants you wanted. Moneys have exchanged hands, and the right agents are in possession of the ships."

"All three ships?"

"Yes! Would you please trust me for once?"

"Trust but verify. I'll call you later. Goodbye." Fayed hung up and found the number for his compliant helicopter pilot, whom he dialed.

"Lieutenant Mahmood, sir."

"Come to my quarters."

Five minutes later, three loud knocks issued from the cabin's door. "Lieutenant Mahmood, sir. I request permission to enter."

Lifting a gray bottle to his lips, the commodore spat and then snapped. "Come!"

Wearing a flight jacket, the young helicopter pilot entered, closed the door, and stood at attention. "Lieutenant Mahmood reporting as ordered, sir."

"Very well. Don't bother sitting."

The young officer gave a smug look but remained silent.

"I have reason to believe that the mercenaries will soon claim to have detected an Iranian submarine. If they do, I will want a helicopter to investigate and to corroborate their claim."

"Corroborate?"

"You'll detect something suggesting a *Kilo*, but you won't be able to pinpoint it exactly, and it will get away. Is that understood?"

"It is, sir. But, I..."

"Shut up."

Gulping, the pilot obeyed.

"If you're worried about the money, I'll make it worth your effort."

"Right, sir, but–"

"Shut up. Leave before I change my mind. And be ready for my order to fly."

The pilot departed.

During the next hour, Fayed grew agitated and mumbled to himself. "This is taking too long. I should prod that bastard."

He lifted the phone and called Damari.

The call went to voicemail.

Fayed considered using a tactical channel to demand the status of the *Specter's* clearing of the waters around Aden, but he wanted to appear unconcerned.

But he also wanted to appear interested.

He sought a fine line, an impossible fence to straddle in theory, but possible in the game of subterfuge.

Lifting a receiver from a wall mount, he pressed a button to call the bridge.

"Officer of the Deck, sir."

"Has the task force commander mentioned the status of the

Specter's clearing of our waters?"

"No, sir. Nothing since the last report of nothing new, which came almost twenty minutes ago."

"When's the last time you requested an update?"

"Uh... never, sir. Commodore Damari's staff reports to me every half an hour."

Fayed recognized thirty-minute intervals as sufficient, but he wanted to express the right amount of urgency. "The *Specter's* been searching long enough. Contact the task force commander and ask for updates every fifteen minutes until this is done."

"Aye, sir."

Hanging up, Fayed expected his request to be rejected. But having asked it supported his illusion of curiosity, despite knowing the outcome he'd fabricated.

Two minutes later, his phone chirped.

Fayed lifted it. "Fayed."

"Sir, officer of the deck. The task force commander declined. He says he hardly gets updates from the *Specter* every few hours, based upon its tactical freedom. He'll stick with updates every thirty minutes."

"I see."

"Sir, shall I put you through personally to the task force commander?"

Fayed assumed a magnanimous tone. "No. There's no need. Thirty-minute updates are quite sufficient. Carry on." He returned the receiver to its cradle, and then he withdrew his phone to read international news.

What struck him was the global panic from a virus. As a master of optics on his career's rise, the Saudi commodore knew that every issue had two sides. He chuckled as he digested the one-sided reporting.

Where were the historians reminding the world it had survived the Black Plague? Where were the debates comparing data from conservative and liberal sources? Where were discussions about the balance between virus safeguards and shuttering the world?

They were nowhere, and he could fathom only one answer–censorship.

And media censorship suited him. The more that people feared their social distancing radius, the less they would care about his maritime coup.

As if global fate favored him, he sensed his power growing.

Snapping him from his thoughts, the wall phone chirped, and he answered. "Fayed."

"Sir, officer of the deck. You might want to come to the bridge. The *Specter* found something."

On the *Makkah's* bridge, Fayed received a helmet from his underling.

Unaware of his commodore's ruse, Commander Hijazi's face was stern. "Enemy submarine detection by the *Specter*, datum bearing two-one-nine, range forty nautical miles from the task force's center."

Fayed slipped the inseam band of his Kevlar protection around his skull and then adjusted the chin strap. After several steps, he let his presence brush aside *Makkah* crewmen, and then he checked a display.

As the *Specter's* search had endured beyond expectations, all ships that had steamed ahead of the Zinjibar group had back-tracked from their push into the Gulf of Aden. United with his full task force–and it was his, despite feigning Damari's ownership–he pursed his lips to suppress his knowing smirk.

The vital presence on the tactical display was the presumed Iranian submarine the *Specter* had detected. "Get the commanding officer."

Fayed watched his chief of staff meander through the white-shirted people staffing the combatant.

When Hijazi returned with the ship's husky commander, the broad-shouldered man asserted himself with a gritty voice. "Commodore Damari ordered all ships to battle stations, sir, and I took the liberty of concurring for our ships. Do you believe we should pursue the submarine?"

Fayed faked concern. "That's a good, conservative decision. We'll stay at battle stations. However, our mission is Aden, not a submarine. I'll recommend to Damari to pull the task force back ten nautical miles, order the *Specter* to safe waters, and send a helicopter over the datum."

Raising a finger in protest, the *Makkah's* commander stifled his comment as he opened his mouth. Lowering his hand, he softened his features. "Aye, sir. I concur. Ten miles, one helicopter."

Fayed ordered Hijazi to give the recommendation to the Yemeni commodore, who instantly agreed.

Half an hour later, the *Specter* had confirmed its safe distance from the datum, and a video rolled in from the helicopter where the American commander had sniffed an Iranian submarine an hour earlier.

After lowering its dipping sonar into the depths over which his aircraft hovered, the pilot called out. "Fifty-hertz tone, resolving the bearing!"

A *Makkah* watchman offered a rote acknowledgement.

Over the background noise of thumping rotors, the pilot yelled again. "No bearing! The fifty-hertz tone is lost. Repositioning two miles to the south."

Another rote acknowledgment.

Over the next two hours, the pilot made reports of repositioning, but his crew failed to regain the fifty-hertz tone.

With the helicopter returning to the *Makkah*, the ship's commander approached his commodore. "There may have been an Iranian submarine out there. If so, it may still be there, or it may not be. Either way, I say, we move forward."

Pretending to be lost in deep contemplation, Fayed looked to the overhead and nodded. "Indeed, this is a risk, but we have a mission. I won't let an Iranian submarine stop us."

The stocky commander smirked. "Alright, sir. I can support that."

Fayed faced Hijazi. “Recommend to Damari to put the task force into an anti-submarine formation, assign waters outside our search area to the *Specter*, and take anti-submarine zig legs to our siege location.”

CHAPTER 16

Andi Amir shook his head. "How do you do it, sir?"

Beside him, Damari scowled. "You know how I detest vagaries. Speak succinctly."

"How can you speak rationally with that jackass, Fayed?"

"I'm used to scum like him. I've seen enough deceit in my lifetime."

"Like when you were on staff duty, serving our former so-called leader?"

"The admiral?"

Amir grunted his affirmation.

"I never trusted him."

Amir felt better about having overthrown his former commodore's regime. "When we took over the navy..."

"Don't mince words. We mutinied. We revolted. If we should ever face trial, we'll have to admit guilt."

Amir's comfort faded. "After all we've done, all we're doing, to save our country... our families?"

"We're only people of shared opinion on one side of an argument. I don't know who has authority to judge us, but being ready to accept judgment is implicit in our acts."

Feeling the noose of treason tightening around his neck, the *Tarantul's* commander scanned the bridge.

While the Aden task force navigated the last twenty miles towards its siege formation, there were few sailors and little activity in the space. The corvette's crew showered, napped, and ate in preparation for the siege's pending test of their endurance.

Noting himself out of earshot of the nearest eavesdropper, Amir objected. "But we're doing the right thing!"

The Yemeni commodore surprised him. "Have you ever read Victor Frankl?"

"Uh… no, sir."

"He was a Jew imprisoned in Nazi Germany."

"You read the works of a Jew?"

Damari shrugged. "We must know our enemies, and I wasn't reading to learn history. I was reading to learn philosophy, and even your enemy can speak the truth."

"I suppose so."

"Regardless, his points resonate with me. He said that a man must find something beyond himself for a purpose. Without an external purpose, there is no motivation to live."

The *Tarantul's* commander found some agreement. "That only strengthens our argument. We're fighting for others, for our families."

Damari's face was peaceful. "That's why I supported you in the revolt. My conscience is clean, and so should be yours, whether or not we die in battle or hang for treason."

Agreeing, Amir wondered why he felt uneasy.

Damari continued. "Those who cannot find something beyond themselves turn their attentions and affections inward. They are the most pitiable creatures."

Amir digested the wisdom. "Egoists."

"Narcissists. Sociopaths. Call them what you want. But sadly, they go mad seeking power, and usually they're the ones in charge."

"Those are the ones we fight against!"

Damari linked his philosophy to his earlier comments. "And once they're removed, new narcissists will replace them, and they'll be the beasts who judge us."

"That leaves us in a trap with no way out."

"Perhaps. But would you prefer the sanity of serving others, or would you prefer the madness of serving only yourself?"

His mind overloaded, the *Tarantul's* commander slowed the flow of philosophy. "I had no idea you were a man of letters."

Damari snorted. "You asked how I could deal with Fayed.

That's how. I see the same narcissism in him I saw in our admiral and in the faces of many people in power. Only by knowing my conscience is clean can I face such monsters."

"And that keeps you calm, even when Fayed is lying?"

"Somehow, it does."

Switching topics, Amir leaned closer towards his boss' ear. "And what about dealing with shame? A British woman just saved our lives. The shame is–"

Damari snapped. "Don't."

"But my crew, sir. Some suspect–"

Damari leaned into his underling's ear. "I said 'don't'."

"Aye, sir."

"Let them suspect, but her voice is never broadcast, since she speaks through a translator. Our sailors believe the executive officer is the commanding officer, because that's what they want to believe. Let them."

Amir had never lied about the *Goliath's* commander, since none of his sailors had asked. Those who had glanced at her image in a display assumed her the executive officer, the woman being subservient to the man beside her. "Okay, sir. I'll let it go."

"Good. We have more important matters. Give the bridge to the officer of the deck and join me in the wardroom."

In the wardroom, a few officers sat around the dinner table in various states of animation ranging from talkative to catatonic as they devoured after-meal pastries.

Amir cleared his throat. "Take your deserts to go, gentlemen. Give us the room."

Within seconds, the room emptied of unwanted ears.

Giving traditional deference to his underling's status as the ship's commander, Damari yielded the table's head to Amir and sat by his right. "Where's the remote?"

Amir spied the wall-mounted display's controller on a shelf that housed pictures marking the *Tarantul's* history within his fleet. Most of the recent photos showed his crew overcoming pirates that had threatened innocent vessels.

He handed the controller to his boss. "Here, sir."

Damari pointed the device at the screen and fumbled through a pixelized keyboard to enter a password. After completing the security entry, the commodore clicked an icon that invoked a secure window. "Let's see if he's there."

"Who?"

"You'll see. He told me he'd be available about this time."

After half a minute, the mercenary fleet's French leader revealed sharp features. Beside the Frenchman sat a man whose swarthy skin suggested his role as an Arabic translator.

As the mercenary spoke, the swarthy man echoed his sentiments in near real-time Arabic. "Captain Damari, it's a pleasure. I see that you've brought Commander Amir with you. Gentlemen!"

Surprised by the French interlocutor, the *Tarantul's* commander hoped to learn something important by remaining silent.

Damari replied. "It's good to see you, Mister Renard. You suggested some news?"

Riding a two-way translation, the Frenchman answered. "I have intelligence that will serve us. First, let me be blunt about some older news. You probably suspect that the *Specter* and *Goliath* faced an Iranian *Kilo* while rounding Cape Agulhas. I'll confirm for you that this is indeed true."

Damari voiced his opinion. "I had suspected, but with the subterfuge of intelligence reports, I didn't bother to ask. I'm not sure how it's germane to our siege."

"We thought the *Kilo* might have followed the *Specter* and *Goliath* to our present theater of operations. However, I've verified that all Iranian *Kilo*-class submarines are accounted for. One is in dry dock, one is in Chah Bahar, and the last, the one that challenged us, is being tracked by forces I cannot reveal."

Amir wanted to question the location of the third submarine, but Damari signaled his unquestioning trust of the mercenary. "*Kilos* may be accounted for, but what about the *Ghadirs*? There are enough of them to blanket the ocean."

"If I may boast, I've been serving you secretly to the north. Where I've advertised constant escorting of the humanitarian aid convoys, I've instead tasked the *Wraith* with interdicting *Ghadir* movements into the Arabian Sea."

"You're sure you've covered all ingresses? A solitary *Ghadir* skulking by the *Wraith* could end our siege badly."

"I trust my commanders, and they're the world's elite. However, if I may shift back to the *Specter's* discovery of a submerged threat. My commanders rarely make mistakes, and that's not boasting. I wish it were, but it's a truth, and it means something nefarious was emitting a fifty-hertz tone below a thermocline."

Seeking defiance in his commodore's body language, Amir saw only agreement as Damari replied. "Fayed is capable of a ruse like that. It's nontrivial to carry out, but I can conceive of many possibilities."

"Indeed. I don't know how he fooled the *Specter*, but I know he did and that he's lying about submarine detections. We must ask ourselves why he's doing this and how do we counter him. I have theories but am open to discussion."

His mind racing with conspiracy theories, Amir blurted out his first pedestrian thought. "Maybe he's trying to divide us by giving us something to argue about."

The Frenchman's eyebrows rose after the translation. "I've already dismissed that possibility. If that's his intent, he's failed because he's united us against him."

Damari tried next. "But I'd venture that he's setting us up to either believe or disbelieve in the future presence of an enemy submarine, depending which deception serves him best."

A shadow fell over the mercenary's face. "Precisely. And since I don't grant him the possession of a true submarine, I suspect he intends to feign the presence of one, likely with the intent of causing fratricide against the *Specter*."

Wagging a finger, Damari replied. "Yes. That's the most logical possibility. But let's remember that he could use a fake submarine report to send our ships in specific directions, into unseen dangers. as part of a trap."

"True. But fortunately, we can counter either ruse rather simply."

Amir volunteered his unsolicited doubt. "How?"

The Frenchman smirked. "When Fayed claims a hostile submarine, we acknowledge it in all feigned earnest. But in reality, we do nothing."

Damari groaned. "Uh... doing nothing will reveal our distrust. We'll lose our informational advantage."

"Not necessarily. We can counter with ruses of our own. If he urges you to run, you'll fake radio failure–all of your ships, as will my fleet. It won't be believable, but it will buy us time."

Damari frowned. "Time for what?"

"To fight him."

Leaning back in his chair, the commodore folded his arms. "You'd jump straight to hostilities?"

"If he pulls another ruse of a faked submarine, I would consider it an act of sabotage, which is an act of war."

After a deep sigh, the commodore assumed a grave tone. "I can't disagree with you. And I agree with your presumption, which is that we must decide now how to react, instead of making our decisions during his sabotage."

"I don't address this issue lightly, but I suspect we'll face it."

Damari contemplated aloud. "I'm mentally comparing our firepower against his, and I'm seeing a rather even match in antiship missiles..."

"In such trafficked confines, hitting a neutral ship would risk a disaster for the Saudis. They're trying to appear saviors–not destroyers. Therefore, you should not risk it either, for the same reasons."

"Thinking of only guns, then, we're... dare I say it? It would be hopeless.

"Not necessarily. With the element of surprise, the *Goliath* can cripple cannons at a conservative rate of two per minute."

Damari grimaced. "Even so, the Saudi's have four cannons, all of which are more modern, reliable, and faster than ours. A well-aimed ten-second barrage destroys our largest ship. You seem to be prescribing a bloodbath."

The Frenchman slid a cigarette into his mouth and lit it, increasing his dramatic flair. He exhaled smoke. "I'm quite used to using a submarine with torpedoes aimed at my adversaries' hulls as a bargaining tool. No shots will be fired unless Fayed wants to die by the *Specter*. Given his ego, I doubt he'd risk it."

Damari's chest swelled with a deep breath. "Okay. We'll follow your lead if it comes to it."

Amir stopped breathing as he assessed his commodore. Without protest, his boss devoured the Frenchman's accusations and planning, leaving the *Tarantul's* commander lost for words.

But then he remembered a peculiar phrase the mercenary had used. "Mister Renard, you mentioned a true submarine."

"I did? I'm sorry. Can you remind me of the context?"

"You mentioned Fayed not having a true submarine. What would a false submarine look like?"

The Frenchman replied with authority. "One can tow an object underwater, one can lower a noisemaker, or one can use remote control undersea vehicles as decoys. Fayed can simulate the presence of a submarine with enough credibility to mislead us, unless we agree to declare him a liar ahead of time."

Switching subjects, Damari showed a modicum of opposition. "What about Saudi air power? They'll be working for us in Aden, but a call from Fayed could send them against us."

Again, the French mercenary absorbed the challenge with strength. "From my intelligence channels, I've learned that the Emirates will no longer be a threat and are likely to see themselves as our allies."

Damari grunted. "That's hard to believe. I was concerned that we had really scared them away. Now you suggest them as allies?"

"Our resistance against the UAE was one factor of many, but their choosing of sides for whatever multitude of reasons is becoming evident. They'll soon be informally against the Saudis after they sign a proposed peace agreement with Israel."

Amir swallowed saliva and coughed it up. "Sorry." Noticing

himself as the only one talking, he continued after several heaves. "The Emiratis hate the Saudis, but enough for open warfare?"

The mercenary smirked. "Their clash over your country has created a good deal of angst. To be certain they act upon their emotions, I've arranged a generous payment for UAE air cover of our dubious Saudi air cover, so to speak. I doubt we'll need it, but it's an option nonetheless."

Damari gave his underling a harsh look and then faced the screen. "Mister Renard, we appreciate your hard work. We'll continue the siege as planned but consider any Saudi submarine report false unless proven otherwise, and I'll trust the air battle to you."

"Thank you, Captain Damari. I promise you that you're making the right decision."

"We'll reconvene on our public channel for further coordination of the siege. Damari, out." The commodore shut off the screen and looked to the commander. "You doubt him?"

Amir was concerned. "What if he's lying to us?"

"About what?"

"I'm not sure, sir. All of it? Some of it? Just enough to make the lie believable?"

"Why would he? President Hadi may have his faults, but he was right to hire him. Renard has a history of loyally serving his clients."

"Maybe that's true, but I can't help suspect a lie."

"Why so paranoid?"

"Because lying seems to be the nature of the world."

CHAPTER 17

Watching a video, Danielle frowned. "They learn fast."

Beside her, Taylor enlarged the view of the Saudi helicopter's camera feed. "You're not kidding."

Assigned to neutralize multiple roof-mounted batteries like that of Zinjibar, she saw her first target's preparedness. Multi-layered sandbag revetements protected three anti-air launchers and their human operators from the *Goliath's* attack.

"The Houthi aren't your average terrorists."

"And they've gotten so friendly with the Separatists that we can't tell them apart."

She hoped to avoid more killing. "How many rounds do you suppose we need to shoot to knock one of those down?"

"Hell, Mike. Your guess is as good as mine." She checked her communications window to verify her muting on the task force's channel. Her private channel with her boss remained open. "Pierre? Are you seeing this?"

His eyes askance, the Frenchman replied. "I'm watching it now." He faced her. "Not to worry. You have plenty of rounds and replacement barrels. The laws of physics will win out."

"But this could take all day, just for one of them. And I'm supposed to take out all five batteries in the city."

"If it takes a week, then so be it. This is a siege, not a blitzkrieg. Also, remember not to engage any targets other than those Captain Damari assigns you, unless for self-defense. Let me discuss the sandbag issue with Damari and get back to you."

She nodded and looked away. "Mike?"

"Yes, Ma'am?"

"Pipe this video to the crew and gather some opinions. Should we shoot solid or splintering rounds? Should we try to time two-round salvos on target? Anything else our experts want to consider?"

"Right." He turned and stepped away. "I'll walk this one around in person."

As her executive officer's steps echoed from the stairs, she spoke over her shoulder. "Good idea."

Although she trusted good but limited ideas to bloom from her crew's minds, she wanted to know more.

As she bounced her voice off electronics, the *Goliath's* semi-submerged state formed sloshing water and sunlight into a dancing halo three-quarters up the glass dome. "Ask the task force commander for a view of all five anti-air batteries."

The translator relayed the message and then, half a minute later, its answer. "He will, but he needs ten minutes to get complete footage on all of them."

"Ask him to send footage as he gets it, site by site."

Again, translations. "He will, ma'am."

Minutes later, the next building's anti-air battery appeared with launcher rails jutting above a small wall of sandbags. Then the image grew as the camera zoomed in.

Noticing a common geometry between the revetements of the first two sites, Danielle's imagination took over.

She hailed Renard.

The Frenchman's face showed agitation. "Be quick. I just muted Commodore Damari."

"The first two anti-air battery sandbag parapets are laid out against an attack from the Gulf of Aden. If that's true for all of them, I can reposition in the Red Sea and attack from the flank. The sandbags aren't set up to protect them from the west."

Renard scowled. "Let me get back to you."

The screen went blank.

Wondering why her brilliant idea had failed, she bid her time watching the Saudi helicopter's camera perspective move around the city and prove that the third and fourth batteries shared the defensive geometry of the first two.

She tapped a display and measured the distance to her proposed launch point. Two hundred nautical miles.

An electronic chirp signaled Renard's hail, and the Frenchman's face appeared. "Danielle?"

"Pierre."

"Commodore Damari and I have agreed to have you batter the revetements with your cannons. It will require patience, but it will serve our purposes."

Danielle protested. "I'm only two hundred miles from a perfect launch point. I could get there in ten hours, tops."

Renard softened his features. "It's a good idea, but it won't work."

She chose her tone wisely. "May I ask why?"

"There's a grave risk of which you are unaware. During his passage, Dmitry discovered that the Houthi monitor the movements of submarines through the Bab al-Mandab Strait. You'd be found, and you'd separated from the task force by a chokepoint."

Her heart sank. "Well, shit."

"It was a great idea. You couldn't have known."

She hated coddling and sharpened her voice into a dagger of defiance. "Got it. I'll plan for a long siege."

Moments after the Frenchman fell silent, Taylor's reflective scalp returned under the dome. "The crew's consensus is to time splintering rounds as two-round salvos. And I like it."

"Any rationale?"

"Not really. A lot of speculation and opinions, but it's all conjecture until we try it."

"Are the gunners ready?"

"They're awaiting your command, ma'am."

"Then let's try it." She bounced her voice behind her. "Tell the task force commander we're ready to begin the siege with his permission."

After a slow exchange, during which the translator seemed to be repeating himself for confirmation, the order came. "The task force commander gives you permission to fire on anti-air site one, and only anti-air battery one. Please confirm."

"Are we ready, Mike?"

Taylor scanned screens, and his tense but singsong tone suggested his final verification was a double check of a double check. "We have visual coverage of the target. Port gunner is ready. Starboard gunner is ready. Satellite telemetry guidance is ready. The ship is at minimum cannon depth, ready to fire, ma'am."

She bounced her voice off the dome. "Tell the task force commander I confirm permission to fire on anti-air battery one, and only anti-air battery one."

Upon the translation's roundtrip, the interpreter was enthusiastic. "Commodore Damari wishes you... it best translates as 'happy hunting'."

She lifted a handset to her mouth. "This is the captain. We're engaging the first target in Aden, anti-air battery one. This could take minutes, or it could take hours, depending on our accuracy and whatever kinetic hell we can inflict. Gunners, aim well, coordinate timing between yourselves, and commence fire!"

A fractional second apart, two hypersonic cracks sliced the dome's silence.

Taylor teased her. "Kinetic hell?"

"Mull it over until you like it. Either that, or shut up."

"I'll be mulling it over, ma'am."

During the salvo's twenty-second flight, Danielle swallowed her guilt and tried to think of anything but the human carnage in Zinjibar that had vandalized her memory.

Proving her worry unnecessary, the sandbag parapet shuddered twice before spewing clouds of dust. But it held.

Ten seconds later, the next salvo yielded the same results.

Then so did the next.

Danielle feared her cannons were strengthening the defenses by packing the bags tighter. "Cease fire! Cease fire! Standby for damage assessment."

The cannons fell quiet, and the two in-flight salvos landed without noticeable damage. But as the dust clouds cleared, Danielle noticed a stream of dirt. "Mike, is that a dying sandbag?"

Taylor pointed at the growing stream. "God willing."

Proving its sound construction, the revetment remained vertical, but it sank upon the vacuum of its emptied bag.

Danielle was hopeful. "If we can weaken it with six salvos, we can bring it down with sixty."

"I agree. This should work."

She ordered the railguns back to life and watched the revetments buckle under her barrage. Behind the wall, soldiers threw fresh bags onto the failing barricade, but their supplies were limited, and the railgun rounds outpaced their efforts.

After two dozen salvos, layers of sandbags toppled, and the soldiers abandoned their post.

Taylor voiced an odd opinion. "Should we stop? Save ammo and barrel life?"

"Huh?"

"They've run. Those launchers require manual control. If nobody's standing by them, they're useless."

"They'll come back the second we aim the guns elsewhere, and we've got plenty of spare ammo and barrels."

"Yes, ma'am."

She watched her barrage continue until the invisible hypersonic shards rocked a launcher and puffed clouds of atomized oil. "One launcher down on anti-air battery one, two to go."

"Right. I feel foolish for asking you to stop."

"Don't get cocky. Something can always go wrong."

Several salvos later, fate mocked her prophecy with a red alarm.

Taylor announced it. "High barrel temperature, port cannon."

She lifted her voice upward. "Cease fire, both cannons!"

A voice rang from multiple speakers. "Bridge, port weapons bay. The high barrel temp is thirty rounds early, but it's not unexpected under heavy use."

Danielle was disappointed. "Can you squeeze thirty more rounds out of it?"

"I could, ma'am, but you'd be risking the mounting bearings, which take forever to replace. I recommend replacing the barrel now. We can do it in ten minutes if we hurry."

She checked an icon of the starboard cannon showing another seventy-two rounds before its expected barrel replacement. "Replace the port barrel."

"Replace the port barrel, aye, ma'am."

Taylor wavered. "Should we keep firing with the starboard cannon? You held its fire, and I think I get why. But, um, why?"

"To make it look intentional. I didn't want to signal that we had a maintenance problem."

"That's what I thought. But we can add insult to injury by hitting with just the starboard gun. Why not signal that the outcome is inevitable, even while we calmly replace a barrel in battle?"

She found his logic sound. "Okay. We'll use the starboard gun until its barrel reaches end-of-life, and then we'll replace it before the next target."

"Then two fresh barrels thereafter."

"Right." She elevated her voice. "Starboard weapons bay, recommence fire. Fire at will."

The supersonic crack pelted her ears. Twenty seconds later, the sandbag wall jumped, and then after eight more hits, a second launcher spewed a cloud. Three more rounds assured the second anti-air hardware's demise, and then the next dozen rounds finished the third launcher.

Danielle barked. "Cease fire!"

The two rounds in flight knocked the already-disabled third launcher off its axis.

While the video hovered over the broken anti-air battery, the translator called out a warning. "Patrol boats... oozes? Oozes patrol boats? The translation is murky about–"

Danielle grasped the cryptic meaning. "*Osas*. *Osa* patrol boats."

The translator's concurrence rose from his tight throat. "Yes! That's it. We have radar information in the datalink."

Though surprised, she found the harbor's resistance expected in retrospect. "Very well."

The interpreter squeaked. "Are we in danger?"

Taylor protected his boss. "We're always in danger. Shut up and let her think."

Instead of thinking, the *Goliath's* commander watched the enemy vessels' icons rise from the datalink. She pointed to graphics. "Here comes the welcoming crew."

Taylor smirked. "You were expecting hugs and kisses?"

"Don't be cavalier."

"Well, shit, ma'am. It's hard to get emotional watching Yemenis fight Yemenis with their old Russian hand-me-down ships. It doesn't feel like our fight."

She agreed, but she also recognized the absurdity of emotions driving actions. "Stowe your feelings. Traitors and terrorists are attacking our clients."

Taylor issued a sigh of partial contrition. "I know, ma'am. But we've been ordered weapons tight on this one. It's almost like Pierre smelled it coming."

Danielle sniffed the stale air while folding her arms. "You're bloody well right, but I want to help."

Taylor's tone softened. "We're spectating on this one."

"Right." A sick feeling overcame her. "Mike, call up the armaments of an *Osa*. I don't remember them having cannons."

His face darkened as he obeyed. "Shit. No cannons. Just four Styx missiles each."

"Three *Osas*. Twelve missiles. If they dare use them, something's blowing up, and fifty-fifty if it's a military combatant or a civilian ship with all this traffic."

"You want to hit their missile launchers, don't you?"

She admitted it. "Yeah. But we'd need targeting assistance to take that shot from here. They're too far over the horizon, even if we come shallow."

"And Pierre's order to await an order from Damari... You think he'd be asking by now."

Listening over her shoulders, Danielle eavesdropped on her interpreter's tense tone.

The translator relayed his meaning in English. "From the task force commander. Target the rebel *Osas* from the *Goliath*! He's sending targeting data. Take them down in any order."

Danielle barked into the screen. "Pierre? You said to stay out of this one. But now I've got Damari asking for help. Confirming permission to engage."

After digesting his own translator's input, the Frenchman scrunched his face in ugly contortions. "Damari's right. Get involved. Now!"

"I'm shooting half-blind. I can't target anything specific. I only have center of mass from radar returns."

"Then use the speed vectors and eyeballing to hit the missiles! Target the Styx missiles!"

Danielle relayed the order, and as her solitary railgun spat its first *Osa*-bound round of speedy metal, she updated her boss. "I've only got one cannon, you know."

"Yes, I noticed. Use it well!"

The cracking cannon stopped after three rounds, and a gunner's voice filled the dome. "Bridge, starboard weapons bay. I have friendly-fire lockout on the *Khalid*. The *Khalid* is crossing my target, and the angle's too shallow to compensate with gravity or vertical guidance."

"Pick another target!"

"Ma'am, I've got friendly fire lockouts on the *Makkah* and the *Tarantul* against the other *Osas*. We're too far away to see enough bearing separation. My next clear shot will come in thirty-one seconds."

She yelled sideways. "Tell the task force commander I can't engage for half a minute due to friendly-fire lockouts."

While the translator's obedience became a background murmur, the Frenchman's lips moved on a monitor. "Don't try any manual heroics. This geometry is far more complex than Zinjibar. Let someone from our clientele be a hero."

She gazed at icons showing her impotence to assist. "I wasn't even thinking of it."

"Good. And stay semi-submerged in case those bastards have

the audacity to... oh, dear god." Renard ogled an offscreen image.

"Pierre?"

"They've launched their missiles."

"All four? From which ship?"

Renard's face was ashen. "All twelve. All three enemy *Osas* have unloaded their arsenals. Submerge, and protect yourself."

Obeying, she called out on the open microphone. "Stowe both cannons! Submerging the ship!"

When the railguns were sealed below decks, she tapped icons to lower the *Goliath* into the seas. Water crept over her head, and she hovered her ship in the rolling swells.

Renard's image became grainy, but his audio remained strong. "Are you still hearing me?"

"Yes, Pierre!"

"But you're no longer vulnerable to stray missiles?"

"No. Just masts and antennas exposed."

His pixeled face aimed sideways. "Good. Twelve missiles are in flight. It's pandemonium."

CHAPTER 18

Sensing the thrill of battle, a chance to violently impart his will, Captain Fayed set aside complex thoughts of lies, deception, and agendas.

Only killing mattered.

Killing those in the Yemeni Navy and even the Houthi his brother had paid to wield three rebel *Osa* patrol craft against them.

His purchased victims, he reasoned, were content–and privileged–to send their bounties to their families as payments for sacrificing their meaningless lives.

Even happier were the former commanders of the three *Osas* who'd sold their ships, which they'd stolen from the rightful Yemeni Navy, to Houthi rebels for the pending attack.

Analyzing the geometry on a display, Fayed confirmed his expectations.

The rebel patrol boats his brother had procured for the Houthi had emerged from nowhere and everywhere, hiding in the busy traffic close to shore. And they remained close to innocent merchant ships carrying food and other needed goods to Aden.

Too close to risk retaliation by anti-ship missiles.

Fayed would seek revenge with cannons after allowing his resources to try defending the Yemenis, whose ships steamed ahead of his flagship, the *Makkah*.

In recapturing their home, the Yemenis had agreed to push farthest towards the natural harbor and deepest into danger. The two friendly *Osa* vessels flanked the Yemeni corvettes, *Tarantul* and *Khalid*, which in turn flanked the central *Makkah*.

Carrying the task force's only anti-air missiles had earned

Fayed's flagship the inner, protected position.

The Saudi commodore watched speed leaders grow from separating icons that represented the rebel Styx missiles. Unsurprised, he smirked as the weapons veered towards the largest Yemeni ships, six at the *Khalid* and six at the *Tarantul*.

His short chief of staff, Commander Hijazi, stepped to him. "Sir, the tactical commander informs you that he's engaging all twelve Styx missiles with Aster missiles, one-for-one, from the *Makkah*."

Tempted to invoke his privilege of 'command by negation' to stop the anti-air defense and let the corvettes perish, Fayed stuck to his plan of appearing heroic.

He let his flagship do its job. "Very well. Let him engage all twelve Styx missiles. But have all combatants with cannons pursue the rebel *Osas*. Get us into cannon range against them. Shoot no anti-ship missiles. And get Damari's permission or concurrence or whatever's needed."

"Aye, sir. I'll move all cannons into range and handle Damari's staff." Hijazi lifted a phone to his cheek, and within seconds, the *Makkah's* prow rose with acceleration.

Moments later, a crewman on the bridge yelled. "Eye hazard! Look away! Eye hazard! Look away!"

Rippling roars thundered through the Saudi commodore's bones, and in the corner of his eyes, plumes of fire became a dozen rising suns baking the bridge windows.

When the silence returned, Fayed watched the smoking contrails trace lines from the *Makkah's* twin eight-cell vertical launch modules onto the horizon.

Trusting his safety, he reckoned himself a deity above the din. Many would die today, but not the master of puppets.

Hijazi seemed concerned. "Can we take them all down, sir?"

"Don't you have faith in your navy?"

"I do, sir. But..." Through the windows, the short officer faced the numerous spaghetti strands of smoky contrails painting the northern horizon. "I suppose we'll know in a minute."

Fayed checked the icons. "Forty-five seconds. We'll know in

forty-five seconds."

Over the loudspeakers, a voice carried hope. "Splash Styx Four!"

Another voice, which Fayed recognized as belonging to a second watchman seated before Aster consoles in the tactical center, shared more good news. "Splash Styx Seven!"

Yet a third watchman chimed in. "Splash Styx Nine!"

But a fourth watchman yelled. "Miss on Styx Two! Miss on Styx Two! Reengaging with Aster Thirteen!"

Commander Hijazi eyed his boss. "Negation?"

With only four Asters remaining, Fayed glanced across the bridge at the *Makkah's* commanding officer, whose silence approved the thirteenth anti-air missile. "No. Let it fly."

The bridge crewman again yelled. "Eye hazard! Look away! Eye hazard! Look away!"

A solitary artificial sun shone forward of the bridge.

While Fayed watched icons disappear on a display, he heard reports of more Styx missiles falling from the sky.

Thinking most anti-ship missiles would fall, he suppressed his inner elation as the negative reports came.

The next voice was tense. "Miss on Styx Eight! Miss on Styx Eight! Reengaging with Aster Fourteen!"

After those with veto power within the chain of command remained silent, the next propulsion plume cast its light over the *Makkah's* forecastle.

The next voice was more tense. "Aster Thirteen cannot reach Styx Two! Styx Two has escaped!"

His adrenaline pumping, Fayed joined the bridge crew in gazing at the targeted *Tarantul*. Seconds passed, and then the report came.

"Splash Styx Two! Splash Styx Two! The *Tarantul* took it down with its close-in weapon system."

Hiding his chagrin, Fayed clenched his jaw but relaxed it upon the next report.

"Miss on Styx Five! Miss on Styx Five! Reengaging with Aster Fifteen!"

Seconds ticked away as Asters took down Styx missiles, leaving two of each missile specie in flight.

"Splash Styx Eight! I got it with Aster Fourteen!"

Fearing the attack would fail, Fayed wished for the worst.

And he got his wish.

"Miss on Styx Five! Miss on Styx Five! Styx Five has escaped!"

On the horizon, the fleeing *Khalid* rocked sideways, and dark, billowing clouds rolled upward. A deadly silence filled the bridge as a harrowed voice announced the obvious. "The *Khalid* has been hit amidships, port side."

Fayed feigned solemnness while giving a theatrical order to Hijazi for all to hear. "Recommend to Commodore Damari to send his *Osas* to render assistance to the *Khalid*. Get a helicopter from the *Boraida* to search for men overboard and another dedicated to medical evacuation. Get the *Boraida* ready to receive casualties."

The chief of staff was grim. "Aye, sir."

"And keep chasing those rebel *Osas*. Send them to the bottom!"

Looks of indignation on the bridge became faces of determination.

The chief of staff held his phone away from his face. "I'm coordinating with the task force commander. The *Tarantul* has already attacked and neutralized the western rebel *Osa*. I'm assigning the northern rebel to the *Hitteen* and *Faisal*. I'm assigning the eastern rebel to the *Makkah* and *Tabuk*. The corvettes *Hitteen* and *Tabuk* will be in range first."

"Very well."

Over the next fifteen minutes, chasing down the *Osas* inside Aden's confined harbor proved trivial. Built to launch missiles and run, the rebellious patrol craft lacked cannons, making them helpless without their Styx missiles.

The Saudi corvettes turned them into burning hulks.

While watching one rebel *Osa* burning and sinking, Fayed received an anticipated question from his chief of staff. "Sir, the commanding officer of the *Hitteen* questions if he should render aid to the rebel *Osa* survivors."

Removing men with possible insights into his conspiracy suited Fayed. "Let them perish. We have more important matters. Return to formation."

"Aye, sir. There will be no aid for our enemy. However, I inform you that we've lost the *Khalid*. They're abandoning ship. Do you wish to alter the formation?"

Fayed glanced at aerial footage showing the burning Yemeni corvette listing hard in its battle for buoyancy. "No. We have cannons to spare. Reform but assign the *Khalid's* targets to this ship. We'll handle them from the *Makkah*."

"I'll see to the assignments, sir."

"Also, get Damari to have the *Goliath* recommence attacks on the anti-air batteries."

Three hours later, two additional rooftop batteries smoldered from the railguns' pounding, and Fayed recognized the first open corridor for air support to enter the city.

He grew impatient. "Get an update from Damari."

His chief of staff seemed hesitant but obeyed. "I'll send word to him, sir." Hijazi turned and lifted a phone to his check. Within a minute, he verified the damage. "Commodore Damari confirms that anti-air batteries one, two, and three are neutralized. The northern flying corridor is open."

Fayed wanted Saudi ground troops in Aden to liberate its populace from door-to-door Houthi and Separatist occupation. The hearts and minds of the Yemeni people needed to favor his kingdom, and by proxy, him–the man who would promise safe fishing havens and steady commercial shipping within the seas he usurped. "I'll let the general know."

His chief of staff gave a knowing look, affirming a milestone in the siege.

Stepping away for privacy, Fayed dialed the number he'd been anticipating as his first victory lap of many.

A well-connected and powerful army general replied. "What news, Captain Fayed? I'm waiting to retake the city."

"And so you shall, sir. I'm sure you've seen what the mercenary railguns can do."

"Of course, I have. Impressive. Clean. Minimal collateral damage. But are my air corridors open?"

"At the moment, only the first corridor from the north, sir. I've taken out the enemy anti-air battery coverage in that sector. But I assure you it's open, and the others will open soon."

"That's a sketchy assessment from high-speed buckshot. If I don't see bent and burning metal, I get doubtful. Are you certain those batteries are neutralized?"

"Sir, even if the hardware is salvageable, their crews can't operate them for fear of the railguns. You're free to fly."

"And what of the ground targets?"

Fayed explained the delay. "Sir, we were attacked by rebel patrol craft that apparently sided with the Houthi."

"And the Houthi and Separatists holding this city have enough tanks and trucks to resist me. I don't need excuses. I need your naval gunfire support."

"We lost a Yemeni corvette in the rebel attack, but we have plenty of firepower. I'm having ground targets reassigned. I assure you we'll attack per plan. It will be for our glory, sir."

"So be it. I'll have aircraft airborne in twenty minutes. I'm trusting you, but I'll personally hand your testicles to Mohammad bin Salman if this fails."

The line went silent.

To avoid friendly fire, Fayed passed word to Damari about the pending Saudi air assault, with a reminder to keep the *Goliath's* railguns aimed away from their allies.

Twenty minutes later, Fayed watched a video of army gunships overflying the city. Followed by a transport helicopter, one hovered over a tall building to visually verify the silenced battery.

Without nearby anti-air batteries, the Houthi managed a solitary shoulder-launched weapon from a neighboring building's window.

In a flurry of flares, the gunship sent hot targets in one direction while banking away. The missile sought the aerial torches, and the helicopter turned on its attacker.

Two streaks of orange shot from the gunship's rocket launcher, and a cloud of dust from the window signaled the assailant's demise. The gunship rose again and escorted a transport aircraft towards the taller building.

Above broken anti-air launchers, the Saudis hovered to allow soldiers to fast-rope to the roof. Surprising Fayed, they wore Yemeni uniforms, proving the courage of the locals to lead the way. Within seconds, the troops banged their way through an access doorway and disappeared into the structure.

Fayed scanned video feeds of other helicopters risking access to rooftops. None encountered shoulder-launched weapons, and each succeeded in placing troops atop contested buildings.

His chief of staff caught his attention. "Sir, the *Goliath* finished taking down anti-air battery four."

"Very well."

"Also, sir. Our ground forces are moving in. Enemy land targets are leaving the city to intercept. Captain Damari has ordered us to engage the enemy ground targets."

As stolen tanks and trucks of rebel soldiers emerged from their concealment within the city to engage the combined Saudi-Yemeni army, they became easy targets. "Excellent. Let's hope our cannons are well aimed."

The *Makkah* spat its first three-inch round at a target Fayed considered irrelevant.

Unchallenged, the task force's cannons hit, and the city began to fall to Saudi control with an near future of Yemeni soldiers and citizens expressing gratitude for their liberation.

As power shifted in Fayed's favor, he noticed an extra opportunity and inquired of his chief of staff. "What's the status of the *Khalid's* wounded?"

Hijazi bought time. "I haven't checked recently. I'll get an update."

"Do so."

Two minutes later, Hijazi informed his boss. "Twenty-six survivors. The rest are missing or presumed dead."

Half the crew's death weighed on Fayed, for a moment, and then he reminded himself of their irrelevancy in history's larger movements. "Are they in our custody?"

"Custody, sir?"

"Are they being taken to the *Boraida*?"

"No, sir. The *Osas* are taking the survivors to the *Tarantul*. They've set up a trauma unit in their crew's mess."

Fayed wanted Yemeni sailors in his possession as a bargaining chip, but he needed to state a believable reason. "The critically wounded must be flown to the *Boraida*. There must be some men in need of care beyond that of a rusty corvette."

"I'll check, sir."

"Hurry."

A minute later, Hijazi was embroiled in a debate that seemed to stall.

Fayed gestured for and grabbed the phone. "This is Commodore Fayed. Get me Commodore Damari on the line."

An underling acquiesced, and Damari spoke. "Commodore Damari."

"Sir, I commend you for tending to your wounded with such efficiency, but I must offer you the facilities aboard the *Boraida* replenishment ship. It has ten dedicated hospital beds and is ready now with a temporary trauma center."

"I couldn't ask that of you."

Fayed recognized the futility of the Yemeni captain's argument. "It's no imposition. Surely, you have critically wounded in need of urgent care. Aden's hospitals are still with the enemy. I'm sure you have no better option to save your sailors' lives."

Damari's pause conceded the argument, and then he spoke. "Three with critical burns. Two with head wounds. Two with internal bleeding. For their sake, I accept your offer."

"I consider it an honor and a duty to care for your warriors. I'll have airborne medical evacuations coordinated."

Damari's next words were strained. "Thank you, Captain

Fayed."

The line went silent.

Finding himself with victory in hand and free time, Fayed stepped to the bridge wing and dialed his brother. "Jabbar?"

"I've been watching from over the horizon. There's a bunch of rockets and cannons firing all over. What's the status?"

"It's happening per plan. Almost perfect."

"Almost?"

"Yes. Not quite perfect. So, I'll need the package soon."

His brother's response was delayed. "Are you sure, Radwan? I don't want to–"

"You don't want to be a coward."

The younger brother sighed. "Okay. But this is on your conscience. When do you want it?"

Fayed's task force's cannons brought destruction to the Houthi and Separatist ground forces. Another hour or two would suffice to neutralize the enemy, but he padded his estimate to be certain the rebel defenses failed.

"Three hours from now."

The brother's voice softened. "Radwan, you're sure?"

"I am. Don't ask again." He hung up and then called his pilot-saboteur.

"Lieutenant Mahmood."

"It's time. Find me a hostile submarine."

"Consider it done, sir."

CHAPTER 19

Jake read the slow teletype and relaxed. "It looks like everything's going fine up there."

Appearing bored at his station, Henri probed. "Do tell."

Starting on his second gallon of coffee per his liberal estimation, Jake appended the latest low-bandwidth update to his caffeine-jazzed memory. "Uh, starting with the traitors' attack with the Styx missiles, everything's been like clockwork."

The silver-haired mechanic protested. "Perhaps my English is failing me. You said 'starting with' the Styx attack. Do you mean to consider the attack itself as good news?"

"Well, no." Jake backtracked in his tired mind. "The attack was obviously bad. But given that it happened–and nobody's too surprised that it did..." He glanced at the mechanic for empathy, for fear of an uninterested audience.

The Frenchman pursed his lips and shook his head. "Upset, yes. Surprised, no."

"Right. Given the attack, they really screwed it up."

Henri's face darkened. "I don't follow. They sank the *Khalid.*"

"They should've sunk the *Khalid,* the *Tarantul,* and a friendly *Osa,* too." Waiting for a protest that never came, Jake continued. "When you attack ships that don't have their own anti-air missile defenses, you can usually assure yourself a hit with only three anti-ship missiles, if they're well-timed to overwhelm the last-ditch chaff an close-in-weapon defense."

Henri reengaged in the chat. "But the *Makkah* proved its ability to defend the corvettes."

"Not really. What they did amounted to target practice. Each one-on-one engagement of an anti-air missile against an anti-ship missile is usually a coin toss. The more efficient use of anti-air missiles is two-on-one, but the Saudis didn't have enough Asters."

The Frenchman sounded intrigued. "So, the Saudis actually did better than expected, letting only two weapons slip through?"

"Yes, but the poor attack tactics gave them a handicap. The Styx salvos were too piecemeal. It gave the Saudis some second chances you wouldn't expect from..." Jake sought the correct phraseology. "From professional sailors."

Henri summarized the outcome. "And the *Tarantul* enjoyed good fortune with its close-in-weapons, while the *Khalid* did not."

Ignoring the Frenchman, Jake opined. "They weren't sailors. They should've concentrated missiles on each corvette, using waypoints and ripple launches. But they didn't. They were bunglers. That's why the timing was off."

"What are you getting at?"

"I'm not sure those were rebel commanders. It was a fool's errand anyway, if they hoped to survive."

"You think... Houthi rebels? Separatists?"

"A poor attack? All but suicidal? You have to admit it's suspicious."

Henri boosted the mood. "We know this campaign is fraught with suspicion. What's good, though, is that you were about to summarize the happy tidings from above."

Fatigued, Jake let doubt slide into his mind's recesses while he updated his team on the siege. While droning on, he stared at faces in the compartment, missing an incoming teletype.

Fortunately, Henri was attentive. "An update from Pierre!"

Jake snapped his jaw towards the nearest screen.

The order informed the *Specter's* commander of a claimed submarine detection by a Saudi helicopter. It reminded him to ignore the claim and to consider the Saudis hostile from this moment onward. It also commanded him to approach the *Makkah* in preparations for countering whatever devilry Fayed threatened.

"What now, Jake?"

"Launch a communications buoy to Pierre with our position, zero time delay, and let him know that we're obeying. Get tubes three and four ready for the *Makkah*."

"Zero time delay and our position, aye."

Remy turned his toad-head towards his boss. "Julien is preparing tubes three and four for the *Makkah*. Shall we consider the Saudi submarine claim as having any merit?"

"No, but keep listening for Iranian submarines. Knowing our luck, there's one hidden out there anyway."

An hour later, Jake had the *Specter* off the unsuspecting *Makkah's* bow. He expected the swift ship to transit beyond his torpedoes' ranges soon, but he knew the frigate's assigned patrol area. The knowledge advantage seemed unfair, but against a man of deception, unfair advantages were necessary.

Over the next two hours, Jake repositioned his ship into firing locations that optimized his geometry against the predictable *Makkah*. Laborious, the effort drained him.

Until Remy spurred his adrenaline. "Torpedo in the water!"

"Get me a bearing!"

"One-four-two. Now another torpedo. Same bearing!"

"Increase speed to eight knots. Get a buoy ready for Pierre with a tactical system snapshot on a five-minute delay. I want some separation between us and the buoy, in case the Saudis sniff it."

Jake studied the data as icons arose on a tactical display. "Antoine, are you sure about the directional ambiguity?"

"Yes! There's been enough movement on the towed array, and the other direction points towards land."

"But none of it points towards the location where the Saudi helicopter claimed a detection."

"Right. Now, may I please listen to the torpedoes?"

Silent, Jake walked to the guru and knelt by his side. Seeing the bearings to the hostile torpedoes moving behind his ship's location, he was relieved the *Specter* wasn't the target.

Wanting to know which ship the torpedoes sought, Jake glared at the screen. He then stood and moved to the central charting table, where he experimented with assumed torpedo speeds and angles.

The answer became clear. "The *Tarantul*."

After twisting his neck and making eye contact, Remy nodded his agreement of the doomed corvette. "Do you want to go after the shooter?"

For a moment, he wondered if the Saudis had been truthful about an enemy submarine's presence, but then he recalled the geometry. It was impossible. But if he hadn't repositioned the *Specter* near the *Makkah*, the geometry might have fooled him into crediting the phantom submarine with shooting the hostile torpedoes.

Torn, Jake questioned if he should pursue the phantom shooter or stay on the *Makkah*. The answer would come from Renard, but the minutes of delay acquiring that answer might cost him.

He announced his intent. "We'll stay on the *Makkah*."

Surprising him, Remy agreed. "I have Julien listening to tapes on the launch bearing, but I don't expect him to find much. Either the shooter is far away..."

Jake finished the guru's sentence. "Or the shooter isn't a submarine. It's something else."

"That's right." Remy added to his report. "I'm studying an escape for the *Tarantul*, but it doesn't look good. I don't think it can outmaneuver the torpedoes."

"I'm practically underneath a Saudi frigate that wants to kill us. But then again, maybe it doesn't. Too many damned lies." Jake sighed, struggling for internal guidance.

His unofficial psychologist prodded him. "We either leave the Yemenis to their death, or we risk ourselves against well-equipped Saudis of unknown loyalties. Whichever you decide, you must decide now."

"Shit. Bring us to periscope depth, raise the periscope, and get Pierre on the satellite."

As the deck angled, steadied, and then bobbed in the shallows, Jake settled his exposed optics on the *Makkah*. The setting sun painted the warship's upper superstructure pink.

On a screen beside the periscope's display, the Frenchman's face appeared. "I've just read your buoy's message. Two torpedoes with audio characteristics of Russian USET-80s."

"Just like they came from an Iranian *Kilo's* torpedo room."

"But you're about to tell me there's no *Kilos* to be found."

"Right. And these are homing on the *Tarantul*, passively."

Interrupting, Remy yelled across the room. "The torpedoes just went active. It's a hybrid search!"

"Correction. It started passive but now is active."

Renard scowled. "Do you have an evasion course?"

"Sadly, no. There isn't one. The *Tarantul's* trapped too deep in the harbor. It's like the attacker knew exactly where it would be."

The Frenchman snorted. "Circumstantial, but another piece of evidence proving the–"

"Sorry to hurry, but I'm in visual range of the *Makkah*. If you want me to shoot it before it runs me over, you've got about three minutes."

Renard frowned in thought, and then the comforting glint of an anticipated negotiation illuminated his eyes. "Don't get run over, and don't shoot unless fired upon until you hear from me. Stay shallow, and keep your mast raised."

Jake's throat tightened with a fear he considered uncharacteristic. "I'll be detected if I loiter here."

"Don't worry about being detected. Leave that to me."

The screen went dark.

Nervously, Jake watched the *Makkah's* superstructure grow in his optics while the seas increasingly revealed lower sections of the approaching frigate. "Come on, Pierre. I don't have all day."

"Actually, you do."

Startled, the *Specter's* commander looked by his side. "Aren't you supposed to be keeping us on depth or something?"

Henri shrugged. "Light seas, nice automation. Not like the old days when everything was manual."

"I don't like waiting for our daddy to intimidate their daddy."

The silver-haired mechanic grasped the metaphor. "Given who Pierre is, I like our odds. I wouldn't worry. If we need more time, he'll find a way."

"What about the *Tarantul*? I'm half surprised Pierre didn't tell me to forget them and get the heck out of here."

"That's not who we are."

"I know, but you have to admit, this technically isn't our battle. We didn't sign up for Saudis versus Yemenis." Hearing his words, he corrected himself. "But we did vow to protect the Yemenis, didn't we?"

Henri nodded. "That's the spirit."

A dark thought overcame Jake. "Are we assuming that somebody has control of these weapons?"

The Frenchman's eyes grew large. "*Merde*. If it's an ad hoc shooter, there's no guarantee of wire control."

"Dang it. Pierre's negotiating, but what can the Saudis do if those torpedoes are fire-and-forget?"

The toad head swung full axis. "Nothing. They can do nothing. But while you ladies have been discussing politics, Julien and I have been planning an escape."

Intrigued, Jake stood and brushed by Henri. "Show me."

Remy rose from his seat and joined Jake at the charting table. "Not an escape per se, but good enough. Look here. The western rebel *Osa* is still floating. Now, if the *Tarantul* makes its best speed to take station on the *Osa*..."

Jake chuckled. "Classic Renard's Mercenary Fleet maneuver. I love it." He looked towards his translator, who appeared interested despite his uselessness to that moment. "Contact the *Tarantul*. Tell them to make flank speed and take station on the western rebel *Osa's* hull. And remember to tell them why."

After the translator relayed the message, Remy, who had returned to his seat, announced the compliance. "High-speed screws from the *Tarantul*. They got the message."

Jake lifted his gaze from the central chart. "Are the torpedoes following?"

"I need a minute to analyze the bearings."

While the guru assessed the weapons, a chime indicated Renard's request to talk.

Jake invoked his boss on a section of the chart. "Pierre."

Renard gloated. "Don't shoot, my friend. The Saudis are holding court, so to speak, with Commodore Fayed. Apparently, some sailors had confided in the *Makkah's* commanding officer evidence of a conspiracy between Fayed and a helicopter crew."

"No kidding?"

"And, from the seething tones, I suspect that the commanding officer and Fayed are political enemies."

"Huh. We were due for a little luck."

"I was expecting a much more difficult negotiation, but this was an open door. As a gesture of good faith, the *Makkah's* commanding officer has agreed to cut his engines and keep all helicopters away from the *Makkah*, and by virtue, away from you, while he interrogates Fayed."

Jake raised his voice. "Antoine?"

"He's right, Jake. The *Makkah* went dead in the water."

Renard probed. "What about the *Tarantul*? I assume you informed its commander about the torpedoes, since I see it sprinting. I thought you'd said it was futile."

"Well, Pierre. Futile for the average fleet, yes. For us, just the end of another mission. We'll talk the *Tarantul* away from the torpedo after it's acquires the *Osa* wreckage. And we'll even have few minutes to spare."

CHAPTER 20

Three days later, Andi Amir pulled the *Tarantul* into its berth in Aden.

He reflected upon the help the Frenchman's mercenary fleet had rendered in bringing him home.

Exposed and disgraced, the Saudi commodore had employed his wealthy playboy brother to fake the sonar contact which had fooled the *Specter.* From the same fishing trawler, the brother had lowered two Russian torpedoes that were programmed to seek a *Tarantul*-class corvette. Amir swallowed in silent gratitude to the mercenaries for tracking the weapons and sparing his ship.

As the Saudis removed Captain Fayed from his leadership position, they arranged at diplomatic levels to replace the mercenary fleet in escorting humanitarian aid shipments to Nisthun.

Disliking the idea of letting the Saudi fox guard the Yemeni henhouse, Amir feared his homecoming in Aden would be short. Somehow, he knew the Saudis would cross a line and over-impose their will on his nation's maritime lifelines, but that was a future battle.

Today, homecoming.

Aden's new waterfront security forces wore the army's camouflage and carried assault rifles, but given the recent clearing of Houthi and Separatist influence, he welcomed their presence.

He hated coronavirus' dehumanizing masks, but he assumed he'd get used to them. Worse, the security team had swollen beyond his wildest dreams–for one simple reason.

President Hadi had arrived at the waterfront.

With the pomp of a high-profile diplomat, and with smoke

still rising from the siege's smoldering fires, uniformed security personnel dotted the waterfront like flies on dung.

Amir considered his president's presence a headache, but Damari had ordered the entire navy–what remained of it–to don clean uniforms and look impressive in case they landed in diplomatic videos.

But the commodore had assured the crews an opportunity to meet with their families before succumbing to hours of high-stress diplomatic boredom.

From the bridge, Amir watched sailors wrap a rope around a cleat. "How much time will we have with the families, sir?"

Beside him, Damari sighed. "I don't know. Maybe an hour in total, but each man will have less time as they rotate through. It depends how fast the *Boraida* can dock."

Through the *Tarantul's* bridge windows, Amir watched the Saudi replenishment ship ease into an adjacent berth. Knowing the families were on the *Boraida* comforted him, and he silently thanked the interim Saudi commodore, Fayed's former chief of staff, for offering the ship as transportation. "It should have the brow on the pier in about ten minutes."

The commodore glanced at the replenishment vessel. "Give each crewman twenty minutes with the families. Rotate them in shifts of twenty to the *Boraida* so that... never mind. I'll issue the order over the datalink."

Amir feared deprivation of a proper, human-interaction visit his family. "What about protocols for the virus?"

Damari appeared abnormally dismissive. "This virus is one hundred times less lethal than the Spanish Flu, which was ten times less lethal than the Black Death."

"You seem skeptical."

Damari smirked. "I fear that more people will die from poverty and depression than the contagion itself. I understand the media sensationalizes their opinions to entertain people for profit, but its treatment of COVID is ridiculous."

Amir had considered it with less scrutiny than his boss had. Perhaps, he wondered, that was the problem. "Maybe."

"The vulnerable must be protected, but this global lockdown stinks of tyranny."

"I admit that I've noticed nations and major media sources enticing panic."

"It makes perfect sense if you consider globalization."

Confused, Amir protested. "I'd always considered globalization a good thing, for trade and economics."

"Free trade is good, but globalization of governments is not. It strips local people of power to self-govern, and it gives absolute power to the elites."

"Sounds like communism."

"Socialism. Liberalism. Progressivism. Call it what you will. The globalists are using COVID as a weapon for the Great Reset."

The term was new to Amir. "The what?"

"Globalists consider the Great Reset their chance to replace local governorship with their regime. It's diabolical, and they're not hiding it. In fact, they're bragging. Apparently, humanity wants to be terrified into finding salvation in global oligarchies."

Amir found the thoughts overwhelming. "Perhaps. I don't really have an opinion."

Damari blushed. "Sorry. I was ranting."

"No, it's fine. But what of the families, sir?"

"Hug your families all you want. Just wear the masks so the Saudis don't complain."

Amir noticed his boss' chagrin and risked commenting. "If I may... you seem subdued, sir."

"Oh... Just concerned about this ceremony with the president. Everything must be perfect. I loathe such things, but I assure you, I'm fine. It's nothing."

Noting there was an 'it' that the commodore had admitted, Amir knew he'd stumbled upon something greater than nothing. But he let his leader have his peace. "Okay."

Amir turned and looked towards the northern horizon.

He knew the enemy he'd helped expel days earlier loomed beyond his sight. "You're not concerned about the city being overrun by a counterattack?"

"I am, but what of it? I trust friendly ground forces to hold them back. We can't live in fear."

Amir found his boss' points valid and important, but he preferred reuniting with his family over further discussion. "If you'll excuse me, sir..."

Damari replied with a forced smile. "Goodbye."

Amir's visit with his family aboard the *Boraida* came and went in a flash, but the familial love wiped away his burdens.

Until he arrived again in Damari's presence.

Within the Aden waterfront building, a crowd gathered in close bunches despite the pandemic. Masks flew on and off the elite's faces based upon their whims of discomfort, as they scoffed at the virus' risk.

Worst among the offenders was the president himself, who at best treated his face covering like an artificial beard until his aides prepared him for each video and photo opportunity.

The present opportunity for pandering to the camera was a ceremony for the victorious dead. In addition to the casualties from the sunken *Khalid*, President Hadi lauded the heroics of three dozen ground troops who'd fallen in retaking his boyhood home.

Grasping camera time beside the president were several army generals, an air force general, the interim Saudi commodore, and Commodore Damari. While the other military men wore forced images of sorrow behind their masks, Damari appeared honestly despondent.

After the public mourning, bodies shifted about the space, and Amir strode to his boss' side while he tasted his own breath behind a black veil. "You wanted me, sir?"

Another forced smile rose behind Damari's masked face. "I did. Thanks for coming. It's a surprise."

"Oh. That sounds–". The *Tarantul's* commander hushed himself when the president's media manager appeared.

The hurried man used rushed gestures. "You? You're Commander Amir, right?"

"Uh, yes."

"Good. Peace be with you." The manager covered his heart with his hand.

Amir returned the greeting and the gesture. Then from the corner of his eye he saw his wife enter the building. "What's going on?"

Damari blurted out a warning. "Stay here. You'll be able to see her after the ceremony."

"Which ceremony?" Amir then saw his thin executive officer enter the building, followed by other loyal commanders of the fleet's few ships. Making contact with familiar eyes above the masks, he exchanged hand waves with his wife and the other officers.

Before Amir could challenge his boss further about the pending formalities, the president marched by him and instructed the media manager to arrange himself and the two naval officers in front of a film crew.

An aura of awe surrounded the president, for no other reason than he expected it and the underlings of his perpetual circle fed it.

Amir twisted, stepped, and angled his torso like a puppet as the media manager became a master of optics. Lights then came to life, blinding him, but he faced the president as instructed.

As Hadi spoke, the words drifted in and out of Amir's understanding. In a whirlwind of praise for courage, initiative, and skill, the nation's leader stripped Damari of his captain's shoulder boards and then replaced them with those of an admiral.

A proper navy, despite its smallness, deserved a flag rank leader, per the president's sentiment. There was no mention of the coup which had deposed the prior naval leadership.

Then, as a gracious afterthought, the newly minted Yemeni admiral crowned his new chief of staff. Damari stepped in front of the *Tarantul's* commander, stripped him of his commander's boards, and slipped captain's boards onto his shoulders. "I assume you accept the promotion to my staff?"

Shocked, Amir agreed. "Yes, sir. I'm honored."

As quickly as the naval officers' promotions had become a spectacle before the lights and cameras, the media manager whisked Amir away to make room for the next ceremony.

Quick greetings with his fellow officers became a whirlwind of congratulatory gestures.

His head spinning, Amir met his executive officer. "Did you know about this?"

The thin officer smiled. "I did, sir. And if you don't mind, can I have your old shoulder boards?"

"You're being promoted, too?"

"Captain Damari... now Rear Admiral Damari, told me privately." The executive officer beamed with a withheld secret.

"What?"

The executive officer nodded. "Do you think you're still commanding the *Tarantul*, sir?"

Amir realized he'd graduated beyond a naval officer's privilege of sea-based command. As a captain in his tiny navy, he'd lead commanders but never again his own ship. "Oh! It's yours now?"

"You trained me well."

"I did. Take good care of my old ship."

"It's still yours, sir, until formal turnover. But if you want some private time today, I'll look after the crew."

For once, Amir let an underling bear his burden. "Yes. Station yourself as the command duty officer. And thank you." Seeing several bodies standing between himself and his wife, Amir stepped towards her.

However, Damari called to him. "Don't get too used to those."

The *Tarantul's* commander faced his boss. "To what, sir?"

Damari gestured him closer.

Amir approached and lowered his voice. "Sir?"

"To those shoulder boards."

Unsure how to respond, Amir was quiet.

"By the end of the year, you'll be wearing mine."

A future admiralship bent Amir's mind. "I... what?"

"I'll be retiring."

"If I may ask... why, sir?"

Damari gave a cryptic reply. "You asked me earlier how I do it?"

"You're confusing me."

"At sea, you asked how I dealt with a devil like Fayed. I gave you only a partial answer at the time."

Unsure how a pending retirement aligned with dealing with devils, Amir moaned. "Uh... yes."

"I'm dying."

"Oh." The news flew circles around the *Tarantul* commander's head before landing. "I'm sorry, sir. How? Why?"

"Cancer. I've got six months, if doctors know anything. With my new perspective, I pity jackasses like Fayed. They no longer bother me."

"I'm..." In a moment of empathy, Amir suppressed swelling sorrow for the man whose shoulders had buttressed his navy.

"Don't worry about me. I've spent the last few months in deep reflection. I know there's a greater power, called God, and I've humbled myself in proper worship."

Unsure how the sentiment of humility, a simple emotion, could counter the fear of death, Amir was dumbfounded. "Okay."

Damari preached a dying man's philosophy. "I believe in an afterlife, but I didn't for so long. That's a mistake I wish I could go back and correct. It would've spared me so much fear and anger."

Amir understood his boss' serenity during times of strife, but he couldn't envision himself achieving the same perspective.

The dying man seemed to sense the confusion. "If you reject life after death, then every waking moment is a horror. To think that life starts from chance, brings decades of sorrow, and then ends in emptiness... it's madness."

Inwardly squirming, Amir contemplated the sentiments but failed to interiorize them. He tried to end the conversation with a generic dismissal veiled in comforting words. But he couldn't think of any. "I... uh..."

Damari raised a hushing palm. "Don't placate me. I've made my peace. There is a god, and he will receive me as a humble servant in absolute surrender."

A sentiment formed in Amir's mind. "I commend you for your courage."

"Don't dwell on my fate. Use it as a witness to reflect upon your own."

Stunned by his emotional day, Amir issued a weak response. "I will, sir."

Like an itinerant preacher, the admiral bid his underling farewell and departed.

Amir sensed a comforting presence by his side.

He turned and saw his wife. "Honey?"

Her beautiful face was stern. "Take me home."

Unable to shift his thoughts towards familial life, the *Tarantul's* commander deferred to the mother of his children. "Should we bring the children?"

"Let's assess the damage first. The other wives are saying our homes were ravaged. It seems the Houthi knew where military members lived and targeted them, like barbarians."

"Do we even have a house still standing?"

Showing her courage, the kind that women need when keeping families united under oppression, she chortled. "Your guess is as good as mine. Does it matter?"

Her question added to his growing confusion. "No. As long as you and our children are well, I am blessed." Then he reconsidered. "But if the best I can do is bring you home to rubble, what did I accomplish?"

"You protected your home. Maybe not your house, but the homes of your neighbors and your hometown."

He considered the departing mercenaries and the encroaching Saudis. "Sure, but for how long?"

"Long enough to encourage everyone to keep fighting."

CHAPTER 21

In his stateroom, Jake pondered his existence.

Hidden from his crew and partially from himself, an undercurrent of anxiety had exacerbated his command of the *Specter*.

He probed himself and realized he'd always been afraid, but he'd hidden it behind anger. He also reasoned that his anger had been justified, even natural, after the violence he'd suffered.

A stolen career, HIV forced upon him, the lies of the coverup... even fifteen years after the fact, his rage swelled.

But then the swelling had subsided.

He'd forgiven everyone, hadn't he?

He had to.

The god he sought demanded it.

Looking over his years of informal and formal study, he'd grown closer to the Christian god by the simple virtue of knowledge.

But anything he'd call prayer or worship was weak. He was a man seeking truth, whether it be God or not. Getting on his knees and praying was an afterthought.

So, without rigorous religious practice, he wondered where his anger had gone? Could it have dissipated over time?

No. It had haunted him for years without sign of abatement, and only after studying Christ had the anger started to evaporate.

Just from the knowledge.

Truth, adages be damned, was setting him free.

But could he commit his will to believing in an invisible man?

Shaking his head, he cleared his mind and accepted the torment of spiritual limbo. Trapped between denial and acceptance of God, he trusted that pursuing the truth would be rewarded if there were a god to reward it.

Mocking himself for life's long, laborious journey of discovery, he stripped naked and stepped into his shower.

While showering, he spied a blob of dark greenness contrasting the silvery sheen of the stall's metal floor.

The greenness offered a respite from his mental aggravation, and before meandering rivulets could carry away the wonderous discovery, he scooped its squishiness with his toes. With hushed anticipation, he shifted his weight to his opposite foot and then carefully orchestrated his well-conditioned leg and torso muscles to hoist the surprise to his waist.

Like a striking viper, his palm cupped his foot and secured the prize. He then lowered his foot, lifted the reward to his face, and identified it.

Broccoli.

He recalled an adage stating that the closer one gets to the divine, the one more becomes like a child. Launching a game with himself, he cupped the floret in his palms. "A riddle!"

His mind raced for answers about the origin of the flowering vegetable's rogue floret.

Breakfast had been a hearty collection of pastries and meats, lunch had been green jobfish from Socotra's waters, and dinner had been steak and potatoes. All fresh vegetables had been salads, and Jake had not seen any members of the cabbage family being plated recently within his submarine.

This vegetable had not come from any meal that day.

Could it have come up the drain?

No, he concluded. Even if broccoli had found its way onto the *Specter's* menu earlier in the week, cabbages lacked the innate ability to climb up pipes.

The mystery deepened.

He redoubled his efforts to resolve it, and reason demanded that he, after exhausting natural explanations, explore malicious human agency.

Someone had staged the vegetable within his shower stall,

hoping for the anguish of confusion that would torment him. With the joking Frenchmen aboard his submarine, it was his primary theory. Adopting his theory as a working hypothesis, he stepped from the shower with the intent of proving it.

But as he toweled himself, a new piece of evidence appeared. A second, smaller floret of broccoli was on his buttocks.

Jake's beliefs quaked under the scrutiny of new evidence.

Grappling with the mystery like his namesake, the Biblical Jacob who'd wrestled the angel, Jake sought a new conclusion.

With the smaller floret appearing upon his leg, none of the French jokers was capable of planting it there. Jake was certain he would've noticed a Frenchman's hands probing within his pants, around his hips, and onto his shapely haunches.

Whatever the truth, it remained elusive. But he would find it.

Invigorated for his journey of discovery, he slid into his underwear and then grabbed his beige pants.

As he stepped into the passageway's air, dampness on his towel-dried hair chilled him. Alone, he strode towards the control room where he expected to find two people half asleep on the midnight watch of his carried submarine.

As he passed the galley's door, he glanced inside the cramped food-preparation alcove. A bag of frozen broccoli florets with footprints on it appeared in the garbage can.

He concluded that someone had dropped, stepped on, and accidentally opened the bag.

The discovery jogged the memory about darting into the galley to shove foodstuffs into his mouth. After he'd grabbed an apple earlier that evening, he'd spied a cook cleaning the broccoli-laden mess for which the disposed bag served as a reminder.

Jake then remembered having assisted the cook in cleaning the spillage. He stopped, stood, and reconsidered the origins of both shower florets.

The broccoli bag explosion presented a challenge.

If it could explain the shower florets, then Jake's hypothesis of a French revolution was vapid.

The *Specter's* commander found himself in a meta-question quandary.

How should he deal with the newest clue?

If he denied the exploded bag, he'd enjoy the comfort of maintaining his belief in culpable francophone jokers. The simplest act was to ignore the evidence.

But ignoring evidence to preserve false beliefs was insanity.

It was the trap of narcissism, placing one's opinions and oneself above reality. For the floret mystery, he'd avoid the pitfall of outright denial.

Moving to the next trap, he considered how to bend the new clue to his will. The way to preserve his belief in Frenchman hijinks was positing a coincidence. He could deny the causality of a broken broccoli bag and consider it a correlation of happenstance in relation to the shower florets. Simple. Clean.

The concept offered comfort, but it led to a half-truth. Allow the broccoli bag but deny its agency. Deny the smoking gun having fired the bullet.

Tempting, the logical pitfall circled Jake's head but then slipped away. He found it distasteful–something that begged the proclamation of half-truths.

The final option was discomfort.

Challenging his beliefs.

As he examined the broccoli bag with fearless scrutiny, he tasted the bitterness of humility. Admitting his prior theory's error, he freed the francophone jokers from his prior condemnations.

His purpose for approaching the control room shifted with his drifting paradigms of the broccoli-truth.

How could anyone know the truth? How could he be sure of his existence? Descartes had opined 'I think, therefore, I am.' But even if Descartes was right, how could Jake trust the philosopher or be assured of anything else?

Once planning to interrogate the nearest Frenchman, he now opted for a philosophical quest.

He pushed through the door into the control room.

Alone at the sonar seats, Julien listened lazily to the ocean's sounds. At his mechanical control station, Henri read a book Jake couldn't identify from the distance.

The silver-haired Frenchman looked up. "You look freshly showered."

"Freshly showered and alert."

"What brings you here?"

Remembering the mechanic's beliefs, Jake struck. "You're Catholic, right?"

Henri revealed his book as the Catechism of the Catholic Church. "Was it that obvious?"

Sitting, Jake confessed. "Have I ever told you why I hate the Catholic Church?"

"Hate?" Henri closed the book and protested. "You brought a priest on one of our missions."

"It was a favor for my wife." Jake reflected upon the sentiment and clarified it. "Somewhat a favor for her. But I admit I was also hoping to decide for or against the Church on that mission. I didn't quite get there. Still hate the Church, but can't look away."

"I see. Where did you get?"

"Nowhere."

"So, then. Why do you hate the Catholic Church?"

The *Specter's* commander remembered his childhood catechesis. In the wake of the Second Vatican Council, his teaching, like that of many Catholics, was crap. "I couldn't have told you who wrote the gospels after five years of lessons. Either I struggled to learn–"

"You're a nuclear-trained engineer. Did you struggle in grammar school?"

Jake remembered being beaten up for good grades. "No."

"Then you didn't struggle."

"Right. So, I'm pretty sure that Satan himself managed my catechesis. I need more unlearning about the Church than learning."

Henri frowned. "And I thought my training was bad."

Jake sighed and left himself in his psychologist's hands.

The mechanic picked up the clue. "I see you're wrestling with something."

"Actually, I'm wrestling with everything. How do I know if anything's true?"

"Do you want the short version or the long?"

"Short. I'll ask for more if I can take it."

"The really short answer is the natural law and divine revelation. You add those two up, and you get the only truth worth knowing."

"Natural law, yeah. It sounds like common sense, but it isn't."

"It's a finite reflection of God's infinite wisdom in our finite minds. Thomas Aquinas called it 'the participation of the rational creature in the eternal law.'"

"So, everyone has access to the natural law, from God, whether they believe or not?"

"We form our consciences by learning it, or we misshape our consciences by denying it."

So far, the Frenchman's story aligned with Jake's studies. "Then tell me about divine revelation. Why can't I just pick up a Bible and read my way to the truth?"

"That's Protestantism. The theory is that the Holy Spirit guides each reader to the truth, but the reality is that the Holy Spirit has let some tens of thousands of denominations form, based upon different interpretations of scripture."

"That's why I hate the Catholic Church. It's the only institution that claims infallibility. It's the only church claiming to have safeguarded the truth since the dawn of revelation, but it's oozing with evil."

Henri baited him. "Which leaves you... where?"

"Hell, I don't know. In Hell, I'm afraid!"

"It leaves you questioning what you know about the Church's teachings."

"I know it doesn't teach priests to molest people."

Surprising Jake with his stoic reply, Henri addressed the jab.

"The Church is staffed by sinners. There's no claim in the Church that its members are superior to other humans, since God preserves everyone's free will. The claim is instead that they know the right path and that straying incurs Hell's worst torments."

Jake completed the sentiment. "God lets us choose sin."

"Even those within the Church. And in some cases, especially those within the Church. He tests those in the hierarchy harder than the laymen, since they promise to tend the sheep. You'll see priests and bishops failing under the pressure, especially nowadays."

"Why nowadays?"

"Because niceties have made life too easy. When everyone's struggling, we look for a savior. But when luxuries roll of assembly lines for cheap purchase, we stuff God into our back pockets or forget about worship altogether."

"Got it. Modernism. Atheism."

"Which breeds communism and socialism. That's what we've seen since the industrial revolution."

"So, the Church is staffed by sinners who are tempted away."

Henri's tone was authoritative. "Away, for some. Others are tempted to remain within and destroy it from inside."

"Like that abuser, Cardinal McCarrick?"

"Him and many others have infiltrated. And why not? We're a huge target for enemies of God."

Jake shrugged. "Any church is. Heck, any organization claiming moral authority is a target."

"That's why the ravages of pedophilia sully Protestant churches, schoolteachers, and the Boy Scouts. Such horrors occur more frequently and in more venues than anyone dares to admit, but the easy finger to point is towards the Church."

"I wasn't attacking the Church."

"No, but you asked about the Catholic Church specifically. You know about the other churches, because you study the Bible, and that's their only guidance. Yet, here you are, lost."

"Okay, jackass. Set me straight!"

"The truth is a three-legged stool. We have the Bible, we have sacred Apostolic Tradition, and we have the Magisterium."

Jake's curiosity rose. "What's that last thing?"

"The Magisterium is the pope and his circle of selected cardinals who interpret ancient teachings under God's guidance."

"You've had shitty popes."

"Oh, yes! Heretics, murderers, fornicators, liars. The club of sinners applies all the way to the top. That's why we trust God to proclaim infallible truths through the pope's office, regardless of the man's heart or character."

"How often is that?"

"Not often. The last time was 1950, the dogma of the Assumption. Before that was the prior century. The point isn't new teaching, for God had revealed everything by the end of the Apostolic Age. Infallible declarations answer questions as new generations forget ancient teachings."

The disconnects mounted in Jake's brain. "What about bickering bishops? Every time I read one bishop saying something, I read about another bishop saying something else. What idiot would join that Church?"

"Yes, bishops can disagree with each other about almost anything. It's been happening for centuries. The Arian Heresy split the Church in half, if memory serves, roughly seventeen hundred years ago. But the Gates of Hell will not prevail, and the faithful knew whom to follow when."

Picturing disagreeing bishops, Jake was confused. "How? Which chain of command do you follow in a broken hierarchy?"

"You can tell which bishops are loyal to the unchanging word, and which ones have slipped into the heresies of modernism. It's evident for those who look, but you need to study the Church's teachings to know how."

"I haven't probed Catholicism for a while. I'm just starting tonight after... well, after thinking there's nowhere else to look for ultimate truth."

Henri chuckled. "Am I helping?"

"Uh... not sure."

"Have you explored the Marian apparitions?"

"You mean, the Virgin Mary showing up to talk to people?"

"Yes."

"No, I haven't."

"Why not try her?"

"Why her and not God directly?"

"When you study her advice, you'll understand. Only a mother's tenderness can save us now."

Jake snorted. "You're preaching doomsday."

"Indeed, I am. God's too furious with modern indifference to address us without his mother's participation. See what Our Lady has to say, and I promise you that you'll have a change of heart."

CHAPTER 22

Docked in Port Said, Danielle followed Terry Cahill up the steps to the *Xerses'* bridge.

Five days had passed since she'd fired her last railgun rounds at targets in Aden.

On the Mediterranean side of the Suez Canal, she recalled Renard's easier negotiations on the northbound return trip, after the UAE and Bahrain had eased tensions with Israel.

Instead of sneaking through the locks, they'd sent all four combatants through the canal, surfaced, and supported with a generous payment for Egyptian protection.

As the newer ship, the *Xerses* seemed bright and clean. "It's good to see my new ship from the inside."

Cahill grinned. "I left it in great shape for you."

Having toured the newer transport ship's spaces with the Australian, she was ready to give up the *Goliath* and take the *Xerses*, as Renard had planned long ago. "You did. I'm sure the gang enjoyed cleaning it for me."

"Not really." He chuckled. "But I smacked them around a bit. Are you ready to relieve me?"

"Sure. I'm ready to relieve you of command of the *Xerses*."

"I'm ready to be relieved of command of the *Xerses*."

"I relieve you."

"I stand relieved." He extended his hand. "Congratulations."

She shook. "Thanks."

"Why not announce yourself?"

She grabbed a microphone. "This is Danielle Sutton. I have command of the *Xerses*."

He accepted the handset from her. "This is Terrance Cahill. I stand relieved of command of the *Xerses*. Congratulations to

Danielle Sutton."

"Are you ready to relieve me? At the moment I command one too many ships."

Since he'd commanded the *Goliath* for years, his retaking of it was less ceremonious. "Sure. I'm ready to relieve you of the *Goliath*."

"I'm ready to be relieved."

"I relieve you of command of the *Goliath*."

"I stand relieved. I should head over there with you to announce it."

He lifted his phone. "Nah. Just use technology. Say it here, and I'll play it there."

She bent towards his phone. "This is Danielle Sutton. I stand relieved of the *Goliath*. Congratulations to Terry Cahill."

He played her voice back and then slipped his phone into his pocket. "Well then, I'll play this when I get there. Also, I'll have the deck logs updated on both ships about who's in command, and I'll tell Pierre."

She winked. "Hey, isn't that the new kid's duty?"

"Normally, yes. But since I'll be walking by both deck logs on me way to the bridge... the bridge I prefer..." He looked at the *Goliath*, which held the *Specter* and was docked facing the *Xerses* like a reversed mirror image. "I figured I'd do you a favor."

"Thanks."

"But if I find any new scratches in me ship, we'll be exchanging some very harsh words!"

"I painted over them all." She pondered a final tactical consideration before he descended the stairs. "You're not jealous about giving up the MICAs, are you?"

He turned and called over his shoulders while bounding down the steps. "I'll be getting MICAs and a robotic helo upgrade too, if we deploy again!"

She wondered what he meant by 'if', but Cahill was gone.

And she had a more urgent matter–one of the heart.

Knowing that Dmitry Volkov was aboard the *Wraith*, a short walk away across the *Xerses-Wraith* interconnecting brow, she buttressed herself for meeting him face-to-face for the first time in weeks.

But the *Xerses'* bridge remained quiet.

She glanced at the displays before her, but they were darkened while the entire fleet preferred to exercise their legs and interact with each other like human beings.

She wondered where her so-called boyfriend was hiding. He must have heard the announcement of her taking command of the *Xerses*. But Volkov remained distant, and she had responsibilities.

Lifting her phone to her cheek, she sought her executive officer.

Taylor answered. "Yes, ma'am."

"Where are you?"

"Over here. Can't you see me?"

Accepting his playfulness, she looked through the dome windows and saw movement on the *Goliath's* bridge.

Standing beside a smiling Liam Walker, Michael Taylor waved his arm over his head.

"You're on the wrong ship. That's Terry's now."

"Oh." He lowered his arm. "I hadn't heard."

She looked at the waterfront's pavement and saw Cahill embracing his wife, who'd flown in for the port call, as had many family members. Danielle found the loving bond between Cahill and his wife striking, empowered by something deeper than the fondness created by time and distance.

Instead of appreciating the love, she grew jealous and took it out on her underling. "Get over here, Mike."

He seemed to sense her stress, and his playfulness disappeared. "Yes, ma'am. Right away."

She relented her angst. "I mean, finish up with Liam first, and then come here. It's not urgent."

"If it matters, Liam and I agreed to let your crew take the *Xerses* without a proper complete turnover of the *Goliath*. Ladies first, you know. I'm sure Terry and his band of merry men remember everything about the *Goliath*."

Letting go of her love-jealousy, she perked up. "Really? So, we're abandoning ship?"

"Well, ma'am, one of us has to. I've been through plenty of changes of command, but a swapping of two commands is just plain weird. Everyone needs to hold the same job on two ships during the exchange, or else each job on one ship is vacant."

"And instead of an orderly, division-by-division exchange, you decided to swap the crews in one fell swoop?"

Taylor was meek. "Well, ma'am, we don't have all day, and the families are here."

"Understood. I'll look the other way. Just get it done." After hanging up. Danielle was alone. One of the few people without visiting family, she examined her solitude.

But the painful introspection revealed a soul that craved loving bonds beyond human reach, and she turned her thoughts outward again towards personal achievement.

She thought if she could keep pressing forward and acquire enough lifetime successes, she'd reach a plateau of triumph, and all would be well.

Happily Ever After.

It was the dream of Westernized culture, the indoctrinated lie of secular schooling, media, and materialism.

A voice within her warned against the dream, which forced competition and division among humanity, screaming that 'Happily Ever After' was an illusion until accounting for happiness in the eternity beyond one's final breath.

As doubts rose within her about her ingrained, constant, and waking dream, she crushed them with thoughts of self-reliance.

I have triumphed in my past. I am a commanding officer of a warship. I am strong. I will succeed.

Surprising her, a second voice within her protested. "*At what will you succeed?*"

She answered. "*Winning. Excelling.*"

The second voice challenged her logical flaw. "*Circular reasoning. Succeeding for the sake of succeeding is madness.*"

"*Shut up!*"

"In your hour of death, what memories will you cherish?"

"I'll look back upon my victories." The conversation's rising fear of death trumped her empty sentiment. *"Never mind my hour of death. I said 'shut up'."*

But the voice insisted. *"To what will you look forward, if not the void of nihilation? Do you fear the nothingness, or do you fear that the nothingness is a lie, and that your consciousness survives death? Are you afraid that death is not the end, but the beginning of something bigger?"*

Before she could answer, echoing footsteps stripped her from her inner torment.

Volkov appeared at the top of the stairs. "Hello, Danielle."

Flushing fear from her mind, she attempted levity. "Hey, did I give you permission to come aboard?"

"No. But Terry yes, and I here before you take command!"

The attempts at levity waned, and she saw the pain in his eyes. The mental fears of her inner dialogue became visceral pains in her body. "You're not here to give me good news, are you?"

He shook his head. "I'm sorry. I think much about it. We cannot be, if you cannot accept God."

She screamed. "Bloody... !" Pursing her lips and looking away, she silenced herself before unleashing an unretractable tirade.

"We cannot be, where I obey God and you obey... I don't know who you obey."

She stared at him. "It's about obedience? You want a slave?"

He frowned in thought, appearing to translate the English and constructing a reply. "Slaves to God, all of us. Must be. How Pierre says it... ah, yes. Nonnegotiable. Otherwise, all is evil."

"Sorry, Dmitry. I can't believe your ancient fairy tales."

His tone softened. "You know, not all ancient?"

"You're a Bible-thumper." She realized the cliché might elude his understanding. "Your Bible. You live and die by its teachings, but it's two thousand years old at best."

"Ah, yes. But do you know about modern appearances of saints and Jesus, too?"

She'd had enough. "You mean like this morning? Did Jesus come down from Heaven and tell you to abandon me?"

He waved his palm. "No. I not special. But some people are. The saints, mainly the Virgin Mary, but sometimes others and sometimes angels... and sometimes Jesus... appear to worthy people with updated messages of warnings and commands."

"Updated? So, this perfect god you worship that can't change, as you've said before, is changing the rules?"

His frown cast dark shadows, turning his eyes black. "No. Just reminders, with details specific to today. Warnings and miracles to prove the ancient truth before time."

"Really? Then why haven't I heard about them?"

"Because nobody gets rich by telling you. Only spiritual gains. Nobody broadcasting that."

She folded her arms. "Name one."

"Fatima. Portugal. Barely one hundred years old."

The jackass was breaking off a multi-month romance and touting Portuguese myths. "Fatima? I should care why?"

"Miracle of biblical size, predicted to hour, witnessed by seventy thousand people. The sun spins, changes color, and moves against nature, dancing. God getting our attention."

It sounded like a conspiracy or fake news. "Again, why should I care about something that happened in Portugal a hundred years ago?"

He seemed saddened and vulnerable without a hint of anger or dismissiveness. "Fatima one of many in twentieth century. Akita. Cuapa. Kibeho. Rome City. Garabandal. There are some happening today, like the beautiful story in Medjugorje in... how you say... Boze and Hertz-gove."

Having to coach her soon-to-be ex-boyfriend's English added to her frustration. "Bosnia and Herzegovina. Get on with it."

"Yes, there. All reminders of God's truth."

She'd had enough. "Okay. You go enjoy your beautiful stories."

"You want me to leave now?"

She yelled. "Get out of here!"

He bowed his head and departed.

Alone, she wanted to cry, but she judged the display of weakness unacceptable. Hardening her heart against the pain, she let affections for Volkov drift from her thoughts.

Christians were idiots, she reasoned, like all simpletons duped by religious lies. Little could be worse than believing in myths founded in legends that led to wars and oppressive rules, and the Christian religion's oppressive rules had just duped an otherwise desirable man into dumping her.

And with Volkov went her last real opportunity for starting a family. Her biological clock ticked away, counting down her chance of bearing her own children.

She couldn't give up this easily.

She was a winner, after all.

Wondering if she could rescue him from his fantasy, she began to construct a logical argument to pull him back to the freedom of rational secular thought.

There was no evidence for his god, other than myths, conjecture, and hope. And the supernatural was impossible. It was that simple. That was the argument.

Then, the concept of hope tormented her with a stark reminder that she mocked him for his, but she herself had none.

Without a god, there was only one short life on earth, filled with suffering and misery, peppered with moments of joy, but always with the looming certainty of death.

She wondered what philosophy could rescue her. Deeper, she pondered why she'd never considered this, or if she used to reflect upon it but had shut down her examination for the horrors it had revealed.

Upon her last breath, everything she'd done in her short life, a spec against the size and endurance of the universe, would be forgotten.

Nihilated. Like she'd never existed.

To be washed away as nothing.

The idea terrified her.

Wanting to throw a tantrum, she reminded herself of her

inner strength. She was a commander of a warship, and she could face any battle.

But how to battle the invisible enemy of death?

Swallowing her last vestige of pride, she let her stark desperation force her receptiveness to Volkov's plea.

She lifted her phone and found websites dedicated to the apparition. "Fine. Bloody hell. I'll give it ten minutes."

Three hours later, she was seated in a chair, engrossed in the first book she'd been purchased after researching the Miracle of the Dancing Sun, which affirmed a plethora of miracles at Fatima.

Her mind was opening.

Her heart was softening.

Unsure if she'd shut her mind again after her examination, she silenced her inner voices and kept reading.

Knowledge... examination of evidence... thinking beyond the narrative of secular schooling... the experience itself seemed, for lack of a better word, religious.

As she digested multiple layers of the story, she saw enough new light to carve out common ground for a future discussion with Dmitry Volkov.

And from this tiny glint of illumination, hope.

THE END

Epilogue 1

Two weeks later, Pierre Renard entered the dining hall established for pilgrims atop Mont Sainte-Victoire, in the southern Provence region of France.

Having paid a premium to climb during the pandemic which had closed the mountain, he enjoyed privacy, except for the required park ranger escorting his group, for overtime pay at Renard's expense.

Assembled before him, key players of the fleet he'd spent fifteen years growing from nothing sat together for possibly their final meal together.

His fourteen-year-old daughter brushed by him. "Excuse me, papa. I'm starved!"

"Yes, go." While she joined her fifteen-year-old brother, Jacques, and their mother, Marie, Renard examined the people before him.

Smiles appeared on jovial faces.

Seated with their wives, Antoine Remy, Claude LaFontaine, and Henri Lanier seemed wiser men than those he'd recruited to an *Agosta*-class submarine long ago. They'd strengthened their spines in the cauldrons of combat. He'd given his old friends countless adventures, and they'd be friends eternally.

Next to Henri sat Jake Slate with his wife, Linda. Sadness covered the fleet's original commander, but there was a sense of serenity. Having offered Jake an outlet for his ancient anger through vengeance, Renard realized the younger versions of themselves had been fools in stealing a Trident submarine long ago.

Vengeance was an evil that fueled evil anger, but it had taken them both fifteen years to learn the lesson. And it had cost hundreds of lives. But Renard acknowledged his past errors and noticed his charmed underling enjoying the same freedom of conscience.

Opposite Jake, Terry Cahill leaned into his wife, Ariella, and playfully adjusted morsels of bread and cheese to her exact disliking. She tapped his hand, and he withdrew it with a smile.

Something had happened during the Yemeni deployment to push the couple closer together, and Renard hoped that Cahill could endure the boredom of the *Goliath's* mothballing by focusing on his bride.

Amid visible tension, Dmitry Volkov sat beside Danielle Sutton, in a strained but earnest attempt to coexist. Knowing his commanders' dispositions, Renard speculated upon the issues seeming to separate the romantic duo.

Her firecracker grit balanced his stoic strength, or perhaps they clashed. Either way, he could only hope they'd resolve what needed resolving.

Perhaps time away from the fleet would help.

Seeking solitude, he turned and ascended the final escarpment to the peak.

A panorama, the entire world appeared below him at his beck and call. Reflecting, he tallied his immense victories against his few failures and reached a haunting conclusion.

He'd reached the top, but he was dissatisfied, and there was nowhere else to go.

After losing his first family to a drunk driver, he'd vowed to protect himself from loss. His new family, which he'd started as a powerful man in his mid-forties, enjoyed the best security forces and private luxuries.

But what of it? What mountains might they climb of their own volition unless he allowed dangers and harm to befall them?

Crunching rocks garnered his attention.

Assessing himself, Renard noticed he was kneeling.

Looking handsome in his approach into manhood, Jacques stood above him and spoke in their native French. "Don't get up."

"Thank you. It would have been laborious for this old man."

"I'll come down." Jacques knelt.

Renard hadn't seen his son kneel in recent memory. "What's on your mind, son?"

"What's next for you, Father?"

"What do you mean?"

"For our family. You're always gone, and Mother, Murielle, and I live like hostages in our own home. And with COVID, it's only getting worse."

"It's a wonderful home. I've given you every..." Renard caught himself. "You want freedom to make your own way?"

"Yes. I'm no longer a child."

A pit formed in Renard's stomach with a father's demand for offering his son accurate guidance. "If it's not yet obvious, I'm keeping the fleet in Toulon for a long time. Possibly forever."

The young man's face lit up. "Really?"

Renard realized his son needed his father's time. He then wondered what else he'd been blind to while pursuing achievements. "Yes. The crew suspects. I'll tell them after lunch."

"Wow. You're sure?"

"Don't tell anyone, but I'm already soliciting buyers for the ships."

Jacques frowned. "Didn't you steal one? Shouldn't you give it back?"

Renard squealed. "Who told you?"

"Who do you think? Mother!"

Chuckling, the Frenchman chuckled. "Oh, will we have words, she and I."

"Don't blame her. We know more than you think."

Renard questioned if he knew any true secrets. "I see."

"But why now, Father? What's changing your mind?"

"Right is wrong. The world is upside down. I wouldn't know where to apply pressure."

"Oh."

"If we deploy again, there must be an enemy to fight. Right now, the global battle is about information and disinformation. It's about science, pseudoscience, and outright lies. Our fleet is useless against such monstrosities."

"I know what you mean. I can search for a subject on one search engine and then get completely opposite results on another. It's like the world is one cesspool of agendas."

"And I'm lucky my son knows it."

"Then where's the truth, Father?"

Renard scanned the valley again and saw beauty, but beauty alone could lie while masquerading as truth. He needed something better.

His son pointed upward. "What about that?"

Renard looked over his shoulder at the nineteen-meter-high *Croix de Provence,* the cross which symbolized the Christian faith. "Do you have any Bible study tools?"

"I don't, but I know a few kids in school who do. I can get the apps and websites from them, no problem."

"Good. When we get home today, you and I will see what we can learn about it together."

Epilogue 2

A year later, Jake knelt in a pew before the Blessed Sacrament at Saint Thomas Chaldean Catholic Church.

The illusion of his former country's superiority over any past empire shattered, and he wondered how America was any better than the Babylonians, the Romans, or the Canaanites.

In the country he'd served before it spat him out, truth was elusive, mass media shaped narratives and censored opinions, and a selfish people shunned the virtues founded in its constitution under God.

Looking back upon his unfair expulsion from the United States Navy sixteen years earlier, he considered it a gift.

To defend his nation's flag, one had to step outside its shadow, meet God, and understand why only adherence to God's truths made the flag worth defending.

But the nation had divided itself.

The apparent split was between right and left, between conservative and liberal. But the deeper conflict was Christian morality versus secular humanism.

Without God, one side killed the weak, undesirable, and unborn for convenience, flouted nature's decree of two sexes, and blessed lustful gratification as 'love'.

But he admitted that the left was consistent within its dogmas. Godless people had to make themselves gods, each declaring his opinion a truth, and self-proclaimed gods had to pursue self-gratification.

They played into the hands of the ultimate rebel, the devil, by following Satanist Aleister Crowley's edict 'do as thou wilt'.

The other side obeyed God, whether intentionally or by accidental intuition, except when the radical violent right allowed their anger to overcome them.

But didn't God call for violence when necessary? Wasn't the Bible and the history of Christendom filled with arms taken up against the powers of darkness?

Trusting his bishop – one who, unlike many counterparts,

had resisted the temptation to willingly lock church doors for the first time in history– Jake would hold back on raising arms until his ordinary would demand it.

And he prayed it never happened.

He hoped the country would recover and reenter peaceful dialogues. Otherwise, he saw few ways to evangelize the neopagans who disagreed on the very definition of humanity.

Dismayed by the fruits of his meditative prayer, he blinked and reconsidered the revelations. Was he seeing doom where there was none? But the truth he perceived by kneeling below the world's only Truth told him the pending terror was real.

Nobody could predict the decade, much less the year or date. But it was coming.

Like the Soviet Union a century earlier, the encroaching darkness of atheism, masked in names like socialism, progressivism, and liberalism, was unfurling itself in America.

Like communist China, where the torture and genocide of Uyghurs in labor camps echoed that of Stalin's worst atrocities in Russia, censorship, fake news, and blind hatred controlled the elites.

Kneeling before the Truth, Jake wondered how long his country had housed and hidden such evils. Had it been swelling for decades, as Our Lady of Good Success had predicted at Quito? Had it been waiting to burst forth as the millennium's third decade began?

The Marian apparitions since Quito, Ecuador told the story, having predicted the world's demise for centuries.

Our Lady said the Catholic Church would bend from within, though never break. She said at Quito, four hundred years earlier, that the Church would see lukewarm priests and failure beginning in the nineteenth century.

She said at La Sallete in 1846 that cardinals would oppose cardinals, bishops would oppose bishops. At Fatima in 1917, she echoed it almost word for word. Then at Akita, in 1973 she said it yet again.

With a failing Church, the faithful had to see through the

evils of its own heretical clergy–its wolves in sheep's clothing. The horrific impact of molesters, heretics, and thieves, and the weakness of other Church leaders to oppose and correct such abuses clouded the deposit of faith.

Like a bludgeoned boxer, the Catholic Church was facing the seventh second of a 'standing eight count'.

But within the deep history of the Church, God's Truth survived intact and would always. But one had to learn it to recognize secular lies and those from ordained heretics.

Beside him, his wife nudged him. "You said only ten minutes. It's been fifteen."

"Uh... I'm good. Can we stay a little longer?"

"Sure."

He returned to his contemplation and noted that one apostle, Saint John the Evangelist, had stayed with God at the cross, while ten ran and hid after the twelfth had betrayed the Church.

The same ratio rose in Jake's mind, because those clergy who championed the truth numbered a small minority, as did those touting heresy. But the majority were lukewarm, avoiding discomfort and seeking the human invention of compromise. Guilty for their silence, they would pay.

And so would all of humanity, without a sea change of repentance.

Our Lady said it many times.

At La Sallete, France in 1846: "If my people will not submit, I shall be forced to let fall the arm of my Son. It is so strong, so heavy, that I can no longer withhold it."

At Fatima, Portugal in 1917: "Various nations will be annihilated..."

At Rome City, Indiana in 1956: "...my children in America. Unless they do penance... God will visit them with punishments hitherto unknown to them."

At Akita, Japan in 1973: "...if men do not repent ... It will be a punishment greater than the deluge, such as people have never seen before. Fire will fall from the sky and will wipe out a great part of humanity... survivors... will envy the dead."

At Cuapa, Nicaragua in 1980: "Man is hastening the arrival of a third world war."

And perhaps the most insightful warning was from repeated apparitions to Fatima's surviving seer. Barring mass repentance that had yet to be realized by yearend 2020, Russia would spread her errors throughout the world.

Her errors that Our Lady noted in 1917 coincided with the October Revolution, which toppled the monarchy, the churches, and natural families by establishing communism.

That same communism engulfed China, threatened Western cultures, and harkened a day when most churches might have to retreat underground.

More warnings from Our Lady circled Jake's head, but each jewel of wisdom from the Virgin Mary's appearances since the dawn of Marxism formed a consistent message.

Repent or perish.

But whom could he warn? Who would believe among the oceans of nonbelievers?

The evidence was within their consciences, and they ignored it towards their eternal doom in a very real and crowded Hell.

Worshipers of the one true God, whether they adore the Blessed Sacrament or simply see their savior in the faces of needy people they humbly serve, will suffer in this life but rejoice in the next.

Haters of Jesus will seek salvation through human inventions, declaring themselves a god among human gods, and will endure Hell's eternal torment.

Those who think they're centered between the worshipers and the haters will be surprised upon death to learn that middle ground is a myth, placing them among the damned.

On must seek truth, which is life and God, in humility, or one must seek self, human inventions, and ultimate torment.

Mentally quoting his favorite movie about Our Lady of Lourdes, he knew the answer. "For those who believe in God, no explanation is necessary. For those who do not believe, no explanation is sufficient."

Jake knew which side to choose, and kneeling before God's Truth, he chose it.

He wanted to help others learn the truth and decide. Somehow.

Because they had to decide.

Decide.

Decide.

Decide!

About the Author

After graduating from the Naval Academy in 1991, John Monteith served on a nuclear ballistic missile submarine and as a top-rated instructor of combat tactics at the U.S. Naval Submarine School. He now works as an engineer when not writing.

Join the Rogue Submarine fleet to get news, freebies, discounts, and your FREE Rogue Avenger bonus content!

ROGUE SUBMARINE SERIES:

ROGUE AVENGER (2005)
ROGUE BETRAYER (2007)
ROGUE CRUSADER (2010)
ROGUE DEFENDER (2013)
ROGUE ENFORCER (2014)
ROGUE FORTRESS (2015)
ROGUE GOLIATH (2015)
ROGUE HUNTER (2016)
ROGUE INVADER (2017)
ROGUE JUSTICE (2017)
ROGUE KINGDOM (2018)
ROGUE LIBERATOR (2018)
ROGUE MERCENARY (2019)
ROGUE NEPTUNE (2021)
ROGUE OUTLAWS (2021)

WRAITH HUNTER CHRONICLES:

PROPHECY OF ASHES (2018)
PROPHECY OF BLOOD (2018)
PROPHECY OF CHAOS (2018)
PROPHECY OF DUST (2018)
PROPHECY OF EDEN (2019)

John Monteith recommends:

Graham Brown, author of The Gods of War.

Jeff Edwards, author of Sword of Shiva.

Thomas Mays, author of A Sword into Darkness.

Kevin Miller, author of Raven One.

Ted Nulty, author of Gone Feral.

ROGUE OUTLAWS

Braveship Books

www.braveshipbooks.com

The tactics described in this book do not represent actual U.S. Navy or NATO tactics past or present. Also, many of the code words and some of the equipment have been altered to prevent unauthorized disclosure of classified material.

ISBN-13: 978-1-64062-108-4

Published in the United States of America

Made in the USA
Columbia, SC
04 February 2021

32225879R00138